ABODE

By Morgan Sylvia

Cover Design © 2017 by Elderlemon Design

http://www.elderlemondesign.com/

ISBN-13: 978-0-9980679-7-1

ISBN-10: 0-9980679-7-0

BLOODSHOT BOOKS

READ UNTIL YOU BLEED!

ABODE

MORGAN SYLVIA

Acknowledgments

Although writing is a solitary art, there are many people are involved in the creation and release of a book. I've had an amazing support system, and am deeply grateful to everyone who has helped me and inspired me. I would like to thank my boyfriend, Asa, for ongoing love and support, coffee refills, and for regularly making me laugh so hard I cry; my parents, for unending love and support; my writers' group, Tuesday Mayhem Society (Peter Dudar and April Hawks), for advice, encouragement, laughter, and camaraderie, and also Amy Dudar, for her hospitality and support; Pete Kahle, for bringing this book to fruition; Kealan Patrick Burke; the New England Horror Writers; the Horror Writers of Maine; Lady Endgame; Tisha, Gypsi, Robin, and my Tampa metal family; the House of Doome; Nayte Wilson; the Craigs; Barry Lee Dejasu; David Price; Tom Deady; Scott Goudsward; Tony Tremblay; the Taco Society; James A. Moore; all of my friends and family; Aleksandr and Antichrist Metalzine; and all of the amazingly talented and creative artists, writers, and musicians who have inspired me along the way. I also want to thank all those who support the arts. I am also eternally grateful to anyone who makes good coffee, craft beer, and music.

- Morgan Sylvia

Chapter One

You don't know me.

You probably don't remember any of what I am about to tell you. At least, I wouldn't expect you to. Then again, who knows? Maybe you do retain some memory of me, however dim, however vague. Some fragmented, distorted image survives perhaps, hidden deep in your subconscious. I thought I saw a flash of recognition in your eyes when I bumped into you that day at Quincy Market. A slightly haunted look. Questions. As if you knew me, but didn't know how.

I thought I saw fear. And then you turned away.

I followed you. With me, there was no doubt. No question. The very moment I saw you, I knew who you are and who you were.

There are no coincidences. That was no chance meeting.

Maybe you saw me again that day at the diner, though I tried to keep out of sight when I followed you. I am no secret agent. I'm sure my attempt at tailing you was horribly inept.

I realize this must all sound very strange.

Before I proceed, let me assure you, I mean you no harm. Quite the opposite, in fact; it is only for your own safety that I am writing you to you at all. I don't want to intrude on your life. I don't want to cause you any pain. I only followed you to find out how to contact you again. Not that that was a smashing success. Those hang up calls at your office? That was me, chickening out. The three no-show appointments from new patients you had last month? That was me as well. I finally decided to write you through the email address on your website. It seemed less intrusive that way. It also gives me a chance to take these jumbled memories and at least try to string them together into something coherent.

Also, to be honest, if I were to try and tell you these things in person, I would choke on the words. Even your name sticks in my throat. I cannot speak these things aloud, though they haunt me still. There are names I dare not speak, for to utter the names of those dark beings is to give them power. Even to think of them is dangerous.

But there is a truth that must be told.

Let me preface this by saying that I am very happy to know you are alive and well. I cannot say how much comfort it has given me to know that you are here, on this planet, in flesh and blood, and, to judge at a glance, healthy and happy and (I hope) doing well. The night after our encounter, I felt the first peace I have known in years.

I would suspect, given that you work with sleep disorders, that you also suffer from nightmares, that you wake in the night sweating and shaking, as I do. I would not be shocked to discover you recognize from those night terrors some of what I am going to tell you.

I wonder if you, too, dream of a man in a black wide-brimmed hat, in a shadowy northern forest. Or of his daughter, the black-haired witch, Sarah. The twins, perhaps. Of dour Josephine; poor, mad Isabelle; or gentle Agnes in her wheelchair.

I will not ask these things, though I wonder about them. Your secrets, your memories ... those are yours to keep or share. I ask nothing of you, save the time you will take reading this.

If you are easily frightened, if you cannot stomach horror movies or ghost stories, you will not enjoy reading this. Perhaps you will be tempted to just delete this email and chalk it all up to a chance meeting with a lunatic. I wouldn't blame you.

Before you do that, though, please understand one thing. You are in danger. Your entire family is in great danger. There are things that walk this world that have no love for humankind. And there, in the dark woods of the north, once rose a bloodline that dealt with these beings, these entities, if you wish.

This may sound crazy. I cannot argue that. I agree, actually. It not only sounds crazy, it is crazy.

But that doesn't make it less true.

I sat on a bench outside your office for most of the next day, trying to decide what to do. I wasn't sure whether or not I should approach you, or, if I did, how to approach you. I kept thinking about going into your work and asking for you, but I couldn't find it in myself to do that. So I simply sat there, hour after hour, until finally the daylight faded. When you left the office that night, you walked right past me. I didn't follow; as I said, I was still debating what to do. But I watched you walk away.

That's when I saw him.

I knew him the moment I saw him, just as I knew you. There is no mistaking him, for the aura of malevolence he projects is as palpable as heat or cold or a strong perfume. He stepped out of an alley as you approached it, and watched you walk away. He looked right at me, and then turned and walked through a wall. Every cell of my being reacted in terror. My skin prickled into goosebumps. The back of my spine tensed, and my muscles coiled like springs.

As though running would be of any use.

That is no human being.

That is a thing there that looks like a man, takes the guise of a man, but has never been human. It has never worn flesh. It masquerades as human, but whether the human face he wears was that of his servant, master, or victim, I know not. I only know that thing is hatred embodied, a malevolence so intense it carries itself into the physical realm.

You and your family are in great danger.

What I am going to tell you may frighten you. It should. It should terrify you. It sure as hell scares the shit out of me. I have spent countless hours and countless dollars on therapy. Shrinks, retreats, gyms, booze, pot: you name it, I've tried it. Nothing worked. I still wake in the night drenched in sweat, with the sheets clinging to my skin.

There are beings that walk this earth which have never been human. I dare not think of these beings at night; I can only begin this compilation in the brightest daylight. It is a dangerous undertaking, to document such instances as the ones I am going to recount. And I have battled myself for days, wondering whether to proceed or just walk away.

But I cannot let you face this thing alone and unprepared.

I hope I am making sense. Well, in a literary way, at least. There is no true sense to be made of the things I am going to tell you. Only that the universe is more dark than light, and that the beings which inhabit that darkness, those primordial lords of hatred, want nothing more than to see us suffer and die.

I know, I know. Madness, right? You're probably rolling your eyes, calling a friend. The conversation will probably start with you saying, "You won't believe this crazy email I got today ..."

I can't pretend to know the secrets of the universe. I haven't unlocked the codes of life and death. I can barely make sense of my own life. I am—I'll admit it—a raging alcoholic, completely incapable of sustaining a healthy relationship. Those are the scars I was left with.

I don't have all the answers. Just a lot of questions.

If you drink, you might want to make yourself a strong one before you go further. Or coffee, if you prefer. If you have a reading nook, I suggest you go there. Chocolate? Music? Candles? Purring cat? Loyal dog? Make yourself comfortable. Cook yourself up a big batch of macaroni and cheese, heat up some soup, or order a pizza. (Is pepperoni and onion still your favorite? I wonder about these things ...) Put on your comfiest sweatpants, and hell, if you have stupid slippers, best get those too. You will need all the comfort you can get.

I don't want to scare you. But you have to know the truth.

I guess I should start at the beginning. You were my little sister once. I don't know if you believe in reincarnation. I didn't know that I did, until I saw you again.

You'll find a Maine address sunk into the header of this document. Look it up on Google Maps. There is nothing there but an empty, overgrown lot now, but you may find it familiar nonetheless. I've attached a photo.

It's where you died.

Shall we begin?

Chapter Two

I guess I should start at the beginning.

This is the hard part.

I have delayed for pages now. I just deleted an entire page about today's weather, when three words (cold autumn rain) would have done just fine. I could wax poetic about the chill in the air or the smell of burning leaves, or ramble on about the intensity of New England autumns, and how fall paints the north in colors of blood and fire. I could tell you about my struggle to stay sober, my painting career and the crappy jobs that support it, or the string of failed relationships in my rear-view mirror. It isn't that I necessarily want to talk about any of these things. I simply find it harder to revisit the golden days at the start of the ordeal than it is to reexamine the nightmare itself.

Even now, my thoughts try to shy away from the subject at hand.

The past waits, menacing, a malevolent shadow hiding in the darkness at the center of my soul, a vortex waiting to pull me under again.

I determined long ago that there is no great wisdom to be gained from those memories, no sense to be made, no answers to be found. I have come to terms with the knowledge that I faced true evil and lost. That is a weight I bear. The scars I carry block any chance of my possibly being able to convince myself that it was all a dream. There is no comfort in the truth. I accept that.

But I have never accepted your death.

This is not the true beginning of the story. The tale truly begins in 1629, when a man named Jeremiah Kent arrived in what is now known as Maine. Jeremiah married a French settler named Marie Dumas. They settled in what was at the time untamed wilderness, on the parcel of land that we would come to inhabit over three hundred years later.

The darkness that inhabits that property was there long before them.

I've pieced together bits and pieces of his history, which I am still compiling. I'll get to that later. These things ... these things are not for today. Today is chilly and damp, and I've set my mind to one task: describing our early lives, and our arrival at the house.

So we begin.

You and I spent our early years in a small but cozy yellow raised-ranch house on a corner lot just outside of Boston. My memories of those early days are a kaleidoscopic blur of mixed images: melting purple popsicles and tire swings, the jungle gym at the park down the street, roller skates, cartoons, and board games. Home was a fenced back yard where we rolled around in clover patches and ran barefoot through soft grass Dad cut with a rusty, push-type lawn mower. We had a swing set with slides and monkey bars. You loved it, though I preferred climbing the maple tree on the front lawn. We had a playroom downstairs, complete with overflowing toy boxes, fake wood wall paneling, and an avocado shag rug. On Saturday mornings, we used to watch cartoons down there, while eating cereal and candy. Mom and Dad got us all the requisite toys, as well as scratch n' stiff stickers, pet rocks, and other playthings. That room was our little haven: it was comfortable and cozy, with its overstuffed sofa and huge lamps. It was safe. It was familiar. It was ours. You did all the normal things any little girl would do, in those years. You played with your Barbie dolls and fashion plates, and filled coloring

ABODE

books with scribbled Crayon creations. You drew lopsided hopscotch blocks on the sidewalk in pink and purple chalk, and you had a crush on the blond guy from *The Dukes of Hazzard*. You took ballet and gymnastics classes, and sold Girl Scout cookies. You were a fairy in a school play one year, and a singing tomato the next.

We both belonged to local Scout troops. We went to Disneyland every spring, and Cape Cod every July. Our summers were filled with ice cream cones, miniature golf games, swimming, barbeques, and water parks. We attended family reunions too, gatherings of more aunts, uncles, and cousins than I could count. We played horseshoes or cricket while nibbling burgers or hot dogs, and cracked open lobsters Mom bought right from the dock. Autumn was Halloween and trick or treating, and jumping into piles of leaves Dad raked up. In those days, people weren't afraid to let their kids go door to door. This was before people started poisoning chocolate and putting needles into candy bars. And winter? Winter was skating and sledding, hot chocolate and snowball fights, clumsy one-piece snowsuits and mittens connected with string. Spring was the season of sunshine and mud and Easter chocolate, baseball games at Fenway Park, and the exhilaration and freedom of finally being able to run around outside after being cooped up indoors all winter.

These things bubble up clearly through the hodgepodge of murky memories that followed them. The wheel of the year, as I recall it, turned peacefully in those years.

In other words, we had a perfectly normal childhood.

Then Dad lost his job.

You, of course, didn't understand the importance of that, or get why Dad wasn't happy to be out of work. Neither of us did, really. I remember asking if we could finally go to the Grand Canyon, since Dad had more free time now. I thought jobs were like school, where time off was actually a good thing. I didn't understand why Mom and Dad looked so glum. You played with your toys, named your stuffed animals, and asked Dad if he could become an astronaut.

Eventually we began to understand what that job loss truly meant. It meant macaroni and cheese or canned spaghetti for dinner almost every night. It meant peanut butter and jelly sandwiches for lunch instead of ham or turkey and cheese, and generic brand cereal for breakfast instead of bacon, eggs, and toast. It meant Kool-Aid instead of juice (which neither of us minded), and it meant we couldn't go to the movies or roller-skating on weekends. We had to tell our friends we wouldn't be joining them at camp, and your birthday was scaled down from a weekend at the water park and beach to a backyard barbeque with cake Mom made from a box and balloons she inflated with her own ragged breath.

Then the next bomb dropped: we were told we would be attending public school that year, rather than private. We were too young to care about what that meant for our education. We only knew that we wouldn't see our school friends anymore, and that we would wear regular clothes instead of uniforms. Like our classmates, we looked down at the public school kids a bit. We were foolish enough to think that we were somehow better.

I sulked for days.

We went to the beach a lot that summer. We went to the park and the public swimming pool. We skated, splashed in the sprinkler, swam in our friends' pools, and basically just amused ourselves with activities that didn't cost anything.

ABODE

It was the best summer of my life. At least, the first part of it was. Those days were sunlight, were precious in their simplicity.

Then the other shoe dropped. We were told we would be moving to Maine.

The reason for the move was pretty cut and dry; Dad got a new job, one worth relocating for, working at a mill up in Mersport. He got the house dirt cheap. He must have driven up one day to see it, but I don't recall any mention of that. I just remember that he came home one night and bluntly informed us that we would be moving immediately. He wanted us to be we settled before the new school year started.

It was a complete shock. To a child who has only experienced one home, moving is a pretty big deal. It's uprooting one's whole world. It's upending the universe and everything in it.

I certainly wasn't happy about it. But you were the one who threw a fit. You cried. You screamed. You kicked Dad, broke a lamp, refused to eat, and basically screamed your lungs out. You even threw a glass of milk against the wall and broke it. This wasn't like you. You were—from what I can recall—generally a pretty well-mannered, happy kid. At least up until that point you were. I occasionally found you annoying, and I thought you spent too much time playing with stupid dolls, but I never hated you the way some kids hate their siblings. Your reaction really startled me. I had never seen you act like that. I don't recall you ever throwing a full-out tantrum, at least, not since you got past the toddler phase. But that night you cried and screamed so much that you actually lost your breath. Mom and Dad were completely taken aback, and spoke in hushed, worried tones. I remember watching it all and feeling sad for you.

I wonder now if you sensed what was coming.

It was me you came to for comfort. You put your little arms around me and sobbed, and a protective big brother was born.

I somehow found the nerve to inform Dad that no, we weren't moving. I got beat pretty bad for it. It wasn't the first time Dad had hit me. I'm not sure where one would draw a line between punishment and abuse, or which side of it that incident would fall on, but I remember just telling Dad to hit me again, it didn't matter because we weren't moving.

I'm glad, now, that I did that. It gives me some tiny comfort to know that I tried, to the best of my nine-year old ability, to stop it.

I ended up sulking in my room with a bag of frozen peas on my eye.

Mom came in to talk to me. The fresh welts on my back still stung, and she put salve on them. "You have to be patient with your father," she told me. "This hasn't been easy for him, leaving his job."

"He didn't leave." I was still sulking. "They *fired* him. Bobby's dad told him all about it."

Mom tried to hide the truth. But she couldn't: it was in her eyes, and in her voice, which was quiet and tense. "It's complicated," she told me. "Things change. Nothing lasts forever. Our time here is done, and it's time for us to move on from this place."

That only angered me more.

"There are jobs *here*," I said. "He didn't even try."

"Sometimes a fresh start is the best thing someone can do," she said. "What if you love the new house, the new school?"

"I won't," I said. "I'll hate it. I don't want to go."

ABODE

Mom's face hardened slightly. "You're going to have to face things you don't want to face, in life. You'll have to do things you don't want to do. Go places you don't want to be. Someday, at least some of those choices will be up to you. But this time, it isn't." She stood up and went to my bedroom door, then paused, looking back at me. "There'll be no more backtalk or whining about this move. We're going, and that's that. You and your sister will start packing your toys tomorrow."

Those words ring in my head to this day.

I wonder now if I hated that place before I ever laid eyes on it.

Needless to say, my nine-year old wiles did nothing to change the situation. We packed up the only home you and I had ever known in preparation for the move to the Great White North.

All of our toys and clothes—even our pet rocks—went into cardboard boxes Mom picked up from the grocery store. Within a matter of a few short weeks, our home had been completely dismantled. The morning we left, I walked through the empty rooms one last time. The only signs of our presence were the stain on the living room carpet where you had once spilled hot chocolate, the cracked window pane that stood as a reminder of the day that I—after ignoring about a thousand warnings—threw a ball inside the house, and the marks Mom had made on the kitchen wall to mark our growth.

I hated knowing that the things that made up my world could be so easily dissembled. That things could fall apart so easily. Looking back, I guess that was my first realization of how fragile life is. The lives we build can be torn down within hours, or even minutes. Dust in the wind, as they say.

There is nothing left of that place now. The house is long gone, razed to make way for a dirty gas station that sells stale nachos and cheap cigarettes. I stopped there once, not too long ago, and didn't even realize where I was until I drove away and passed the park down the road. As far as I can tell, the men's room now stands right where your bedroom used to be. The backyard where we used to play is now covered in cracked pavement and litter.

Dust and bones and ash. That is all that remains of those days, of our former lives. Of you. I'm the only one left to tell the tale, and you're the only left to tell it to.

One hot, sticky August day, we all piled into the station wagon, with Buster, our Border Collie, and Lucky, our fluffy orange tabby, and drove up I-95 to our new home. I remember the trip pretty clearly. We stopped at a fast food place for lunch. You and I both got little plastic toys with our meals, and we spent the rest of the trip playing with them while the radio played songs by The Eagles and Fleetwood Mac. Mom and Dad both seemed happy, if a little nervous. They fussed over details (Would the movers break their wedding china? Would Mom be able to plant a garden? Should they have left the shag rug behind?) and discussed taxes and furniture and snowplows.

It seems like a thousand years ago.

It seems like yesterday.

We crossed the big green bridge in Portsmouth, and then we were in Maine. I didn't notice much of a difference at first. Less houses, more trees. But as we drove further and further north, into the wilderness, I felt as though we were leaving civilization behind, and going back through time. We saw more and more pine trees, and fewer deciduous ones. The woods pressed thick against the road, a wall of forests broken occasionally by rivers or thick tan bogs where dead trees reached skeletal branches into a pale blue sky. We drove past the traffic, and had the road nearly to ourselves. Each exit seemed more remote, and less interesting, than the last.

After what seemed like forever, we finally turned off the interstate, navigating a series of roads that unfurled through rolling green hills, past dairy farms and antique stores and, of course, more woods. We passed ancient stone walls, burnt-out barns, and the occasional general store, and drove through towns with little brick-front downtowns that were so small we went through most of them in less than five minutes.

The first thing I noticed about Maine was that it seemed to be mostly made of pine trees, half-burnt barns, and old cemeteries. Even now, whenever I visit Maine, I'm struck by the abundance of cemeteries. It seems you can't drive more than a mile without seeing some old, crumbling graveyard. Many are small, and, while some look well-tended, most of them look forgotten.

You noticed it too. "Why are there so many dead people here?"

"What?" Mom frowned.

"There's a cemetery on every road!" You pressed your hands to the window glass, and looked at her over your shoulder. "Do people die here a lot?"

"People die everywhere," Dad snapped. "Don't ask stupid questions."

Mom shot him a look, and said something under her breath. I thought you were going to have another fit, but instead you just settled back into the seat and picked up your Barbie doll.

We stopped for ice cream at a roadside place with red painted picnic tables and big metal trashcans painted in bright colors. I got Chocolate Swirl; you got Tutti Frutti. We tried to eat it before it melted, but despite our valiant efforts, we both ended up with sticky fingers. The place had an outdoor fountain with a spigot, and I remember Mom washing your hands there. You looked at her, blinking from the sun, and asked, very seriously, how long we had before it got dark.

"Oh, sunset isn't for a while yet," Mom said. She dried your hands with a napkin. "We have plenty of time. It won't be dark until almost nine."

"Why? Is the darkness afraid of summer?"

Mom just sighed and fed you a generic reply. It struck me as an odd question. I suppose that's why I remember it.

We left the ice cream place behind and moved on.

It too, is gone, now, abandoned.

We drove further and further into the wilderness. There are huge tracts of unbroken forest in Maine, even today. That primeval wild is quiet, unusually devoid of large predators. At least, those made of flesh. As we drove into the forest, I had a strange sense that the land was aware, that the woods were, in themselves, watching me.

Eventually we drove through what served as Mersport's downtown, which was really little more than a cluster of brick stores concentrated over a few blocks. The town offered a fairly typical selection of small businesses: a drugstore, a salon, a bookstore, a travel agency, a department store, a bank, a jeweler's, and a pizza place. From there, we turned onto a road that took us even deeper into the country. We passed mirror-calm ponds and fast-moving streams, acres of fields, lumberyards, centuries-old farmhouses, and the burnt husks of wooden barns. The trees crowded close along the side of the road, a wall of greenery shielding the wood and its secrets. In other places, blueberry barrens stretched out over rolling hills, or grassy pastures fell away toward dark distant woods. There were no more big shiny stores, no more movie theaters.

When we started passing houses with woodpiles, I felt like we were traveling back in time.

"This is the middle of nowhere!" I complained. "They still chop wood here, like it's a thousand years ago."

"We'll burn wood this winter, too," Dad said. "Cheaper that way. And guess who gets to help carry it?"

I kicked the seat.

"Keep it up." Dad caught my eyes in the rear view mirror. His voice was calm, but there was rage smoldering in his gaze. "Keep it up, and you'll carry every stick of wood we burn all year."

I was quiet the rest of the way.

After what seemed an eternity, we crossed a bridge, passed an old mill, and turned onto a road that wound even deeper into the woods. A few miles down, we started up a huge hill. I strained my neck, trying to see over the hump. The car, overloaded, strained to crest the hill. We made the top at a crawl. The land leveled out a bit, and then rolled downward, and we started picking up speed again. But not much. Dad held off on the gas, because we had reached both the end of the road and our destination.

A snapshot becomes clear among a kaleidoscope of memories; that first glimpse of the house, its dark silhouette a sharp contrast against that bright summer day. Just before Dad turned into the drive, we passed an old, dead tree, a huge oak. A flock of black birds took flight from its branches.

"Here we are, kids," Mom said brightly.

The house did not, at a glance, seem like anything out of the ordinary. All in all, it was a fairly typical New England farmhouse, box-shaped and big. It had three stories, but was more tall than wide. The property was roughly boxed in by oaks, maples, and pines. A tangled hedge wall of wild roses, berry bushes, and burdocks and a short stone wall held the surrounding woods at bay. The place was somewhat rundown, and had a desolate, neglected air. Cobwebs hung like veils over cracked, grimy windows, hiding the shadowy unknown of the house's interior. The chocolate-colored paint and white trim were chipped and peeling, and the half-dead shrubs surrounding the house had been all but enveloped in weeds. The yard was completely overgrown, and resembled a meadow more than a lawn. A huge dead tree stood sentry in the front yard. It looked skeletal, a dead thing reaching bony fingers for the sky.

Behind the house, the land sloped up, became forest. Across the street, a large field gently rolled down and away from us, cleared centuries ago for crops and pasture. A few twisted apple trees were all that remained of an old orchard. Further down, we could see a dark smudge of trees, with a clear, serpentine line in them that announced the presence of a stream or a river.

It was completely silent. There were no birds, no sirens, no voices. We were too far away from the main roads to hear any traffic. The only sounds that broke the stillness were the hum of a few tree frogs buzzing and the wind moving through the trees. Ours was the last property on the road, which reached a dead end just beyond our driveway.

In later years, I became strangely adept at spotting places that host paranormal activity. I can be driving down a street for the first time, when I will suddenly notice a place that seems slightly amiss. Invariably, I will turn my head and see a relatively normal-looking home, its windows dark, its shadowy interior perhaps a

ABODE

little blacker than it should be. And something in me shudders in terror, knowing.

I feel uneasy now, looking back on that moment. I recall a sense of wrongness, but I can't say for certain that the memories of what transpired later haven't colored my recollections of that first day. At the time, I was just . . . unimpressed.

"It's a dump," I said disdainfully.

"It's three times the size of our old house," Dad said.

You didn't like the place any more than I did. You started crying, and quickly worked yourself into such a fit that Mom didn't seem to know what to do. At one point, you were crying so hard you almost choked. "I don't wanna live here," you kept saying. "I wanna go home."

Dad picked you up. "It is going to be just fine, honey. This is our home now."

You screamed to be put down. He obliged, startled, and you stood still, as though frozen in place, simply staring at the house. At the third floor, to be exact. I don't know what you saw there, if anything.

"It looks dirty," I said. "And old."

"It *is* old," Dad said. "She was built in the 1800's. These old houses have strong bones, and a lot of character." He pointed at the chimney. "See that? The chimney is made of stone taken right out of the river."

"Just looks like rock to me."

Mom was no more enthralled than we were. She eyed the house warily. I could almost see her making a mental list of all the work that had to be done: the scrubbing, the mopping, the sweeping, the painting. "You said it needed a little work. This place is falling apart."

"Cosmetic," Dad said. He flipped through his key ring. Even I could tell that some of his cheeriness was forced. "She's sound. Good roof, good foundation. Wiring tested out fine."

"It will cost thousands to get this place into decent shape."

"And we will still have made out like bandits." Dad kissed her. "Don't worry so much. You can have a garden." He pointed toward the yard, which was an overgrown tangle of brush and wildflowers. "That spot over there looks perfect. And we can put an outdoor pool in next year."

"I want a pool *now*!" I cut in. "When can we get the pool?"

"Right as soon as you learn to tie your shoelaces without me having to tell you."

I looked down, grumbled, and tied my sneaker laces.

Snapshots.

Moments fallen away into time.

Buster yanked the leash out of my hands and took off around the side of the house. I ran after him, but I didn't have to go far. As soon as I came around the back of the house, I saw him. He stood at the doors to the root cellar, growling.

I saw those doors, and, well, I know I didn't like that. A hole leading into the ground. No thanks. I never liked underground. My earliest nightmares were of tumbling down a deep, dark hole and falling straight into hell. Caves give me the creeps, and mines terrify me. Even basements freak me out. Below ground, below the reach of the sun … that is the realm of the dead.

There are few things I am sure of in this world, but this I know: only the dead belong below the surface of the earth.

Buster started barking loudly. I grabbed his collar and tried to pull him back, but he had about fifty pounds on me and I couldn't budge him. Dad came around the back and grabbed his collar.

"What's he barking at?" I asked.

"Probably an animal down there," Dad said. Mom joined us as we went back toward the front door. You trailed along behind her, clutching Lucky, and stood there, still sniffling, as Dad fiddled with the lock and key and then opened the door.

"Go on, kids," Dad said. "Go pick your rooms."

You and I took off like, well, like little kids going to pick rooms out. Dad tied Buster to a tree, so he wouldn't get in the way or run off. His barking was the soundtrack to the rest of the day.

The house is no longer standing. You can still see some of the property features if you look up the lot online. The foundations are still visible, and the driveway paving is still there. The garage still stands, though the roof has collapsed. The lot is once more overgrown, even more so than it was that day. You'll find—or perhaps have already found—several photos attached to this email, but only a few, the ones I got from Uncle Mike, were taken inside the house.

There were three doors. If you walked in the front door, you would find yourself standing in an open parlor/entry way. The stairs were immediately on your right, and had an old-fashioned wooden banister we used to slide down. If you walked straight ahead, you would find French doors on your left, opening onto the living room. Continuing on, you would pass through the dining room. The dining room opened onto a small hallway on the right. This held the side door, the one closest to the garage. This little alcove—or tiny hallway, if you prefer—also contained a closet, and the door to the cellar stairs, which ran directly beneath the other stairs. If you went past the alcove/hall and dining room, you would pass a pantry and a bathroom, and then walk into the kitchen, where the window over the sink looked out onto the yard. A door to the left of the sink led onto the back porch.

The house had one of those round tower-like attachments, with windows all around it. The bottom portion sat off the living room. The top floor was a bedroom. You went straight for that one, without even looking at any other rooms. I opened door after door. None of the rooms felt particularly inviting. They all had old, busy wallpaper and dark wood floors. I finally ended up picking the room by the attic stairs, mostly because it had a sort of closet beneath the attic stairs. I thought at first it would make a really cool little secret hideaway. Being nine, of course I was all into secret hideaways. I remember Dad telling you that you could stay in the round room in summer, but when it got cold, you'd have to move, as that room wouldn't have much heat. You protested a little too much, and he made you take the room beside mine.

I heard all this, but I wasn't paying too much attention. I lugged my suitcase up the stairs, and brought it into my new domain. I crossed the room and stood looking out one of the windows, gazing at the strange, wild land before me. To someone who had always lived in a busy city neighborhood, it just seemed empty. I couldn't see anything but trees and fields. On the other side of the river, I could just barely make out the shape of another roof, but there were no other neighbors in sight. For all practical purposes, we were alone in the world. It felt like we were on another planet.

ABODE

I turned and surveyed my bedroom, and then decided to check out the cubbyhole under the stairs. However, when I finally opened the latch (it was rusted shut) I didn't like it at all. It was cold and black and it smelled like a grave. I could see things at the far end: an old chair, a suitcase, two trunks, some old tools, a big glass milk jug that was caked with fine dust, and some other odds and ends. The rest I couldn't quite make out. I didn't like the look of it: it spoke of an earlier age, of another time, an era I didn't belong to. I shut the door and pushed the old armchair Dad had brought up to my room in front of it.

Mom called us back down to the yard. Dad was taking the camera out of the station wagon's glove compartment. "Come on everyone," he said. "Family photo."

I'm sending two photos, one of a handful I have. The only reason I have these is because Mom had decided to have some duplicates made, and had brought the negatives back to the photo shack. They were still there on the night of the fire. Somehow, Aunt Janet ended up with them. The first photo (Picture One) is a shot Mom took of you and I unpacking boxes. You were closer to the camera than I was, close enough that the small birthmark on your right cheek is visible. That birthmark also shows on your old school pictures.

I saw an identical birthmark on the profile photo you have on your website.

I've also attached the photo of the four of us (six, if you include Buster and Lucky) standing in front of the house. I still remember us taking that picture. Dad set the timer on the camera and scrambled into place. In the photo, you're clutching your favorite Raggedy Ann doll, squinting slightly. You had your hair in pigtails that day. I'm wearing a football jersey and a look of annoyance. Mom's smile looked slightly forced. Buster is a brown and white blur; he was straining at the leash, his attention rapt on something in the forest.

A smudge in one of the third-floor windows bears the distinct shape of a human face: a young woman, her pale face framed with dark hair. An analyst could examine the photo, and say the image is a trick of light, the reflection of a cloud. It could be a flaw in the negative, or a spot that happened during processing. But I haven't the luxury of skepticism. Don't get me wrong: I'm not gullible, by any means. I've seen plenty of faked paranormal footage and charlatan psychics. Were it only the photo, I would be more than happy to dismiss it as a trick of light against cellophane.

Her name was Isabelle.

Chapter Three

It isn't easy for me to revisit these things. To revisit is to relive. You leave a dark path, you don't want to go back down it. You run as far and as fast as you can in the opposite direction, and smother those recollections in any way possible. Burn them, exhale them in fragrant smoke, bury them, chew them up, rip them, cut them out of your skin, swallow them ... anything and everything you can to leave them behind. If you're tough enough, maybe you'll face your personal demons on your own ground; at the gym, in a studio, on a mountain path or in a dojo. If you aren't so strong, you'll choose the easy route, as I did, and drown your demons in alcohol.

I am a recovering drug addict and alcoholic. I started drinking at a very young age. I had already spent a thousand nights at the bottom of a bottle by the time I reached legal drinking age. I'll spare you the sordid details of that dark phase of my life, other than to say I fought long and hard to get to where I am now. Sobriety is a battle I still fight every day. It's a struggle that never ends, a war that falls into occasional lulls, only to flare up again, even uglier and angrier than before. I won't lie; I've found liquid comfort and liquid courage, along with liquid rage. But the respite, as so many are, is always a lie. You pay a price for that numbness, for those brief moments of clarity you grasp as you are sucked, spinning, down the flush of your own life. What won't you sacrifice for those few, precious minutes of feeling good? Those short, blurry moments you have before the room starts to spin and the vomit spews forth, that brief moment of calm before the rage takes over.

My dance with inebriation always ended the same way. At some point, inevitably, I would find myself staring at my foul, puke-covered memories, and sink further into self-hatred. I couldn't face the truth, so I ran. And then I dove headfirst into a bottle.

You can't run away from memories.

Such a simple truth, and yet so hard to accept.

The bottle is only a mask. The pipe is an illusion, a flimsy promise of a brighter hour, a medicine that poisons you. The only gift of the needle is numbness, a pretty lie, one that comes with a cost much higher than that of the drug itself. I see that now. I see many things now, things I couldn't face or comprehend when I was younger. It took me 12 years to get sober after decades of inebriety. It took the loss of too many relationships to name. It took jobs and friendships, and a lot of moments that make me wince now when I think of them.

I've come a long way. But sanity is a fragile thing.

I suppose we all have lessons to learn. We all have to face the strings that come attached to the flesh we are born into. The burdens of being upright, someone once called it. I only wish my truths hadn't been so

-dark

-evil

-hungry

Losing you was devastating. I have nightmares about you to this day, the little sister I couldn't protect. You were a pale, fragile flower that had just begun to bud, only to be lost to eternal night. I clawed my way back to the normal world, but in doing so, I've had to leave many things behind. Everything, really: everything I was, and could have been. But the nightmares never stopped. These are the dreams of blood and fire. Part vision, part memory. Dark images I never witnessed sear my thoughts, my dreams, my reality. I see you in a body bag, pale and silent. I see you engulfed in flames, your flesh burned and seared, your mouth open in a final silent scream. I've seen you cut apart, dismembered, ripped into a torn mass of bloodied flesh. I've seen the mess made of the things your skin once contained. I've seen you drown in a tub of your own blood. I've seen you hanging from a tree. Sometimes you are a pale shadow in the woods. Sometimes you are a rotting corpse in a cold, northern graveyard. Often, in these dreams, you are reaching for me, your pale tiny hands pushing up through damp, spongy soil.

Sometimes you are only bones, and the shadow of flesh.

In the worst dream of all, you stand pure and whole. With them. They stand around you, behind you. Jeremiah. Elizabeth. Josephine. Isabelle. Sarah. Agnes. The twins. There are others, too. Their stories and faces are lost in time, but their names survive. Those names are etched onto the crumbling, moss-covered tombstones in the spongy soil in the Kent family cemetery.

See? Even now, I am delaying.

We moved into the house on Woodfarrow Drive August 4th, 1977. You were six, and I was nine.

I was the only one that ever really left.

Chapter Four

It began slowly.

We spent most of that first week just unpacking and settling in. Those days return to me now in a blur of fragmented images: cardboard boxes and various piles of our belongings, the newspapers Mom had wrapped our dishes in strewn everywhere, cold bologna and cheese sandwiches, and the radio blaring what is now considered classic rock but at the time was modern: Fleetwood Mac, The Eagles, Pink Floyd, Steely Dan. Even now I get chills when I hear 70's rock. Actually, there's a lot about the 70's that sets my nerves on edge. I absolutely hate orange and yellow, puke green, and just about every shade of brown. Yellow dishes make me cringe, and I wince every time I hear the theme from some once-popular sitcom. Needless to say, I'm not a big classic rock fan, either.

My memories of those early days in the house are shattered, scattered juxtapositions of darkness and light, comfort and terror. Those recollections are like a long reel of film that suddenly comes into sharp focus, and then dissolves into a blur of shadow and sunlight. Certain things stand crystal clear in my memory. I remember the kitchen the best: the worn-out, yellow and brown patterned linoleum on the kitchen floor, which must have been there since the 60's; the dark brown cabinets; and the walls, which were sort of a beige-yellow color. I remember other tiny details of that house, too, things that come to me all too easily when I close my eyes: the dark wood paneling on the stairway and in the living room, the dark reddish-black wood of the dining room table, the glass window cutouts in our dark brown front door, and our old green shag rug, which Dad put down in the living room.

As we settled in and arranged our things, I remember waiting to feel at home. I thought at first that maybe it would just take time. But every time I stepped through our door, I felt uneasy. The air seemed thick with a silent presence, and I became more and more aware of feeling as though I were being watched. There was a heaviness to the atmosphere in that house that never lifted. It was nothing we could really put a finger on, but I think we all noticed it right away.

Only small things happened at first. Broken dishes. Paintings falling from the walls. Some doors wouldn't stay open, and others wouldn't stay shut. I heard voices in empty rooms, and felt a cool breeze brush past on a sweltering hot day. Once, one of my toy cars fell off a shelf of its own accord. Moments later, a crow flew into my bedroom window. I remember being startled, and sensing that somehow something wasn't right. But the sun was shining, and the world outside was green and gold with summer. So I brushed these things off and just went on about my business as though nothing had happened.

Some instances weren't so easily dismissed.

I was in the kitchen one day, making a sandwich, when I heard the thud of something falling. I turned to find an apple rolling across the floor, as though some unseen hand had moved it.

Charlatan, you're probably thinking. *Fraud.* These are classic signs of a haunting. Taken right out of a ghost story, or an episode of some cheesy TV show.

I wish they were lies.

Trust me, this is hardly a diabolical plan to end up on a reality show about the paranormal. What have I to gain but ridicule?

Simply writing about this, about you, is a form of torture to me. I feel as though I am bleeding ink and memories, ripping open old wounds.

In fact, that's exactly what I'm doing.

Even now, the shadows in that house cluster around me in my dreams.

My experiences, at that time, had been quite limited. My only knowledge of ghost stories was from cartoons. Mom and Dad never let us watch scary movies. Sure, I'd seen some classics, like *Dracula* and *Frankenstein*, at friends' houses during Halloween sleepovers. And you? You could barely get through a Scooby Doo cartoon without crying. But those hauntings took place in huge, elaborate Gothic castles, where knights in rusting armor stood sentinel against the unholy things that crept through the night. Those stories featured pretty girls in white dresses; strong, brave heroes; and distinguished older gentlemen. More importantly, in those classic tales, there was always a way to defeat evil. A cross, a pale beam of sunlight, garlic, a silver bullet. Something.

In reality, there are no such relics. None that I've found, anyway. And we had no heroes. No one helped us. No one came to our rescue. What we faced, we faced alone. I can't even say that we dealt with things as a family. Our unit fractured and shattered and, like a glass, once broken, it could never again be whole.

But that was later.

I remember sensing tension building slowly, the way water heats up slowly before it boils. I didn't even think, at first, that our run-down home could be worthy of harboring the souls of the restless dead. I didn't even know that was even possible. Ghosts were no more real to me than Jedi warriors or cartoon dinosaurs. They were fascinating, but completely imaginary.

ABODE

Or so I thought.

We tried to reassemble ourselves, though we were a long way from the place that had always been our home. Dad set up the basement room as his studio, and spent more and more of his time there as days passed. Mom busied herself in decorating and housework. You and I, well, we just played.

Some people say that ghosts are nothing more than imprints, leftover energy patterns made from a human's electromagnetic fields. Others swear that they are souls trapped between worlds, caught here because of an untimely, violent death or a task left unfinished. I don't know which of these things is true, if either of them. I only know what I saw.

You and I were together when we encountered the first one. That moment is still very clear to me, despite the passage of time. We were playing Chinese checkers. I even remember what you were wearing: rust-brown bell-bottoms and a yellow tee shirt. Your hair was in pigtails held with yellow plastic barrettes. I was reaching for a bright blue marble when I felt the air chill suddenly. I just happened to look up.

She was standing in the doorway, a dark, shadowy figure in a long dress that dissolved into nothing just below the waist. She floated toward us, and passed *through* us. I felt completely paralyzed. My vision darkened, focused on a single spot, like a tunnel, and around the edges I saw only static.

This all happened really quickly, in the blink of an eye, as they say. Then she was gone, and I looked at you, and I saw, that first time, not terror in your eyes, but placid acceptance.

"Did you see that?" I asked.

You nodded. "That's Agnes," you said. "She was in a wheelchair. That's why she had no legs."

Then you jumped my checkers, and won the game.

I tried to ignore the event, to pretend it hadn't happened. But the heaviness in my gut told me something was very, very wrong.

Those early incidents were mild. But they made us anxious. They kept us on our guard. They sparked the first dim glow of fear, and, in doing so, opened the door.

The dead were, as it turned out, the least of our worries.

The true terror in that home never wore human flesh.

✳ ✳ ✳

After we moved in, we had a few weeks of summer vacation left before school started. Seeing as we hadn't yet made any friends to fill those sweltering hours with, you and I were pretty much left to our own amusements. We spent a lot of time outside, playing on the swing set, riding our bikes, and exploring … all the things children don't get to do today. That makes me sad, actually. If there's one thing I do appreciate about my— our—early childhood, it's that it happened before the world went mad, before the threats of predators and lawsuits and heavy traffic and all of the other looming threats that fill our world drove children indoors. But this was the 70's, and, like most parents, Mom and Dad barely blinked at the thought of us running around unsupervised. Actually, most days you and I were unceremoniously booted outside, sent off to entertain ourselves while Mom busied herself with housework, game shows, and soap operas.

Had we lived closer to town, no doubt I would have taken up with kids my own age, and spent those summer days playing soccer or baseball. You may have found friends to play dolls and tea parties with. But, as it happened, you and I were all we had.

ABODE

You always stuck close by me, following me around even when I didn't want to play with you. I thought your dolls were stupid, and had already outgrown the Lite Brite you loved. You didn't care that I didn't like your toys, or that I preferred toy cars, soccer balls, and comic books to dolls. We often met in the middle, playing board games like *Candyland* or *Chutes and Ladders*. You were, in a nutshell, the epitome of the tagalong little sister.

Looking back, those last summer days were green and gold. Autumn was blood and fire. Winter was bones and snow and ash. We were gone before the springtime melting began. But, during those first few weeks, we stood on the edge between the normal and paranormal, between madness and sanity, between dream and nightmare. We sensed that something was amiss, but we were still innocent, naïve. We certainly had no idea that we were about to plunge into the abyss.

At first, we mostly stayed in the yard. But, as the memory of the ghost we had seen faded, I convinced myself that I had dreamt it, and found myself more and more drawn to the woods.

We'd never had access to a true forest. Our old neighborhood had a few lots, but it was rare to find a patch of wood you couldn't see houses through in winter. We'd gone camping and to parks, of course, but those were manicured places, neatly divided into specific areas. They did not belong to the wild, anymore: they had been tamed, prettied up, made safe.

This was different. This was the wilderness: untamed, natural, ancient. Primordial. The woods were full of secrets and mysteries, and I was immediately drawn to them. Once I dared to venture beyond that stone wall that acted as an unofficial border between our land and the forest beyond, I became fascinated by the hidden faces the forest showed me. Boulders and deadfalls, patches of swamp and hidden glades: these things pulled me like a magnet. I grew almost addicted to the smell of pine, and the patterns of sunlight and shadow entwining on the forest floor.

The world is full of interesting nooks and crannies, when you are a kid. A fallen log, a stone wall, a stream, a boulder; these things fascinate us in our formative years, as we begin to learn about the world and its pocks and wrinkles. Before we learn how cruel and ugly life can truly be, the world is truly an amazing place, full of wonders. I picked up rocks to find out what creepy crawly things were slithering around below them, and made you scream more than once by pretending to eat them.

Soon the forest began to play tricks on me.

In my early explorations of the property, I found many trails, a maze of paths winding into the mysterious wild. I followed these old paths to ice-cold brooks and clear burbling streams, to mysterious bogs and silent meadows. Every day brought a new adventure. At first, I thought it was great.

Then I noticed that it was very, very hard to find the same trail twice. I spent days trying to locate a track I had followed previously, only to end up, time and again, back in the same spot. I didn't realize, at first, that this wasn't normal. I only thought it was an aspect of the woods that I didn't yet understand. Something I needed to learn.

Inevitably, I got lost. One August night I only found my way home as the last traces of pale grey light were fading from the sky. Mom and Dad were both in a panic. You ran to the door and hugged me. I mussed your hair, teasing you, but was secretly glad that I hadn't taken you with me.

After he finished switching me, Dad told me that our house faced east (sunrise) and that moss grew on the south side of trees.

ABODE

Mom, overhearing this, insisted it was a myth. Their conversation quickly devolved into a fight. I remember how this upset us. We were accustomed to them bickering, but we weren't used to hearing them scream at each other the way they did that night. I think it was the first time you heard the words *Fuck, Bitch,* and *Asshole,* and really knew what they meant, because you asked me about it the next day.

I barely felt the welts Dad left on me that night.

A few days later, Dad gave me a compass. "East," he said, jabbing his finger toward the rising sun. He did this out of Mom's hearing, and I knew he was, in his way, having the last word. He pointed at the road before our house. "This whole damn road runs north and south. If you get lost, listen for traffic. If there's no traffic, just go east. If you go north, there's nothing but woods for a couple hundred miles. Go south: woods and mountains. Go west: woods and swamp. You don't want to get lost in the Allagash, boy. You won't come out alive. Go East. East, toward the rising sun, or away from the setting sun. East, you'll come to the river or the road. If you can't see the sun, look at the moss. And if you ever get lost in winter, make yourself a little den out of pine branches and snow." He made shaping motions with his hands, and I realized that, though it wasn't even noon, he was already drunk.

He noticed my questioning look, and apparently thought I didn't understand what he was saying. "Like a little fort. You won't be comfortable, but you won't freeze. Maine winters are no joke. There's no gas stations in those woods. No neighbors. Lot of places for a boy to get lost." He looked toward the sun, squinting. "Or, follow a river or stream." He paused. "Did *any* of what I just told you sink into that thick skull of yours?"

I nodded and said something vague, then scampered off into the woods. His words were meant to scare me, but they only made me more curious. I couldn't wait to get back to the shady world that awaited me beyond the yard.

I think I wanted to get lost, even then. I wanted to emerge in someone else's yard, where some other father would, instead of berating me, throw a football to me, or teach me how to change the oil in a car. A father that would spend time with me, and talk to me like I, well, like I mattered.

As it turns out, Mom was right: moss grows on the north side here.

I only occasionally took you with me on these adventures. For the most part, you wanted to play with your dolls or swim in your little pool. You never really liked the woods. This worked out fine for me: I usually preferred to be by myself anyway.

One day I had to watch you while Mom and Dad went into town. Of course, I took you into the woods with me. You were a little scared, mostly because you had somehow gotten it into your head that poisonous snakes and giant spiders lived in the forest, and that the fallen leaves hid holes and quicksand that would swallow both of us up forever. But you didn't really argue. You just went where I told you, when I told you, chattering like a little bird. I feel bad now that I never really gave you a choice: I just told you that we were going to play in the woods that day.

It was hot that day. The air hung thick and sticky, heavy with humidity. We tramped into the woods, wandering from spot to spot. I showed you how to eat honeysuckle, scared you by picking up a centipede and pretending to eat it, threw a fat worm at you, and then protected you from a bumblebee. We saw something brown and furry scuttle past us, and argued about whether it was a bear, a raccoon, a rabbit, or a squirrel. Then we got into a debate about beavers, groundhogs, and woodchucks, and the differences between them. This led us into whole woodchuck-chucking-wood thing, and laughed at each other's attempts to get through the riddle. I still remember that, for some reason. Probably because it's one of the few good memories I have about that place.

I can't recall how long we were out there before we found that old logging trail. I just remember emerging from the shadows of the woods and finding what seemed like a road in the middle of the wilderness. Trees had been removed from a long but narrow swath of land on a jagged, rolling hill, which dropped away in waves before us. Because so many trees had been uprooted, the soil was very loose, as though it been turned with a giant tiller. I noticed a few signs of recent activity in the area; rusted chains, footprints. I saw hoof prints here and there, and thin trails that I thought must have been made by wagons or carts. But no people. No machinery. There were no tire treads, though this for some reason didn't seem either relevant or unusual to me at the time.

It was high noon, on a bright summer day, as we stood there. But something about that gash in the earth unnerved me. It seemed like a wound in the forest. I suppose it was. I don't consider myself a tree hugger or a bleeding heart, but that place made me uneasy. Jim Morrison's words rang through my head as I stood there, staring at the patch of logging carnage.

What have we done to our fair mother?

I looked at the hills on either side of the trail, where black shadows clustered in the daylight, and felt as though they had secrets. The touch of fear traced cold fingers down my spine, that feather-tickle that warns us something is amiss. After a moment, I realized what it was.

The forest was dead silent around us.

There were no birds in that spot. No squirrels chased one another through the branches. No tree frogs buzzed. Nothing moved. Nothing stirred. The forest around us usually rang with the haunting calls of chickadees, but here there was only silence.

It suddenly seemed like a dead place, and I had the distinct feeling that no human being should set foot in it.

At least, none living.

A cool breeze touched my cheek. It was the very first touch of winter, which was still far away. A promise of ice and cold and snow to come.

"He wants us to leave," you said suddenly.

I turned to look at you. You were wearing a pink shirt and a little ball cap, and your hair was white-blond in the sun. You were a tiny thing, but you looked at me with an expression far beyond your years.

"Who?" I asked, looking around. I saw no one. Heard no one.

You stared intently into a patch of trees. "The man in the hat," you whispered. "He's watching us."

I felt cold, suddenly, though the day was stifling hot. "Where?"

You pointed. I looked in the direction you were pointing in, my gaze following your finger. At first, I saw only a shadow.

Then I made out the shape of a human form. Or, what I thought was human.

Jeremiah.

I did not know who *he* was then.

I wish I didn't know now.

ABODE

His name, when he wore human form, was Jeremiah, though I didn't know that at the time. I didn't know who—or what—he was. I only saw a man in a dark suit standing at the edge of the tree line, watching us. I could not see his features, for the wide-brimmed hat he wore hid his face in shadow. He did not move or speak, but he caught my attention as though he had cast a spell on me. He projected—emanated—a feeling of malevolence and hatred so thick it gave me goosebumps.

That was the first time I knew that I was in the presence of something evil.

I rubbed my eyes, and he was gone. Every nerve in my body was on edge. I had no idea, then, what I had seen.

A cloud crossed the sun, casting the world into shadow. "Come on," I said. "Let's go home." I turned to go back.

"It's this way," you said, pointing in the opposite direction.

We argued, and then I let you have your way, certain that I would prove myself right. But we followed the path you chose, and emerged from the woods only a few minutes later, just a short distance down the road from our house. It made no sense to me, as we had set off in the opposite direction and walked for hours.

But when, I questioned you, you just shrugged. I remember your words, clearly. "Time flows differently here," you said. "He controls everything."

I just stared at you. I remember wondering how to break it to Mom and Dad that you were completely insane.

You just walked right past me, and then ran to play on the swing.

The next day, I set out in the same direction, and found the path we had started out on. Walking down it, I found myself on a thin trail that looked absolutely nothing like the trail we had followed the day before. The earth was unmolested, the trees growing thick and strong. I couldn't find the logging area.

This made me curious, because by then I had explored the area several times. I found another trail, and followed it for a time, until it started getting dark, but I never found the logging area. I didn't see anyone, though at one point I heard a horse in the distance. Eventually I grew uneasy—not to mention hungry—so I gave up and headed for home.

My luck was no better the next time I tried.

I spent several days crisscrossing the area, trying to find the logger's swath or the track, to no avail. Every day I went into the woods. And every day I found different landmarks. Different trees. Different paths. I tried marking them, but rarely found my markings again. Once I carved my initials on a tree. I found those again, but they were much higher up, and they looked weathered and worn.

For some reason, it did not immediately occur to me that I should find the same scenery by heading out in the same direction each day. I guess I chalked up the inconsistencies in the landscape to my own poor memory.

One day I found myself on the shore of a cold lake, looking across the water at a strange mountain. The mountain was grayish purple, as distant mountains are, but its colors seemed slightly different from those of the others around it. It had a strange hue, and seemed, from a distance, to be more rock than tree. I saw a small island in the middle of the lake, but knew it was too far to swim to.

A few days later, after heading in the same direction, I found myself in a swamp. I was able to make my way across a good part of it by hopping from one mossy tree stump to another. I looked

ABODE

behind me, and realized I could not see how to get back. I went forward, and then walked around the edge of the pond, crashing through burdocks and cat-o-nine tails and thoroughly soaking my sneakers. It was almost dark when I finally made it home, and I received the belt for my carelessness.

Another time I came across a strange pit that had apparently been hewn out of the natural stone. It had a weird shape to it, almost like that of a hoof. Someone had etched strange figures into the granite. I couldn't make much sense of them: they were an unfathomable mix of beasts and runes I didn't recognize.

I know, you would think that these things would have scared me, and I won't try to say that I wasn't a bit frightened, but at that time, at least at first, my curiosity overcame my fear. The only place that really gave me the creeps in those early days was that swatch of cleared land.

Sometimes in my dreams, you are there, in that sinister patch of wood on the other side of that logging track, standing in the shadows, just out of the reach of the sun.

With him.

Chapter Five

It is now three days since I left off. It hasn't been a great week. Some jerk on a cell phone rear-ended me the other day, and, even though the X-ray showed nothing, I've had a pounding headache ever since.

I have so many questions for you. My thoughts burn with them.

I want to know, of course, what you remember of your former life. I would love to find out if you remember that time, or any of us, at all. Those would be the first things. But I have a million smaller questions as well. I wonder if your food tastes are the same, if you are still left-handed. I wonder if you loved the same Disney movies and fairy tales in this life as you did in the last. Do things return to you in dreams, in déjà vu? Did you remember any of this when you were young, even if those memories have faded since?

I Googled you, the other day, and I paid a stupid amount of money to one of those internet research sites to gather background information on you. It isn't that I mean to pry. As I've said before, I mean you no harm. It's just that there are so many things I want to know.

The answers have I found only lead me to more questions. More mysteries. Things that make my head spin, and find me curled up in a fetal ball, crying, in the brightest hours of the day.

You named your eldest daughter Annabelle. That was Mom's name.

ABODE

Your birthday, February 18th, is the same as, well, the day you died. You were born, to the day, a year after the fire. (Where were you during that time? In some realm where the dead and the unborn wait together? Or in a grey fog of nothing? Did you choose to come back? Or did someone—or something—send you?)

The birthmark in your old kindergarten school photo matches the current one on your bio page exactly. As does your hairline.

I also noticed that in your bio page you mention that you love Italian food, especially pizza, and that you do ballet to keep in shape. You loved your ballet class when you were little. And pizza and spaghetti were your favorite foods.

You have an orange, fluffy cat and a dog named Buster, a Border Collie. As did we.

Mom and Dad were both artists. You loved to draw. And, judging by your bio, so do you.

Some may see these things as coincidences, tiny, insignificant details. I see threads, connecting the present to the past. Even now, after only a fleeting contact, I see so many parallels.

I understand that you aren't entirely you. But some part of your core being, perhaps the energy that was in you when you were born, was once my little sister.

I'm not the first to believe in reincarnation. Some remain dubious, but there are some cases that are hard to ignore. Take little Edward Austrian, who remembered details of life in the muddy, rat-infested trenches of World War I. The little boy hated dreary days, and often complained that the bullet in his neck hurt. He gave specific details about the life of a soldier who had died of a shot through the throat on a rainy day.

42

There is also the child who remembered living the luxurious life of a Hollywood star. He knew tiny details about the life of an actor he claimed to recognize as himself in a film from 1923. And then there's the case of Shanti Devi. You may have heard of her. She remembered living another life, over a hundred years earlier, and knew so many details about the woman that an official commission concluded she had been reincarnated.

There are many, many other cases, each more incredible than the last. Of course, some of these show up in gossip rags next to the amazing three-headed woman or the mermaid a fisherman dragged up from the sea, which is probably only a wooden carving done by some guy in Florida. I believe that there is a grain of truth behind even the most outrageous lie. All of these stories can't be fake.

You were always an old soul. You'd been here before, you know, even before you became my little sister. You spoke German before you learned English. That would have been fine if we had, in fact, been German. We weren't. Nor were any of our friends or family members. But you, nevertheless, kept saying German words. Mom told me once, after you died, that you frightened her half to death by describing the catacombs below Paris. "We went there," you said. "We hid among the dead. I got lost in the dark."

I watched a documentary about Paris just a few months ago, which mentioned, albeit briefly, the fact that both German and Allied forces hid in the catacombs.

I hope you chose to come back. To find me again.

I suppose we'll never know.

I'm not sure, given the choice, if I would decide to come back. I think I'd rather fade away, dissolve into the comfort of unbeing. What if it's never over? What if there is no end? Just eternity?

ABODE

Moments fall from us like drops of water: trying to hold on to time is like trying to catch raindrops. But just as water falls into the ground, to emerge in a lake or river, evaporate, and again become rain, I believe that we are all on an endless journey.

I don't think all of us are reincarnated. I don't know what happens to those that aren't. The first law of science holds that nothing can be created or destroyed, but can only change form. That mantra, which belongs in the realm of science labs and school textbooks, is one of the few things that ever gave me comfort.

Because it's the only way any of this makes sense.

I cannot begin to tell you how much it soothes me to know that you made it back from the unknown realm. You defeated death and won. And you were just a little girl.

Do you remember any of it? I wonder.

And, although I'm thrilled to know that you live and breathe, I still cannot rest easy. One terrible thought keeps crawling, spider-like, into my days, even in the calmer moments. A thought that has, more than once, been the only thin thread keeping me from killing myself.

I have this sickening feeling that Jeremiah will be waiting for me beyond the grave.

Chapter Six

One of the earliest signs that something was not right in our home was the footsteps in the attic. We all had heard them, plain as day. Since my room was nearest the stairs, I guess I experienced them the most. Almost every night, I heard the distinct sound of someone moving up and down the attic stairs, which shared a wall with my room. The first few times, I assumed it was just Mom and Dad putting away boxes. It took a few weeks for me to realize that it wasn't them.

I had to get up one night to go to the bathroom, and I passed their room on the way. They had left their bedroom door open a crack, and so as I walked past I glimpsed their sleeping forms. Dad was snoring loudly, so there was no question about where he was. Mom was a distinct form on the mattress beside him. I did my business and went back to my bed. The room had gotten colder. I dove under the covers, shivering, and listened to the wind through the trees until I grew drowsy again. Just as I was about to fall asleep, I heard the steps coming down from the attic.

I could hear Dad snoring, so there was no chance that it was him. I knew the steps weren't Mom's; she always scurried up quickly up or down stairs, and she wasn't heavy enough to make that much noise. Besides, she always wore sneakers or slippers around the house.

I turned up my little radio, trying to drown them out with the sounds of Dr. Demento.

I remember we sat down to supper one night (spaghetti), when we heard the distinct *thunk* of footsteps crossing the floor or, to us, ceiling). All four of us were at the table, so there was no chance that it was one of us making the noise.

You looked frightened. "Who's that?" You asked.

Mom had gone pale. "Daniel?"

Dad put his fork down and went upstairs to check. We heard him climbing the stairs to the second floor. Impossibly, at the exact same time he was going up, we heard the steps going down into the cellar. This was followed by the heavy thud of a door closing in the basement.

Mom was by then as white as a sheet.

We heard Dad coming back down the stairs. As soon as he walked into the kitchen, the steps once more were above us.

Then they—it—moved down the wall. Straight down the wall, as though that thing was walking across the wallpaper. Its tread was heavy enough to make the paintings tilt, and to rattle the dishes in the cupboard.

"What was that?" Mom demanded. She looked at each of us in turn, as though we were playing a joke on her.

You looked up at her, calmly. "He's gone into the cellar now," you said. "He's gone back into the dark."

No one answered you. Not even me.

We finished our spaghetti in a thick, terse silence.

Another night, not long after that, I was standing at the kitchen sink, doing dishes. We must have been in the house a few weeks by then, maybe a month, by then. There is, or was, a window above the kitchen sink. This offered a view of the yard, with its unfamiliar trees and slopes and brush piles and boulders, and, beyond that, the forest. The sun had just fallen below the horizon. There was still a bit of pale, pinkish-gray light in the sky, but it was pitch black beyond the tree line.

I happened to glance up and saw, clear as day, two red eyes glaring at me from the darkened woods. I froze in terror, and my flesh prickled into goosebumps. I kept staring. I wanted to move, but I couldn't. I was rooted in place. The eyes stared back, burning into me. I felt hatred emanating from it, a rage so thick it was actually palpable.

Then the thing moved, and I had a glimpse of its shape as it slipped back into the woods. The creature seemed to be made of blackness, as though it had somehow been formed of night itself. It seemed part beast and part man. It bore the faint outline of a human, but its legs were like those of a deer or goat.

Once it was gone, I regained control of myself, and immediately started screaming. Mom came running, and did her best to calm me down. You followed her, asking question after question. You seemed more curious than frightened.

"I-I-I saw a-a shadow monster in the forest," I said. I didn't usually stutter, but I was terrified.

Dad followed Mom into the room, and reached us in time to hear this. "Just a deer," he said. "Nothing to worry about."

I shook my head. "It wasn't a deer. It had red eyes and-"

"Oh, for Christ's sake," Dad went to the fridge for a beer. "Enough of that nonsense. There's deer all over these woods."

"I know what deer look like," I said. "It wasn't a deer. It was a monster."

"Grow up and stop acting like a baby," Dad snapped. "There's nothing out there but wild animals."

"No more scary movies for you," Mom chided. "You're scaring yourself silly."

I saw that it was pointless to argue, so I pretended to believe them. I pretended Dad was right. But I knew damn well that deer didn't have eyes that glowed like embers. And they sure as hell didn't walk on two legs.

I suppose Dad got some flak from Mom for snapping at me, since he went to town that night and got us pizza for dinner. You, me, Mom and Dad, and even Buster and Lucky, settled into the living room, in front of the TV. We watched some sitcom—I think it was *Mork And Mindy*—while we ate. I remember feeling as though we were in a little bubble of safety, like there was a force field around us, protecting us. You and I were safe, stretched out on that hideous avocado shag rug, one of the last ties to the comfort and coziness of our old home. Back then, I thought Mom and Dad could protect us. I felt safer near them. We both did, I think.

I stayed up as long as I could that night, but eventually I was ordered to go to bed. I turned my nightlight on and lay down in my bed, under the afghan Grandma had made me, painfully aware of every creak and groan the house gave off. Every sound the woods made at night seemed sinister and eerie. The moonlight coming through the tree outside my window cast strange shadows on the wall, and I lay there watching the play of darkness and light, both fascinated and terrified by the strange shapes the shadows made. Outside, the wind picked up as a storm rolled in off the coast. The branches scraped against the house like bony fingers. The sound made me think of skeletons, reaching up from a cold, dark grave to scratch at my windows.

Eventually, I closed my eyes.

That was the night I had my first nightmare about Jeremiah. I remember it still.

That dream haunts me to this day.

That is one thing you and I experienced together. Almost every night we lived in that house, you and I had dark, bloody dreams. At first, we didn't speak of them. But as the dreams grew stronger, we began waking at the same time, you and I, both of us screaming at the top of our lungs.

"Tell me your dream," I remember saying to you, one morning, when you came to me in tears. "I'll take it away."

You looked up at me, your pale blue eyes full of innocence and hope. "Can you?"

I nodded.

I of course had no power over your nightmares. But I could make you think I did. You were very, very gullible back then. You believed anything I told you. When I insisted that cats were actually aliens, you spent an hour trying to get Lucky to pass on a message from his home world. I told you that lizards were baby dragons, and that there were elves living in our attic. I told you that caterpillars were really evil wizards, and that bumblebees had killed all the unicorns. You ate it all up, every outrageous thing I told you.

Most of the time, I was being a mean older brother. But that time, I really was trying to help.

You believed me, as always. And you then described to me, piece by piece, the same dream I had had.

In that first dream, you and I went down into the cellar, and found a door there, leading into the hill. Or, I suppose, under the hill. The door was closed, but I saw a ring of reddish, fiery light behind it, as though the door opened onto an inferno. In my dream, you opened the door and walked through it, but it shut behind you. When I reached out and touched the doorknob, I burned my hand.

ABODE

The pain carried through to reality. I remember Mom and Dad rushing in as I woke screaming. The burn, when I looked at it, bore the outline of a strange insignia. I bear a pale scar to this day, though the scar itself happened later.

These are the things I carry with me, even through the paler hours.

Chapter Seven

Days passed, grew into weeks. Little incidents piled up. Bigger occurrences started to happen. Each day died slowly, a lingering death. This was a time of shadows and noises, of unknown smells and figures moving in the trees at night.

We heard footsteps in empty rooms. Or voices. An object would move inexplicably, or a door would open or close, seemingly of its own accord. Something would fall from a wall or a shelf, though nothing touched it.

At first, the strange occurrences we had experienced were isolated incidents, cushioned by the days and even weeks that separated one event from another.

The lulls didn't last. It always started again. Every incident was worse than the last, as though it/they/he was growing stronger.

The things we experienced at this point were frightening, but they were not, at least not then, daily happenings. A door might slam, or a cupboard would silently swing open. We would hear footsteps, or perhaps smell something unusual. Then days would pass without incident, and the tension would ease a bit. Sometimes we would hear only one or two footsteps or a brief murmur of voices. Sometimes there was nothing at all, only a thick, oppressive silence.

The scariest things weren't the actual incidents. A dish falling off a shelf is hardly the stuff of nightmares. What frightened me at that point was the sense of an evil presence nearby, the heavy feeling that we were always being watched. I became more and more afraid of the possibility that something malevolent and unseen moved in the nooks and crannies of our house, slid through walls.

Mom kept herself busy with housework, but she grew pale and tight-lipped. She said little, but I saw her wring her hands as she looked out into the woods at night, and she took to wearing a crucifix, which she had never done before.

Little good that did her.

We were all uneasy. Even you. You didn't like to go up the stairs alone, and soon wouldn't stay in any room but your own by yourself. You followed me around like a little shadow, clutching your toy dolls.

I was in the backyard with Buster one morning, kicking a soccer ball around, drinking a bottle of Moxie. I kicked the ball past the tree line. When I ran to get it, I saw the path, clear as day, a dark line cut into the trees, almost like a tunnel leading into the shadowed green silence of the woods. I had never seen it before. I remember standing there, puzzled, wondering how I had overlooked it all this time.

The trail went straight into the wilderness, crossing over the hill behind our house. Where the lawn met the forest, the tree line was black, as though the woods were plunged into eternal night.

I had the sense that the forest was waiting for me.

That I was being summoned.

I turned and faced the other direction, and saw the morning sun, still several hours away from being overhead. Through the screen on the kitchen window, there came the familiar sound of glasses clinking as Mom did the breakfast dishes in the sink.

Then I walked into the wilderness.

I wasn't curious so much as drawn. I don't recall thinking about whether or not to explore the path. I just went, as though called. I had a strange sense of being propelled, pushed almost, as I walked past my ball and into the woods. I recall feeling as though I was a puppet, and something unseen was pulling my strings, manipulating my arms and legs.

The path led me up over the hilltop behind our house, and then down the other side. Although I had explored the woods quite a bit, nothing around me looked very familiar. I was in new, uncharted territory, and I looked around with the eye of an explorer.

I felt as though I had stepped into a dream, for everything around me had a strange, almost dreamlike quality.

I saw a break in the tree line, an empty space beyond the branches that belied either grassland or open water. Curious, I drew closer, leaving the path to cut directly through the wood. I found myself standing on the banks of a small pond that stretched across a valley. It was more of a bog, really. The water was dank and murky with mud and debris, and the moss grew thick over the rocks and fallen pines along its banks. I don't know how long I stood at the edge of that water, but I could sense power in that place. Here and there, dead trees reached up from the water, like skeletons. And far in the distance, I saw the top of a large, oddly-colored hill peeking over the trees.

I walked down the bank, and came across a noose, hanging randomly from a tree. I do not know whether I named that bog, or whether the woods or the forces within them gave me its name, but I knew where I was. *Dead Man's Pond.*

I walked to the edge of the water and looked down at my reflection. I thought for a moment that I saw something behind me, but when I turned, there was nothing there.

In time, I turned back, returned to the path, and continued on.

ABODE

The track brought me up a curve that rose with the climb of a fairly steep hill. Here, the footing was mostly pine needles. The air was hushed and still. I found myself at the top of the rise, in a circle made of stones. In the center lay a huge, strange boulder with a split in the middle. I have rarely seen rocks that big. It was cracked, and I could see blackness in the fissure. Beyond, the trees cast long black shadows that seemed to whisper and hiss with dark, forgotten secrets.

Around the next bend, I stopped short.

A cabin stood before me, nestled deep within the woods, framed by two white pines. It was very small, just one room, I would guess, and looked very, very old. Paint that had once been white was now dingy and peeling: the boards that framed the doors and windows had faded to the color of dust. Odd and random pieces of junk lay in front of it; an old wheelbarrow, a broken bench, some rusted tools. A single wooden chair sat on the porch. It looked old and worn and abandoned, a forgotten relic.

The cabin was pitch-black inside. I could see nothing through the windows. Just darkness.

There was something there, in those shadows. I couldn't identify it. I didn't want to. I only know I felt—or sensed— something malevolent stirring within that place, watching me. The energy it gave off was predatory, and yet the cabin itself seemed to gather an oppressive air of doom around it, as though terrible things had happened within those walls.

I saw movement in the window, the faintly distinguishable form of something pale and grey.

I stood frozen, unable to move. Terror gripped my stomach in an icy hand. My throat tightened. I felt my heart pounding like a drum in my chest. My eyes were fixed to the darkened windows. Again, I saw the shadows shift as an undefined shape moved within those pitch-black shadows. My skin shriveled into gooseflesh.

I felt my right foot step forward. Then my left.

A loud, terrible voice boomed out over the sullen wild. "Bless us, oh Lucifer, before you destroy us. *Ave Weresh*."

With that, the spell was broken. A flock of birds rose from the trees, and the sky filled with black wings. I suddenly was in control of myself again. I ran all the way back.

It was pitch-black outside when I got home. The clocks said it was nearly midnight, but I didn't believe it. Mom and Dad were frantic with worry.

I cannot explain the time frame. I remember the morning sun, the soccer ball tucked against my side. I remember walking into the woods with that sun against my back, and then running back across the yard in pitch blackness.

I would have sworn I had only been gone a little while, an hour at most. The bottle of Moxie soda in my hand was still cold, and when I took a sip, it was still fizzy.

I was sent to bed without supper. I went to my room, tried to read, but couldn't concentrate: the words and pictures of my favorite comic book just weren't connecting in my jumbled thoughts. Finally, I stood and went to the bathroom window, which looked over across the back yard. I tried to see the path, but darkness made the woods a shadowy, featureless nightscape, and I couldn't discern much.

The next day, when I finished my chores, I went straight to the back yard.

The path wasn't there.

ABODE

I spent the next several afternoons in the woods, looking for the path that led to the pond and cabin and that strange rock. I crisscrossed back and forth across the area, and eventually found myself again before that strange, dark lake.

I thought back, trying to remember landmarks, and recalled that the cabin had been flanked by two white pines. Two similar trees stood in a spot I knew that wasn't far from the house, so I set out through the woods again.

Sure enough, I found them. They were a lot taller, and much wider. And between them, I noticed a flat area. I stepped forward to investigate, and found a foundation, where the cabin had once stood.

I realized that the woods I had visited at night were younger than what I stood in now. Some of the trees still stood: others had fallen. New ones had grown.

It sounds crazy, I know. But I was seeing the same land as it had appeared at different times. In one spot, there was a wash where a bank had collapsed. I had already seen it in various stages: new, overgrown, whole, within the space of a few days. But I hadn't understood what I was looking at.

This was not the only time that this strange phenomenon occurred to us. There were other moments, but I will come to those soon enough. The first, I have already touched on: the logging road. It was years before I truly understood what happened and realized that, in those moments we stood among the loose soil of the gash, we were looking back through time, at land that had once been cleared, but had, in the intervening centuries, grown wild again.

You would think that, even without completely understanding what was going on, these odd incidents would have been enough to keep me out of the woods, but I guess I was more curious and confused at that point than scared. The terror set in later, when I thought back on the moment. It sets in now, revisiting it. But at the time, I thought it was kind of neat. I continued my explorations, and kept finding trails that would apparently appear one day, only to disappear the next.

I heard things, in that forest. Voices. Whispers. I heard branches crack, as though stepped on, when nothing was there. At the time, I chalked these things up to my unfamiliarity with the area. Perhaps I was too foolish to be scared. I thought I was just getting lost, or walking too far. I told myself I had dreamed it. I told myself I was mad.

Maybe I was.

Maybe fear colors all my recollections.

Maine has a lot of uncultivated land. There are still forests that have never been cut down, thick patches of woods that have always grown wild. Dozens—if not hundreds—of old paths, trails, and roads weave through that wilderness: hunter's tracks, logger's roads, deer paths, ATV trails. Many of these are forgotten, and a good number of them are now abandoned and overgrown. Some lead to Canada. Others wind toward tiny, remote towns like Jackman. Some go nowhere.

Some lead places one should not dare to step.

Chapter Eight

The next thing that happened to me still scares the crap out of me to this day. I have goosebumps, even writing this.

I had found a lot of cool trees, but there was one in particular I liked to climb. It was close to the house, only a short distance beyond the tree line. I thought it looked like a giant centipede rearing up from the earth, which I thought was great. I liked to use its 'legs' as a ladder.

One particular day, I decided to climb it, and go higher than I had before. I got a good ways off the ground and looked over our land. I could see the house, and even look at our parents' bedroom window. I had only been there a few minutes when the sun went behind a cloud. I looked to the east, where the shadow of a coming storm darkened the sky. Somewhere in the distance, I heard the roll of the thunder drum. (That's what I called it then.)

I was sitting in the branches, resting against the tree trunk, when I heard a loud crack behind me, the sound of a branch breaking underfoot. It seemed to come from directly behind me. This would have been bad enough had I been on the ground. But I was in a tree, several yards above the ground.

As I turned my head to look behind me, I felt two hands on my back, shoving me forward. Suddenly I was airborne, my stomach lurching and heaving in sudden panic. Terror reached an arm down my throat, clenching itself around my insides and bowels. You know that feeling you get on a roller coaster, when you just start to move down over the edge? That's what it was like.

It was sheer luck that I landed how I did. I hit the ground just beside a large boulder. I very easily could have cracked my head open. Instead, I landed feet-first in a pile of leaves. My legs didn't break my fall entirely: they crumpled and I slid, falling backwards, smacking my head against the ground.

The world changed for me in that moment. It became a threatening, menacing place, filled with unseen dangers and unspeakable evil.

It's never quite changed back.

I got my bearings, and then shakily stood up. I heard another crack behind me, and didn't turn to see what it was. I sprinted back for the house, my spine tickling with terror. There was something behind me. I heard it. I felt it.

I did not dare turn around.

Mom was in the kitchen on the phone with a friend. She must have seen the terror on my face, because she froze, mid-sentence. "Angie? Let me call you back later. Ok, bye." She hung up the receiver and crossed the floor to me, scooching down to get to my eye-level. "What happened? You're white as a sheet."

"I-I . . . I just . . . I just . . ." I couldn't talk. I was just stammering and sniffling.

"What is it? Are you hurt?"

I looked at her face and saw the worry there, and knew I couldn't tell her the truth. "I fell out of a tree."

Mom went into, well, Mom mode, checking my head for bumps and asking me a million questions. I was telling her for about the fifth time that I was ok when we heard Dad's car pull up into the yard. Mom gave me a kiss on the forehead, stood up, and straightened her hair. "Go boil some water," she said. "I'll make you a hot chocolate."

ABODE

Never mind that it was 90 degrees, if not hotter. I loved hot chocolate. You and I both did. Actually, we liked a lot of the same things; hot chocolate, mac n' cheese, cereal, grilled cheese sandwiches with tomato soup, strawberry ice cream, chocolate milk. These things were staples of our childhood. The normal part of it, at least.

These are the things that bind me to you now.

I dutifully went back through the house to the kitchen, and put a kettle of water on the stove. While I was waiting for it to boil, I glanced out the kitchen window, looking into the yard. I thought I saw someone—or something—moving through the trees, but it was gone before I could really make out what it was.

I just stood there, staring into the woods, until the whistle from the kettle drew me away.

Mom made hot chocolate with extra marshmallows and, I suspect, a shot of liqueur. I began to feel warm and relaxed, and could have almost convinced myself that I was safe, if I hadn't still been able to feel the spot on my back where I had been pushed.

The next day, I saw the bruises in the mirror. They were almost perfect handprints, except for one thing. Each hand had seven fingers, instead of five.

Chapter Nine

One of my clearest memories—and one of the ones that pains me the most—is that of Grandma's first, and only, visit.

I was sitting on the back porch one morning with a glass of orange juice and a *Spiderman* comic, watching the woodchuck that lived in the debris pile behind the garage. Cute little guy. I couldn't help but giggle when I saw him waddle across the yard. The trees were still green and gold, with only a slight tinge of red here and there. Autumn was still a few weeks off.

I hadn't gone into the woods since that day. But every time I looked in that direction, I saw the centipede tree. It seemed to be waiting for me. Lurking.

The sound of a car horn broke the stillness, splitting the air. Startled, I jumped up and went inside, following Mom through the house to the front door. As Mom opened the door, we both saw Grandma getting out of her tan station wagon. This puzzled me. Usually we knew well in advance when Grandma would be visiting, because Mom always made us clean our rooms and tidy the house before she arrived. I looked up at Mom's face, and realized that she was as surprised as I was. She covered it, though, wiping her hands on her apron before untying it and trotting lightly down the front steps. She moved with a little bounce, as though her mother's arrival had lifted a weight from her shoulders.

"Mom," Mom hugged Grandma, and kissed her on the cheek. "This is a surprise. I wasn't expecting you."

ABODE

"I thought maybe you could use some help," Grandma greeted me with hugs and kisses. She smelled of lavender, baby powder, church, and Ben-Gay.

"You didn't have to do that," Mom said. "We're almost finished unpacking."

Grandma glanced at the house. "You still have a lot to do, dear. This place is a shambles!"

Mom brushed a strand of hair from her forehead. "We're getting there."

Grandma leaned into her car, and pulled out a box that had once held chocolate chip cookies, no doubt from the soup kitchen she volunteered at. The box looked fairly large and heavy, but Grandma held it easily. She held it out to Mom. "Here," she said. "I wanted you to have these."

Mom took it, but didn't open it. I heard glass clinking inside the box as the movement jarred its contents. "Let's go inside," she said. "I'll make some lemonade."

Grandma surveyed her daughter. "You look pale. And you're much too thin."

You appeared at the doorway then, a pale small thing stepping from shadow into sunlight. You were still in your favorite pink pajamas. You rubbed your eyes, then saw Grandma and let out a little squeal of happiness. I remember the way the smile beamed out of you. It was as if someone had turned a light on in your soul. You ran to Grandma and gave her a big hug, and then we all went indoors.

Mom led us all into the living room, which by then was fairly complete. Dad's paintings hung on the walls amidst carefully-placed macramé pieces; our console TV again displayed Mom's collection of owls and a weird, slender brown vase; and

Grandma's handmade lace doilies once more sat beneath our huge, bulky lamps. All this, of course, was set off by our avocado shag rug and brown art-deco furniture.

It was hideous, even by 70's standards.

Mom set the box carefully down on the coffee table, opened it, and took out a newspaper-wrapped object. She went very still when she saw what it was, and the smile fell from her face. She looked at Grandma, concern and confusion furrowing her brow. "Your angel collection? But why? You've been collecting them as long as I can remember."

"Oh," Grandma said casually. "I've decided to move into a smaller place."

Mom looked as though she'd been slapped. "What? When did you decide this?"

"A few months ago. I didn't want to worry you; you were busy with the move. Don't worry, dear. I'm quite happy. The house is a bit much for me. The new place has a cute little apartment. Georgette and Julienna are there already. We'll play cards every day. They organize trips into Boston for plays and things like that, and it's full service. We won't have to cook or clean unless we want to! Doesn't that sound lovely?"

Mom looked absolutely flabbergasted. She opened and closed her mouth several times, as though she couldn't decide what to say. "But you love cooking," she said, finally.

"Can we have your house?" I asked. I had absolutely no tact.

Mom shot me a withering stare. "Go boil some water for tea," she told me.

"I thought you wanted lemonade."

"Fine. Go make lemonade."

"Tea sounds lovely," Grandma said.

ABODE

"Tea it is," Mom said.

You raised your chin, squinting a bit. "But I want lemonade."

Mom sighed. "Just get both."

I just stopped to think for a moment, wondering why I remember the tea/lemonade debate. It was a tiny moment, one of a million everyday things that happened in that house. Even later on, when we were living in a nightmare, there were still bits and pieces of regular life, fragments of ordinariness, everyday events.

I guess it was so normal, so happy, that it stands out against the murky gloom of my other recollections.

I shrugged and got up. I saw a shadow move as I walked into the kitchen, but it was brief and fleeting, so I hesitated for only a moment before continuing on. I made tea for Grandma, and mixed yellow powder into water for you and I, pouring yours into your favorite pink plastic cup. I remember giving Grandma the tea. When she reached out for the china saucer, which had pale pink roses on it, she looked up, met my eyes, and smiled. Her smile seemed slightly forced, as though something was bothering her, but I didn't question it.

Mom sent us outside to play. She and Grandma spoke for a long time inside, while you and I played in the yard. When Dad came home, he fired up the barbeque. We ate outdoors that night, on the old picnic table in the back yard. It was a classic New England summer feast: grilled hot dogs and hamburgers dripping with grease; potato salad with egg, celery, and onion; steamed clams from a small store down the road; and fresh corn and blueberries Mom had bought at the farmer's market in town.

I still remember the sweet, sun-drenched taste of the corn, and the way the butter melted onto it. And I fucking hate myself for that.

I can't recall what color Grandma's eyes were. I don't know what happened to her house, or to the rest of her things. I don't know what she told Mom that day, though, looking at things through the lens of adulthood, I suspect she may have had health problems. These things are lost to memory, where I can never retrieve them. I can't even remember what Grandma's voice sounded like.

But that stupid piece of bright yellow corn is still crystal clear in my mind.

Grandma stayed the weekend. We spent a lot of time drinking iced tea and lemonade, eating the cookies she baked the next day, and playing Spades with a beat-up set of cards. We sat on the porch, eating ice cream from soup bowls, and you proudly showed off your cartwheeling skills. Grandma asked us if we were looking forward to starting school, chatted with Mom about gardens and recipes and how to properly fertilize tomatoes (coffee and newspapers), and spent two nights in the spare room. Then, Sunday afternoon, she gave us both a big hug, and told us to be good, and said she'd see us at Thanksgiving. Then she just drove off. She was gone as suddenly as she had arrived.

I—we—never saw her again.

You're probably expecting me to tell you that Grandma sensed something and fled the house, screaming. That she had a terrible car accident, and never made it home, or called the next day to tell us she'd had a terrible premonition. Perhaps you're wondering if she died unexpectedly that very week.

None of those things happened. What did happen, not long after that, was a massive stroke.

I didn't know when I said goodbye that day that it was goodbye forever. I had not yet been touched by death. Had I known, I would have kissed her wrinkled, velvet-soft cheek, hugged her longer, told her how much I loved her. Instead, I gave a quick, dutiful hug, said I would see her on Turkey Day, and asked her to make chicken drumsticks when we went to visit.

We always think we have time with our loved ones. We think we have time to change, to improve ourselves, to face our problems and heal the things that eat us from within. We think time is our servant, when in fact it is our master. We are mortal, ethereal souls trapped in fragile, imperfect bodies of flesh and blood and water and bone. We are made of atoms that come from the earth, sea, and sky. And long before those things were here, we were stardust, floating in the abyss of eternal night.

Sooner or later, we all return to that darkness.

As a scientist once said, we are dead stars, looking back up at the sky. At mysteries we will never understand.

At the time, I believed, quite simply, that good people went to heaven, and bad people went to hell. At the time, I believed that the earth was an orderly place, and that all its pieces—races, cultures, religions—fit together neatly.

In truth, the borders of our humanity are drenched in blood.

Chapter Ten

In time, bored with the back yard and wary, by then, of venturing into the woods, I decided to go across the street and explore the fields and the woods over there. Perhaps I hoped maybe that the heaviness, the occult thickness that I sensed in the air, did not extend across the road.

I was wrong.

The first time I went across the street I didn't make it very far. The field was green and gold in the summer sunlight. I heard the insistent buzzing of crickets and tree frogs as I entered the field, picking my way past clumps of goldenrod, honeysuckle, and mint as I walked toward the wooded area on the other side. A group of carrion birds clustered around something further down in the field, where the old pasture sloped down to meet the trees and river.

As I drew closer to the tree line, I noticed strange stone formations in the field. One was shaped like a bench or a flat, low, table. A small circle of boulders surrounded it.

A bit further on, I came across a perfectly rounded hay mound. It took me a moment to realize what seemed unusual about it. I could see through it. Stepping closer, I realized that pipes had been driven through the mound. By the ends, which were grooved, I suspected there may once have been lenses in them. One looked directly north and south. I found another that ran east to west.

Beyond, where the field met the forest, I saw a dark hole in the trees. The path looked almost like a tunnel. I had the sense that something was watching, and I felt myself taken by a thick, strangling fear. I was not brave enough to go further that day. I turned and went back to the relative safety of the house. But it didn't take long for me to try again.

Perhaps I was curious.

Perhaps I was called.

On my second venture, I went past the stone circle, and entered the woods. The path was overgrown, but still easy to follow. It led me to a little grove overlooking the river, where I found the old Kent cemetery.

I think that my visit to that cemetery was the first time I understood the essence of death. The main word that comes to mind is numbness. Death is bereft of any sensation. The flesh has become just meat, dead, lifeless. The spirit changes form, and I think in many cases it dissolves. If you stand still in a cemetery, and clear your mind, you can sense that void, the currents flowing through the river of time. You feel that other realm, and how thin the walls that separate it from our own.

I felt death walking through that ancient cemetery. I felt time presiding over the primal forest and the ancient hillsides. I stood there for some time, sensing and pondering the endless, yawning abyss that waits on the other side of our last breaths. For a brief, razor sharp moment, I understood. I felt the history and the power of this cold, northern land.

And then I was just a boy, standing in a graveyard.

Many of the stones were so old and worn that the inscriptions were no longer legible. One moss-covered crypt stood in the center of the boneyard. The rest of the graves were plain, with thin, worn gravestones that bore little or no decoration, beyond a name and date.

I started reading the names and dates on the tombstones. Some were too worn to be legible, but others I could make out. I still remember many of the names. Josephine. Agnes. Marc. Jacob. Martin. Isabelle. Guy. Julia. Elizabeth. Phillip. Anthony. Joey.

There were, in all, forty-three graves. Seventeen of them were children. Only a few seem to have lived longer than a few years, though a handful lived to be about ten or so.

So many children dead.

It is no secret that infancy survival rates were much lower in those days. Miscarriages, stillbirths, and infant deaths were not uncommon. But seventeen is not, by any means, common.

I came across a matched set of stones with little cherubs. Reading the names and dates, I realized the double grave belonged to twins. *Jessamine and George, 1882-1891.*

They had been my age when they died. I felt sad for them, and looked for a flower to put on the grave, but there was nothing blooming in the vicinity.

I noticed another grave, more recent. Joseph Kent, who had died just over a decade before we moved in. He too, was young, only nineteen or so.

I stayed there a little while, reading the names and dates. I noticed that many of the dead in that place had passed in the winter. Looking at the wilderness around me, I wondered how anyone had dared approach it one on one, without the power of modern tools and inventions.

The cemetery seemed timeless, as though a veil had fallen there, blocking it from the outside world. I felt closer to the land of the dead than that of the living. I could no longer hear any birds, crickets, or tree frogs. Not a single leaf moved.

ABODE

I sensed a shift in the atmosphere, subtle, but palpable. I again felt as though I were being watched, and looked around, but saw nothing there. The feeling only grew more intense. The sun dipped behind a cloud, and a raven screamed. I was overcome by a strange certainty that the earth would open beneath me, or that zombies would start crawling out of the ground.

I ran back across the street. When I reached the yard, you were playing jump rope in the yard. You looked up at me, smiling, and asked if I would play a game of Uno with you.

I dream of laughter, of feeling happy when I turn my face to the sun. These things, however, never open themselves to me. It's as though I am looking at them through glass. I am winter, looking at summer through a window.

And you, you are a spring that never bloomed.

Chapter Eleven

You and I started school not long after that. The bus didn't come all the way down our road, so we had to walk to the corner, which took about ten minutes. That was a different time, an era where kids were booted out the door in the morning, and given their own keys so they could let themselves in at night. Mom went with us to the bus stop on the first day, but then, after making sure we knew where to go, she and Dad just left it to us to get to the bus stop and back. Nowadays, they'd likely be arrested for child abuse for giving us that freedom. I understand the reasons for being vigilant against strangers in low, dusty cars that lure children into nightmares with promises of candy. But at the same time … if children aren't trusted to walk two blocks alone, how will they ever gain independence?

I'm sorry. I digress. Maybe I would feel differently if I had children of my own. I don't. My ex-girlfriend and I almost did, once, but she couldn't stay clean, and she lost the baby.

If it had been a girl, I was going to name it after you.

Fragments.

We never had any bad experiences on the walk, at least, not at first. We couldn't wait to grab our paper lunch bags and get on that bright yellow bus. Even early on, you and I were happy to go to school, and reluctant to come home.

My experience as a new kid in school probably was very similar to what millions of other new kids have gone through. I remember the first-day jitters very clearly. I was usually a calm kid, but my nerves were very tightly wound that day. I felt uneasy

ABODE

leaving home, but I was even more anxious at the thought of having to return to it.

My teacher that year was Miss Bouchard. I remember that she was tall and thin, with thick glasses. She almost always wore a green sweater over her clothes, even in warm weather. She baked us brownies and gave us lemonade for our first day of school. We spent that first morning talking and drawing pictures about our summer vacations, getting our new schoolbooks, and going over various rules and drills. Nobody was mean, though no one really made too much of an effort to talk to me. I didn't feel entirely unwelcome, but all the same, I was very much aware of the fact that I was the outsider. Most of the kids in my class had lived in the area all their lives, and had grown up together. I was the anomaly.

At recess, the boys ran out to the field and started kicking a soccer ball around. I sat down and leaned against the building, wishing I had brought a comic book.

A shadow fell across me. "Do you play soccer?"

I looked up. The kid had pale, pale blond hair and brown eyes. His name was Tommy Mathieus, though I didn't know that yet. "Yeah," I said. "Sure."

"Come on." He gave a little wave, inviting me to follow him. I took my place on the field. I don't recall much about the actual game. But I do remember the bell ringing. We crossed the yard, heading back inside.

"Where are you from?" Tommy asked me.

"Near Boston," I said. "We just moved here."

"Yeah? Where?"

"Uh, across the river."

"That river runs through half the state," Tommy laughed.

I tried again. "You know where the old mill is? That road just past it?"

Tommy's face changed. He seemed very interested, all of a sudden. "The Old Murder Road?"

I shrugged. I knew it as a numbered route. The maps called it Woodfarrow Drive. "I guess."

The kid raised his eyebrows. "The brown house at the end of the road?"

"Yeah."

He started laughing. "Wow."

I didn't get the joke. "What's so funny?"

"Your house is haunted," Tommy said. "Keep your creepy ghosts at home." Then, to make matters worse, he turned and yelled at the top of his lungs. "The new kid lives in the haunted house!"

"I do not." I said.

"Do too!"

A redheaded kid—Matt Lessard—grew wide-eyed. "Old Mr. Kent blew his brains out in there. Just like his father."

"Yeah," Tommy said. "There's baby bones mixed into the mortar, and there's a monster in the woods. Witches used to live there. That place is creepy."

I glared at him. "It is not!"

It didn't matter that I completely agreed that the house was creepy. Sometimes you just have to defend your turf.

Ensue childhood fight.

At the end of this, Tommy Mathieus and I were sitting in Principal DeMillon's office, him with a black eye, me with a split lip. Nowadays, we probably would have been expelled and sent to juvie, but back then, things weren't quite so tangled.

DeMillon had a greasy black comb over, thick glasses, and an ugly plaid jacket. He stared down his nose at the papers before him, and gave us his sternest look. "What happened?"

I spoke first. "He said my house is haunted."

"It is." Tommy said snidely. "My brother told me about it. He heard it from his friend, who used to-"

"Enough!" DeMillon silenced Tommy with a stare, and proceeded to lecture us for what seemed like hours about being kind and polite, and never, ever raising fists to one another. I was hoping I'd be able to keep the incident a secret, but just as he was letting us go, he told us he was calling our parents.

I was pretty nauseous by the time school let out. Not because of the fight, but because I was so scared about what Dad would say. What he would do. I had a sick feeling in my stomach, that dread that sinks into you like lead, turning your bowels into a rancid stew of anxiety.

You asked me a million questions on the bus.

"Why did you hit that kid?"

"Because he's a jerk."

"Why is he a jerk?"

"He said stupid stuff about our house."

"Like what?"

You kept asking questions. I ignored you for a while, and then I got annoyed and yelled at you. I said some terrible things, and made you cry. I remember exactly what I said. "You're just a stupid, ugly little baby, and you're too dumb to understand anything."

Those words ring in my ears, even now, and they strike like bullets every time.

As expected, Dad let me have it with the belt.

That night I curled up into a little ball of anger and misery in my bed, hating everything: the house, Mom and Dad, my room, my school, you. I thought about ways to kill myself, and how terrible everyone would feel.

The next day I walked right up to Tommy Mathieus. "You know what?" I said. "You're right. My house is haunted. And I bet you couldn't stay in that place ten minutes without pissing yourself."

I gave him my best cold stare. And in his eyes, I saw exactly what I was hoping for: a glimmer of fear. But it was an empty victory. I felt down for the rest of that day, and for many others after it.

It was the first time I ever remember feeling depressed. The blanket of unhappiness that fell over me that day has really never lifted.

I fear it never will.

Chapter Twelve

Around this time, I started hearing scratching in the walls of my room at night, a faint but distinctive scraping. It isn't unusual to get mice or squirrels or raccoons inside a house in the woods. And at first, that was what I thought: mice. But every night it seemed to get louder and louder. Then I noticed a certain rhythm to the scratching, a deliberate pattern, which no mouse could or would create. It was not the insistent push of little claws making a nest out of wood, but a patterned, staccato scrape of something with rhythm. I can still hear it to this day. *SCRATCH scratch scratch. SCRATCH scratch scratch. SCRATCH scratch scratch.*

Mice do not scratch in tempo. Raccoons do not have rhythm.

It would have been a comfort to tell myself I had imagined it. But I was denied that luxury. Our orange cat, Lucky, heard it too. One night he sat staring at the wall and ceiling for well over an hour with that telltale feline alertness, occasionally hissing. Then, suddenly, he yowled, flattened his ears, and ran away as though he'd been hit.

I am quite certain that cats are a bit magic, and see and hear things we cannot. Like most cats, our furball was always a bit goofy. At our old house, Lucky was frisky and playful. He loved to hide in paper grocery bags and bat at our ankles, and he always curled up on Mom's lap at night. But when we lived in the house, Lucky hid a lot. He would often stare or react to things we couldn't see. To this day, I'm not sure if he was sensing things, or just being a cat.

He had always been Mom's cat. But in the new place, he spent more and more time with you.

When I told Mom and Dad about the scratching, they said it was mice, and told me to stop reading so many scary comics. They made jokes about Lucky's lack of hunting skills. But the very next day, Lucky started bringing us mice. He would line them up neatly on the porch, looking very proud of himself. We watched him stalking his prey in the grass: all business, tense and alert. But when he heard the noises in my room, his reaction was completely different: he hissed and growled and poofed out his fur.

Buster also pleaded my case, for he would often start barking when it started, or look upstairs when the footsteps passed overhead, sometimes baring his teeth and even growling a little.

I mentally added the scratching to the list of strange events, which by then also included doors opening and closing by themselves, food spoiling unnaturally fast, dishes breaking, things being moved around, strange smells, disembodied voices, and, of course, the footsteps.

One night, I was almost asleep when I heard the footsteps moving across the attic floor (or ceiling, from where I was). It was growing chilly, and I was warm and snug and comfy, just on that hazy border between sleep and wakefulness. But that now-familiar tread yanked me back into full alertness. My heart thudded in my chest, and my whole body tensed. I froze, listening intently, and hoping I would hear nothing.

The footsteps moved back and forth across the attic floor a few times, and then stopped directly over the spot where my bed was. I had the sense that whatever was up there was staring at me through the floor/ceiling. That was the first moment I knew true fear. Every inch of my body prickled into goosebumps. I opened my eyes, and stared into the blackness of the shadow-cloaked ceiling. The darkness seemed to be moving. The trees cast shadows from the moon; this was different.

I don't know how long I laid there, afraid to fall asleep, afraid to stay awake. I spent so many hours, so many nights, just lying there in my bed, scared out of my wits, that they all blur together.

The next day—at least I think it was the next day—you and I settled into the living room with some hot cocoa and a game of checkers. I asked if you, too, heard things at night, if you saw shadows move.

I'll never forget what you said. You looked up at me, and nodded. "They come to me at night," you said. "They stand around my bed and tell me secrets. Their voices are ice and bone and dead branches."

I frowned. "Who?"

You looked up at me innocently. "The shadow kids," you said. You were quite casual about it, as though this were perfectly normal.

"What do they look like?" I asked.

"They're all short," you said. "Sometimes they have no faces."

I was equally fascinated and terrified. "Well, what do they say?"

"They want me to play with them," you said. "They're very hungry and cold. But they still want to play."

Dad came home then, and the sound of the door opening brought our conversation to an end.

"They don't want me to tell you any more," you said. Then you smiled, jumped my checkers, and won the game.

More and more strange things were happening, but no one had actually come out and said that the house was haunted. It just seemed like the more uneasy we became, the more things happened. Photos fell from the wall. Doors opened and shut. We'd hear noises from empty rooms, or catch the trailing sound of a voice from a dark corner. An odd smell clung to the home. I didn't identify it until much later: rose water. Sometimes we also smelled wood smoke or burning leaves, but those odors may have been purely natural: it was Maine, after all.

We did not speak of these things. It was almost as though some unspoken rule had been set down. I don't suppose any of us knew how to address it. These were the days of family dinners, and, at least in our family, such matters were not to be discussed. And for a time, things remained random and spaced out well enough that we could retain—or pretend—some sense of normalcy. But our meals grew more and more silent. The unspoken and the unseen hung in the air like smoke between us.

My—our—parents, at least at first, brushed off the footsteps, as they did so many other things. *It's the trees*, they said. Or: *There's a raccoon on the roof. Old houses settle. It's the pipes. It's the wood. It's the wind.*

They said these things to soothe us.

But I know what I heard.

I knew they believed me. They believed you, when you told them about the shadowy figures that surrounded your bed at night. They saw things out of the corner of their eyes, just as we did. But they never admitted as much.

ABODE

They just didn't want to face the truth.

Dad refused to admit it, because he would have had to take the blame for bringing us here. I suspect that Mom stayed in denial simply because she was frightened. More than once, I saw her jump at unexplained noises, or shadows that moved when they shouldn't. But she refused to admit seeing anything strange, at least at first. She wasn't strong enough to deal with such things.

Some days, nothing happened. Sometimes, save for the heavy feeling in the air, the house seemed almost normal. You and I would have cereal and watch our favorite Saturday morning cartoons: *The Jetsons, The Flintstones, Looney Tunes.* I played soccer at school, and you started dance class. Mom chain-smoked and chatted for hours on the phone, and Dad drank beer, painted, and watched football.

The respites never lasted. Before long, something would happen, and destroy our fragile sense of ... normalcy? Peace?

Like the day we found the well.

We were in the backyard one day, helping Dad clean up the yard. It was late summer, probably early September. As we worked through the pile of debris, which was mostly old boards and posts, we found a pile of stones. It looked rather like a cairn, though I didn't realize that until much later. Dad decided the stones would make a great fire pit, and decided to move them. We were enlisted to help. Well, I was, anyway. You mostly carried the little stones from the pile to your little red wagon. But as the pile of stones was slowly dismantled, you paid less and less attention to the rocks and spent more time staring at what was emerging from the land.

A well.

You started screaming bloody murder the moment it was clear what the well was. Dad and I both jumped, and Mom came running. Both of them frantically checked you for wounds or bites. They found nothing, of course. Nothing had touched you. But you were sobbing, tears running down your face. You cried so hard you were literally choking on your screams. And you didn't stop, even when Mom picked you up. You clung to her, your little arms around her neck.

"What is it?" Mom kept asking. "What's wrong?" She had question after question. None of us answered them: none of us could.

After what seemed like a long, long, time, you fell silent. Mom had to ask you what was wrong several more times before you finally spoke. Though your voice was quiet, it seemed the only sound in the world. "That's where the twins fell," you said. "They died. Jessamine and George. He pushed them in."

I stared at you. You hadn't been to the cemetery. At least, I don't think you had: you were always too scared to cross the road alone. And, to be honest, you weren't a great reader at that age. Even if you had seen the gravestones, I'm pretty sure they would have been too much for you to read. You were still struggling with words like *happy* and *round.*

"Twins?" Mom asked you, frowning.

But you offered nothing more. The moment passed: you became more like yourself again. You looked into the sun and smiled, as though nothing was wrong, as though you hadn't been throwing a fit a few moments past.

Then you looked to the sky and pointed. I followed your gaze and saw a perfect V in against the pale blue sky. Birds, flying south for the winter. "Look," you said. "They're going home, where the snow can't reach them."

Mom turned her attention to the well. "Is that safe?"

Dad tried the cover. "It's sealed," He said. I tried to get a better look and he scowled at me. "Stay away from it," he said. "Both of you."

It was one rule neither of us had any problem obeying.

Chapter Thirteen

A utumn Equinox is, according to ancient traditions, the beginning of the dark half of the year.

That day we crossed the line.

I know it was September 21st, because it was the day after Dad's birthday (the 20th, btw) when the next few strange incidents took place. Dad was putting in a lot of hours at his mill job, so he is absent from a lot of my memories of the next 'phase' of events, if you want to call it that.

It was beginning to feel like autumn. The nights were getting chilly, and the leaves were just starting to turn. Mom brought our winter clothes up from the basement, and stashed our shorts and tee shirts in the attic. Our summer toys went into boxes, along with our bathing suits, our lawn sprinkler, and deflated beach balls.

As the weather cooled, things happened more frequently. Dishes fell from the shelf or counter almost every day. Dad mumbled about slanted shelves, and said the house was sagging in the middle, like Mom. (He didn't say this in front of her.)

One day I filled a glass of water and put it on the shelf, to see if it tilted. The water sat perfectly straight; I could tell through the glass.

The glass flew off the shelf and shattered.

I ran out of the kitchen, and seriously considered running away. I even went so far as to pack a suitcase and tie some things in a bandana, which I hung on a stick. Then I walked down the driveway, and start trudging up the road. But I realized before I even reached the end of our street that I had nowhere to go. And even if I had, I couldn't leave you there alone. So, I turned back.

That night, or a night shortly after that, we were eating dinner, when suddenly a foul odor filled the room. It was as though we were sitting next to an open sewer. We all started gagging and coughing, our eyes watering. Mom even called the fire department.

When they arrived, the smell was gone. The stench actually seemed to dissipate the moment the fire truck pulled into the drive. It didn't dissolve slowly, either: one moment, it was so horrible we went outside to escape it, and a minute later, it was entirely gone.

Mom and Dad pretended it had been a skunk. We knew better.

Several things happened over the course of the next few days. We found claw marks on the celling. The lights flickered on and off. Something tore my homework up. And you kept finding spiders everywhere.

Before long, tension filled even the quiet days. We were always waiting for something else to happen. Waiting for the next shoe to drop, so to speak.

I remember one night in particular. I just tossed and turned, hearing noise after noise. I was thirsty, so I decided to go down to the kitchen for a drink of water. As I went down the stairs, I had the distinct, unpleasant feeling that I was being followed.

When I reached the foot of the stairs, I heard a *thunk*. I spun around, staring up into the shadows, but saw nothing. After a few moments, I continued on my way to the kitchen. The leftover part of Dad's birthday cake was still sitting on the kitchen counter, which is how I know the date. I thought about sneaking an extra piece, but I was really thirsty, and my thoughts turned to water instead.

I remember reaching into the cupboard for a glass, and then going to the faucet and turning it on. I let the water run for a moment, so it would get cold. I drank a full glass, and then a half of another. Since I didn't want to have to come back downstairs in the dark again, I decided to take some water back to my room.

I can still hear the gurgling sound our faucet made as I filled the glass.

I turned around and saw a woman standing before me. She wore a black, long-sleeved dress, like they wore in the Victorian era. Her hair was pulled back into a tight, neat bun. I remember that her eyebrows were very thick. She didn't move. She didn't speak. She just stared at me. She didn't radiate hatred as much as ... disapproval. I had the sense that she didn't like us in her house. She didn't like Mom's taste, either, it seemed. As I stood there, she sort of morphed into a smaller ball of darkness and knocked the glass out of my hands. It shattered on the floor, spilling water all over that hideous linoleum.

Then she was gone. I suppose *vanished* is the word. She was there, and then she wasn't. She became a moving shadow, slipping into the night, and I was alone again.

I just stood there, shivering and shaking, for a very long time. Eventually, I decided that I wanted to go back to my room, and I ran all the way up the stairs.

The next morning you cut your foot on the broken glass. I felt horrible, for it was my fault, and tried to cheer you up by giving you chocolate ice cream.

ABODE

I never saw Josephine again.

But you did.

You mentioned her frequently. You told me about her and the twins and, on occasion, Isabelle, whose face was terribly burned. You also spoke about Elizabeth, who you said was crazy, and Agnes, who couldn't walk.

I cannot tell your tale. All I can offer is bits and pieces. I was caught in my own nightmare.

I do know this much.

You saw things the rest of us didn't.

You began having terrible nightmares, as did I. You woke screaming in the night, and when I asked what frightened you, you spoke of pacts and winter storms and desperation. And you came to me one day, your little blue eyes calm and serene, and said that you wanted to be an angel, so you could comfort and protect the shadow children.

"They're scared," you told me. "They're cold and hungry. He makes them do things."

"Then set out food for them," I said, annoyed. I really didn't want to talk to you. I was more interested in playing my new video game.

"They want to play in the sun," she said, "but they can't. The sun will dissolve them, like it does the snow." You looked out the window, where swollen, sullen clouds hung thick in a grey sky. "It will snow soon," you said.

I looked at you, curious, and told you that you were weird and silly. But something in your eyes, something in your voice, chilled me.

You called me a gooberhead, stuck your tongue out at me, and bounced down the stairs to greet Dad at the door.

I cannot begin to explain the guilt I carry on your behalf. I cannot truly relate your entire experience. I know some things that happened to you. Some of these events I witnessed, others you just told me about. But there are many things that I think you never shared with anyone. As I have said, your experiences were not the same as mine. I don't know everything that happened.

But I began to recognize fear in your eyes.

I have a suspicion that, since you were the youngest, the most recently come to us from the beyond, the other realm had not yet loosed its grip on you. I believe that the dead and the unborn wait together in one place, souls twisting and reforming.

You never had a chance.

You were the purest of us, the youngest, the most innocent. While Mom, Dad, and I certainly all had horrific experiences, you were the one they wanted.

And in the end, you were lost to us.

Chapter Fourteen

Grandma passed a few weeks later. I remember the afternoon clearly. It was a dreary October day. You and I were on the living room floor, playing board games. Mom was in the kitchen, making supper. Things had been quiet that day, as far as I can recall.

The phone rang, Mom answered it, and then she was crying.

And we discovered—experienced—death for the first time.

To this day, I don't know if Grandma's death was a coincidence, or if it was connected, somehow, to us moving into that place. She died in her sleep, of a massive stroke.

I only wish your death had been as peaceful.

We drove south for the funeral. That ride, unlike the last long drive, was not filled by songs and toys and bickering. It was silent. You and I just stared out the window, or played quietly with our toys. Mom and Dad barely spoke at all. Every now and then, Mom let out a quiet little sob or a sniffle. Otherwise, it was completely quiet.

Grandma's funeral took place on a cold, rainy day. She was laid to rest in an ancient cemetery, one filled with crypts and statues. It was a peaceful place, but, as in the Kent cemetery, I felt as though I could sense the dead. I felt numbness in the air, a sort of energy, the sense of souls slowly dissolving into the land.

You caught a terrible cold that day. Mom kept you home from school that entire week. I didn't really worry much about you, even when I heard Mom and Dad talking about doctors and pneumonia, but I felt bad that you looked so miserable. I knew you were really sick when you missed *The Muppet Show*. I made you a cute little puppy drawing during art class.

That week at school, we visited an old-time farm, where they did everything just as they had done things in the 1700 and 1800's. I spent the day shoveling sawdust and learning about yokes and plows and harvests. I may have enjoyed it more, but even that, somehow, seemed connected to the house. I recognized some of the items in the old-time barn, for our old shed was full of similar objects. I felt bad that you had missed it: your favorite show was *Little House On The Prairie*, and you were so excited to see how Laura Ingalls really lived that you'd been chattering about it for weeks.

I came home that day and went to your room. It was colder than the rest of the house. I noticed the temperature drop even just stepping from the hallway into your room.

"Hey, Lexi," I said.

You coughed. "Want Lucky," you said. "Want Lucky."

"Ok," I said. I tried to think where I had seen the cat last, and couldn't remember. "I'll find Lucky for you. Here, I drew you a puppy."

As I put the puppy picture—crayon masterpiece that it was—down on your blanket, Mom came up the stairs, carrying a tray with a bowl of chicken noodle soup. She frowned when she saw me. "What did I tell you?"

I didn't know what she meant, so I just shrugged. She put the tray down on your nightstand (which was painted white, and covered with unicorn and rainbow stickers) then put her arm around my shoulder and gently led me back into the hallway.

ABODE

"Leave Lexi alone. I don't want you getting sick, too. Why don't you go play outside?"

I looked out the window, puzzled. It was grey and drizzly outside, one of those dreary autumn days that makes you want to curl up with a book and a blanket. "It's cold."

As soon as I said that, we heard a loud crash from the living room.

Mom immediately headed downstairs. I followed her. One of Grandma's angels had fallen off the shelf. The shelf still stood. The ceramic deer that occupied the space next to the spot the angel had stood in remained unmolested, its glassy eyes somehow seeming to accuse us. Only the angel had moved.

Again, I felt like something was watching me.

"Can you get the broom, please?" Mom asked tightly.

I got the yellow broom from the hall closet silently. Mom swept up the broken angel. She was crying, and I felt bad for her.

"Are you okay, Mom?" I asked.

She sniffled a little bit. "This angel, I remember it from when I was a little girl. We used to put it on the Christmas tree every year."

Another spiderweb crack in her psyche, that would later spread and deepen, and in time lead to her collapse.

Mom swept the last bits of glass into the dustpan and then wiped her nose with her sleeve, which I'd never seen her do before. "Christmas will be nice," she said, her voice straining with forced cheer. "We'll get a big tree, and I'll make cookies. I'll get another angel. No big deal."

I knew she was trying to muster herself and pull it together, but I could see right through it. "I'm sorry about your angel," I told her sincerely.

Mom ruffled my hair and managed a weak smile. "No use crying over spilled milk, right?" She didn't wait for a reply, but just turned and carried the glass bits to the trash bin in the kitchen. Her voice was shaky, as though she couldn't truly manage more than a whisper. But I knew she was trying to sound cheerful. "Would you like shells and cheese for dinner? That sounds good, doesn't it?"

It was my favorite; a delicious concoction that involved Velveeta, macaroni noodles, and tuna fish. I wasn't sure if the comfort food was for me or her, but I nodded. "Yeah," I said. "Okay."

We both went into the kitchen. Or started to, anyway. We'd only made it a few steps when we heard another crash from behind us. Again, the thud was accompanied by the tinkle of breaking glass.

Every hair on my body stood on end. The skin on my neck prickled, as though a ghostly hand was tracing my spine. I felt a hateful presence in the room, watching us. And I had the sudden certainty that if I turned around, I would see something there, in the shadowy dining room.

Mom went white. I saw tears well up in her eyes, and her shoulders shook. But she didn't say anything. She just stood there, quietly sobbing.

I took the broom from her and went to the dining room.

Another angel had broken. This one had fallen from a bookshelf, and landed a good four or five feet away.

ABODE

As though something had pushed it.

Mom thanked me for cleaning the mess, and made me a hot chocolate. She poured herself a big glass of white wine, put some strawberries in it, and started cooking. Her hands were shaking so bad she dropped the can of tuna.

Mom wasn't perfect. She was nervous and fretted a lot, even before everything happened. But she was a good mom. She loved us. She made us baked macaroni and cheese when it was cold, and ice cream cake when it was hot. She drove us around to various events, taking you to ballet and gymnastics and me to soccer and hockey and football. She went to your Brownie meetings and my Boy Scout meetings, and helped us with our homework. The bottle took her in later years, and she fell into horrible insanity, but back then ... back then, she was a good mom.

I felt very sad as I dumped the remains of the second angel into the trash, not for myself, but for Mom, because she just looked so defeated. So I decided, in my puny, prepubescent wisdom, to draw her another angel, as though a child's jagged sketch could replace a family heirloom. I went upstairs to get the drawing box. I knew it was in your room, since you had been drawing and reading Nancy Drew books throughout your illness.

You were playing with dolls on your bed. The soup bowl was empty. (I know you were getting a bit better then, because you were starting to get into being waited on.) The drawing pad and crayons were on your little desk, near the unicorn lamp. You looked up at me, squinting a little. "Have you seen Lucky?"

I tried to remember when I had seen the cat last. "No," I said. "She's probably chasing mice."

"Want Lucky."

"Ok. I'll go look."

"Can you ask Mom if I can have some hot chocolate?"

"Sure. I need the drawing pad for a little bit, ok?"

You just nodded. Your eyes were kind of blank. The sun was setting, and the sky was a sort of pale pinkish-purple color. Twilight was all around you in that room, as though dusk itself was seeping in through the windows.

Time does strange things to me. There are so many things I have forgotten—hell, I've lost chunks of entire years—but that moment is still crystal clear in my memory. Minute details are coming back clearly now, as I revisit this. I can see your toy box, with its pile of Barbie and Ken dolls, and the Cher and Sonny dolls, board games, and stuffed animals. I can see the paint-by-number unicorns you'd stuck to your walls with Scotch tape. I can almost remember the pattern on your pink pajamas.

That is one of my clearest memories of you: a small, innocent child, drawing fairy tale princesses and unicorns as, all around us, the shadows drew closer.

I went to get the drawing pad. When I saw the picture on the top, I froze.

It was a perfect replica of the angel figurine that had just broken. You had somehow managed to draw lines right where the wings had cracked. And the lines were straight, which was very odd, because, well, no offense, but you hadn't yet learned how to stay between the lines in coloring books, and you definitely hadn't mastered drawing straight lines.

Even now, I get chills down my spine thinking of it, and my heart races. I just had to stop writing and take a shot of whiskey to calm my nerves before I could continue. (I've started drinking again, but only a little. Just long enough to get myself through this.)

I think I held my breath as I flipped through your sketchpad, looking at your other drawings. Some were normal little-girl art: smiling, bright yellow suns hanging over lopsided houses and triangular trees, kittens and unicorns, that sort of thing. Others seemed darker, images of doors and slim, bony figures and crosses. There was one of a funeral, with people standing around a single, lonely grave. You drew the twins, in 1800's style dress, holding hands. You had drawn our house, silhouetted in yellow, red, and orange.

At the time, I thought it was sunset.

I didn't ask you about the angel drawing, or any of the others, for that matter. I just quietly ripped a fresh sheet off the pad, took the box of crayons and colored pencils, and went downstairs to draw while Mom finished cooking. As I walked down the stairs, out of the corner of my eye, I saw a dark figure slip past me.

It was only one of many encounters with the shadow people.

I froze, sensing something nearby, but I couldn't see anything. I remember that I stayed at the kitchen table, drawing, for a very long time. I often ended up in the kitchen. It seemed the safest place in the house.

I am going to stop for tonight, because the memories are bubbling up, and the terror is coming back, and I cannot think clearly anymore. Sometimes when I think of what I lost, I begin to shake.

I try not to dwell on these things much now. I try not to remember.

MORGAN SYLVIA

I never brought you your hot chocolate.
I'm so sorry.

Chapter Fifteen

Do you know what true fear feels like? Not the false terror you get from watching horror movies. Not the way your senses sharpen when your car skids on ice and you think you will lose control. I'm not talking about those terrors, though they can be quite visceral. I'm not talking about the panic you get feel when you know you won't make your bills, or the anxiety that eats you up when your boss fires you. I'm talking about the horror you feel when you know that you are in the presence of true evil.

We've so many things be afraid of these days. Terrorists, famine, disease, violence, car crashes, cancer, nuclear war, the death of Mother Earth herself. Yet we still manage to walk around as though we are safe, impervious to the hazards of fire and steel and stone, protected from the invisible, insidious dangers posed by viruses and bacteria and tainted food or water. When you think about it, human fear is a fascinating thing. I once dated a girl who was terrified of the sight of cracked mud. I could never wrap my head around that. I thought it was ridiculous. Now, seeing photos of the droughts spreading across the planet, I wonder if she was onto something, if perhaps she was sensing the horrors of the future, tapping into visions of something we haven't experienced yet.

We all have our own fears.

You were really, really scared of spiders, when you were little. Snakes, too. You freaked out at the sight of earthworms glistening on pavement after a summer rain. And if a small black dot on our walls or ceilings moved, you completely devolved into a screaming, hysterical mess.

Do you want to know my greatest fear? Being buried alive. Being trapped underground, with the weight of the earth above you, below you, and around you, and no way to escape. The waiting would be the worst. To just be trapped there, terrified, with full knowledge of your own impending doom, would be torture. You wouldn't know if you had minutes, hours, or days before death claimed you, and, with no way to tell time, you'd never find out. You'd have no company in those silent, terrible moments, nothing but your own frantic thoughts, and the slow, terrible knowledge that death was drawing closer with each breath.

I can pinpoint the very moment that phobia formed.

It was the day Jeremiah locked me in the root cellar.

Right around then, we started noticing a stench. If you've ever smelled a dead thing, you know the scent. Words don't do it justice, even words like *putrid, wretched, vile,* or *horrible.* It started when you were still sick in bed, because I remember you commenting about it. Over the next day or so, the smell got worse and worse. Finally, Dad pinpointed it to the root cellar. He enlisted me to go help him investigate.

As soon as he opened those doors, the stench hit both of us full force, a foul odor of decay and putrefaction. We gagged and stepped back. It was hard to even breathe, the smell was so bad.

"Stay here," Dad said. He pulled his tee shirt up over his nose and went to get a flashlight. When he came back, he shone the light down into the blackness.

ABODE

For a moment, he was silent. Then: "Oh," he said quietly. "Oh, shit."

"What is it?" I asked. I had backed away from the smell, so I couldn't see into the cellar.

"It's Lucky," he said, his voice tight. He didn't look at me. "Go get me a shovel from the garage."

"How did he get in there?" I asked. The door had been chained and padlocked shut, and there was no other way in.

I think we both came to the same conclusion, though neither of us said it. Someone—or something—had locked him in there.

This is the part where my brain does not want to push further. It could have been Dad, in one of his dark spells. It could have been something demonic.

I don't know which is worse.

"Must have found a rabbit hole," he said.

Bound by morbid curiosity, I stepped forward, and glanced into the darkness, where Dad's flashlight shone on the decaying corpse of the cat. I realized right away that something wasn't right. Dad told me not to look, but it was too late.

Lucky was in pieces.

I only remember the next sequence of events in bits and pieces. I started screaming. My shrieks drew you out of the house, and Buster shot out the door with you. You peeked around the corner cautiously, but Buster, less wary, sped toward us and took up a guard stance at the root cellar door, snarling. He turned into a different dog, in that moment. I had never heard him growl like that.

Mom came around the corner then ... and stopped short at the smell. She put her hand to her nose. "What is that?"

"We found Lucky," Dad said tightly.

Mom's face went white. "What happened?"

Dad just shook his head. "Bring Lexi and the dog back in. *Buster! Cut it out!*"

Mom started crying. She'd found Lucky when he was still a kitten, just a tiny ball of orange fur meowing near a dumpster. The painting had Dad made of her kissing Lucky's little orange face that night was hanging in the upstairs hall. She stepped closer, but stopped in her tracks as Dad snapped at her. "Stay back!"

Mom bristled. "Don't yell at me."

"You don't want to see this," Dad told her darkly. "Trust me. Just get me a trash bag. And some gloves."

You didn't understand. You asked where Lucky was, and then, before anyone could stop you, you ran past Mom and looked down into the cellar.

The next moments were pure chaos. You let out an ear-splitting, high-pitched screech, and then started bawling. Dad yelled at Mom to get you inside, at me to get the damned shovel, and at Buster to get out of the way. A thick cloud of misery enveloped us all. I think our rage rose equally, each of us holding an anger that the others matched and fed.

I got the shovel and handed it down to Dad. Meanwhile, Buster was causing a ruckus in the kitchen, barking and whining and jumping against the window. We heard something shatter as he grew even more frenzied.

A few minutes later, Dad called me into the cellar.

I felt sick, and was afraid of what I would see, but I knew what would happen if I refused. Fortunately, I the only signs I saw of

ABODE

Lucky were a damp spot on the dirt cellar floor, a few clumps of ginger fur, and the black garbage bag, which was no longer empty.

There was absolutely nothing in the root cellar. No bodies, no weird chests, no skeletons. Just spiderwebs and dirt, really. With the exception of a few old tools leaning against one cement wall and some empty wooden shelves, that tiny room was completely empty. But, for some reason, that emptiness terrified me more than anything else in that house. I'm not sure why. All I know was that my skin crawled, and my nerves were on edge. It reminded me of a tomb.

Dad had me hold the flashlight while he checked the door hinge, which was rusty and crumbling. I tried not to look at the dark wet spot on the dirt floor, or the trash bag in the corner. Moments passed in what seemed like an eternity. Finally, Dad stood up, picked up the shovel and the bag with the cat in it, and climbed the cement steps to the world above. I have never followed him so closely in my life.

He immediately went around the corner of the house, heading for the garage. He yelled back at me, turning his head to call back over his shoulder. "Shut that door."

Only too happy to oblige, I turned to close the doors. They lay almost flat against the ground, only slightly angled to keep snow and rain out. The sun was behind me, so I saw my shadow on the dirt floor below.

Then I saw a second shadow. Someone in a wide-brimmed hat was standing behind me.

I froze in fear, but before I could react, I felt two hands on my back, pushing me down into the darkness.

The doors slammed shut above me.

I ran for the doors and shoved with all my might, but they held fast.

I wasn't just scared. I was so completely terrified that every cell in my body reacted. My bowels tickled, and I literally almost shit myself. I felt a strange cold burning on my skin as my nerves became ultra-sensitive. My spine shivered, and my breath came in shallow gasps. I could barely think. In fact, if someone compared my brain waves at that moment to those of a mouse being snatched up by a hawk, or a zebra being chased by a lion, I bet they would be identical.

I immediately started shouting, but I was underground, and Dad had already headed for the garage to get his shovel. My heart thudded in my chest so hard that I feared it would burst.

I heard something draw a breath behind me. Then I felt the touch of rank, icy breath on my neck.

My skin crawled, and I shivered with disgust. The stench was horrible, so foul, that I gagged. But my nausea was nothing next to the terror I felt. I didn't dare turn around. I just shut my eyes and clenched my fist, and kept screaming.

I cannot say how long I was trapped in the choking darkness with that demonic being. I only know that it seemed like forever before the doors opened again. I was crying, sobbing, big thick snots running down my face.

I saw Dad, silhouetted in the light of day. And in that moment, despite all his shortcomings, he was my hero. I thought of myself as a big kid, but I just wanted him to pick me up and hug me.

Instead, he started yelling at me. "What the hell are you doing? What is wrong with you? Do you think this is a joke? I could barely hear you. What if I'd come back and locked the doors? If you ever pull a stunt like that again, I will beat your ass raw."

I ran into the daylight, gulping air.

Dad kept shouting. "Your mother loved that cat! This is no time for a prank!" He threw the shovel at my feet, and pointed toward the tree line. "Go find a nice spot and dig a hole. Make sure it's at least four feet deep. And don't expect supper tonight."

Shortly afterwards, I found myself in the woods again, digging said hole. I was still shaking and nauseous from my ordeal. I tried to focus on what I was doing, but my thoughts kept filling with an orange, fluffy ball of fur that had made us all laugh, and I kept having to stop to wipe my tears away. As I worked, every now and then, I heard your voice, as your cries and wails carried down from your room. It was an eerie sound.

I felt that I was being watched the whole time. I kept looking up, looking around. I saw a shadow move out of the corner of my eye, a dark figure slipping past me, but when I looked, there was nothing there.

Dad came out to check my work, carrying the bag. When he reached me, he took the shovel from me, apparently unhappy with my progress. In a few minutes, he had doubled the depth of the hole. He dropped poor Lucky into it unceremoniously, filled the dirt back in, and kicked dirt and leaves over the top of it. Then he stormed back toward the house.

I made Lucky a little cross out of sticks.

I turned away. I had only gotten a few steps when I heard a sharp *crack*.

When I turned around, the cross was broken.

In my dreams that night, the forest was young again, and the land was covered in blood.

Chapter Sixteen

It's been a few days since I left off. I suppose that won't matter to you; you won't see the gaps in the finished document.

Things have been bad for me, lately. Seeing you opened the Pandora's box of my memories, and my subsequent decision to write out my recollections has stirred up a maelstrom of feelings and fears. I knew this would be hard, but I didn't think it would be this bad. To be honest, I'm not sure I would have contacted you if I had. But it's too late to stop now.

I am having nightmares again. This isn't entirely new. I've suffered from nightmares ever since we moved into that house. But the ones I had after you died were very different than those which took place when I (we) lived on the property. The dreams I experienced in the house were almost painstakingly clear.

As are these.

Some of the memories I had suppressed are coming back to me now. Things that I had locked in a box in a dark corner of my mind are now crawling out of that blackness, slithering into my waking hours. Sometimes, the memories return with no discernable trigger that I can put a finger on. More often, something jars them.

Triggers are nothing new to me. I've been prone to flashbacks since, well, since you died.

But I've never experienced anything like what happened today.

I'm getting a cold; nothing unusual, this time of year. So last night I decided to make myself some chicken noodle soup. When I reached for the red and white can in the cupboard, the second my fingers touched it, I was back in 1978, taking a nearly-identical can off the pantry shelf to give to Mom so she could cook it for me.

I looked down and tiny details jumped out at me: the scuffs on my sneakers, the lines on my rust-colored corduroys, the muddy spots on my shoelaces, the dust on the yellow and brown linoleum floor. I held up my hand, and it was again a child's hand. I was back in the kitchen with Mom.

The kitchen was, to me, the safest place in the house. It was where Mom usually was. It was where the food was. We had all started to eat more than usual.

I handed Mom the can and sat down at the table to read my comic book while she put the soup on the stove to heat.

A few minutes later, I suddenly felt extremely thirsty. It came on very quickly. My mouth grew dry, and I became suddenly and completely fixated on the thought of drinking something cold and sweet. I got up to get a can of soda from the fridge. I had to walk past the stove, but I didn't really look at it. All I could think about was getting a cool, refreshing drink. I remember the swishing sound my cords made as I walked.

The pot of soup literally flew at me. Mom didn't see it happen, because her back was turned. All I remember is walking past the stove. I didn't touch the pot, or anything else, for that matter. The next thing I knew, I felt a searing, white-hot pain on my hand, arm, and side. My skin felt like it was on fire. I started screaming.

Mom went into full 'Mom' mode, immediately rushing to my side and making me take my sweater and tee shirt off. The skin on my arm had turned an angry red, but only my wrist and hand,

and a tiny spot on my neck, were really burned. The only thing that kept it from being worse was the fact that I was wearing a long-sleeved tee shirt and a turtleneck sweater.

We had all taken to wearing several layers of clothing. It was always cold in that house.

Mom cut a raw potato to put on the burn. She kept insisting that I had somehow knocked the pot over, but she was more concerned with the burn itself than how it had happened. She never truly accepted my version of events, regardless of how hard I tried to make her understand. I can't really blame her, though at the time I was very upset by that.

The pain lingered for days. I still have the burn scars.

Remember the nightmare I told you about? The one with the door to hell? The patterns of the burns I got that day perfectly matched the marks I saw on my hand in that dream. I know because I had the same dream again that night, and the night after that, and every night until the burn healed. That's how I got the scar.

In the chaos, neither of us saw you enter the room. Mom was applying the potato to the burn, and we looked up and noticed you standing in the doorway, clutching a doll.

"He's angry," you said. "He wants us to leave."

That's where the flashback ended. I was back in the moment, as suddenly as I had left it. I slid to the floor, pale and shaking, somehow hot and cold at once. I felt a burning pain in my hand, so strong that I clutched my arm against my chest and rocked back and forth like a child.

For now ... let me just say that there are still things I do not know. Time hasn't made it any easier to comprehend or analyze what happened to us. But hidden amidst these dark, bloody mysteries, there is at least one truth, one thing I think I understand.

The demonic presence that rules those woods is not bound by time.

Chapter Seventeen

D ad began to withdraw from us, at this point. He worked
obsessively to finish the cellar, and when that was done, he
spent his time down there, drinking, watching TV, or painting.
His work grew dark during this period. Before, he had drawn
mostly landscapes and nautical scenes. Our home was filled with
his depictions of old sailing ships and New England's rocky
coastlines. But once we moved, he took to drawing shadowy
forests and snowy, moonlit hills. Actually, come to think of it, his
subject matter itself didn't change. He still drew mountains and
lakes and rivers and seascapes. But now, he drew them at night.
For the first few weeks—or perhaps months—that we lived in
the house, he still showed us his paintings. Then, after Mom
chided him for frightening you with a creepy forest scene, he just
stopped sharing them.

None of us mentioned the change.

School became my respite. Although my first day hadn't gone
over so well, over the course of the first month or so I had settled
in a bit and made a few friends. I learned how to fade into the
background. To be unremarkable. I was the kid that lived in the
haunted house. As far as pecking orders went, I fell into the
middle, somewhere between the kid with glasses and the one that
stuttered. At home, I dealt with things by burying myself in comic
books. But at school, I was free, and the weight was off my
shoulders. I could joke and laugh and run and listen to Mrs.
Bouchard talk about the normal world. At school, I was able to
take comfort in the presence of other people. I acted up

frequently. I guess I was so giddy and relieved to be out of the house that I overcompensated, and became a bit of a clown.

Terry, John, Matt, Ruben, and even Tommy were all buddies of mine by then. But the kid I grew closest to was a pale, skinny blond kid named Lane.

Lane was an odd duck. He was neither popular nor unpopular, which, looking back, is really the best place to be. He was as much of a comic book fiend as I was, so it wasn't long before our fascination with the Marvel Universe cemented our friendship. He also had an insatiable appetite for anything that was even remotely scary. Even as a young child, Lane was attracted to darkness. He loved horror movies, books, and comics. His Mom allowed him to see R-rated movies in theaters, and would even walk in with him to make sure the ticket-takers let him in. He had already seen *The Exorcist, Last House on The Left,* and *Dawn of The Dead.*

He told me lots of tall tales. I remember one in particular: he half-convinced me that giant alien spiders lived under the earth. We both spent several recesses staring at cracks in the pavement in the schoolyard, half-hoping to see spider legs sticking out of the pavement.

I told you about this, and for weeks you were scared of sidewalk cracks. You dodged them, stepped over them, or ran around them, no matter where we were. This didn't last long, though. I guess we had enough to fear, without worrying about spiders in the ground.

Lane and I argued a lot. We bickered over *Batman* vs. *Spider-Man*, *Godzilla* vs. *King Kong*, *Battlestar Galactica* characters, *Star Wars* vs. *Star Trek*, pretty much anything and everything we could take opposing sides on. At some point, we apparently realized that we enjoyed these silly little arguments, for we often ended up giggling.

As punishment for talking in class, Lane and I had to stay after school one day and help Miss Bouchard pick up the classroom. We cleaned the chalkboard, sharpened pencils, and straightened the desks. Then we had to copy the same sentences again and again, and study our math flash cards . . . things that were supposed to seem like punishment to young boys. We made faces at each other, passed notes, and tried to gross each other out with fake silly noises. Detention was supposed to suck, but I was having fun.

Until Lane said my house was spookier than the one the Addams Family lived in, and that witches used to live there.

"You're a liar," I said. One thing about youth — we pull no punches when we're young. Later in life, I often backed down from direct confrontation. I hadn't learned that yet. Whatever I felt and thought came right out of my mouth. And in some cases, right through my fists.

"Am not."

"Prove it."

"There's a creepy old well in your back yard," he said. "There's a pile of branches and junk on it."

I blinked. "That doesn't prove anything. You could have poked around — trespasser!"

"My aunt told me about it. It's covered because twins fell into it and died."

I remembered the twins' gravestones then. A sick feeling twisted in my gut. I became more curious then angry. "Really? When? How do you know?"

But he never answered, because Miss Bouchard returned then. We both fell silent, and amused ourselves by making silly faces at one another behind her back.

Dad picked me up at school that day. The car smelled of tobacco and cheeseburgers. He lit a cigarette as we drove, his arm hanging out the window, and asked me, absently, how my day went.

I remember that day mostly because it was one of the first times that I remember feeling keenly aware of how heavy the atmosphere in the house was. At school, I was this happy, free little boy. As soon as we pulled in the drive, I immediately fell into a pit of gloom and misery. I became sullen, and sometimes I took this out on you, pulling your hair, pulling the heads off your dolls, that sort of thing.

The moment I walked in the door I was greeted by the sound of something breaking, which was followed shortly by the sound of Buster barking.

I found Mom kneeling down, picking up the pieces of another shattered angel with her hands. Though she wiped her eyes when she saw me, I knew she had been crying.

I heard a sound behind me, and turned around. You were standing in the doorway.

"We shouldn't be here," you said quietly. "Can we go? We should go."

Mom stood up. "No, honey, we live here. Just an old house." She held the dustpan, and half-turned to go into the kitchen, but

ABODE

then Dad walked in the door. Their eyes met, and I saw animosity there, true rage, for the first time.

Mom hustled you out of the room, wiping her tears away.

It occurs to me that I have said little about Mom and Dad. It becomes harder and harder for me to remember who they were before everything went so wrong, before our world went so dark. The things that happened to us broke them.

Some people are able to crawl up out of whatever hell they have made or found for themselves, and put themselves back together. Neither one of them was that strong.

I find myself looking over the few photos I have of them from happier times. They are mostly Polaroids taken at family gatherings that various aunts and uncles were kind enough to send me after the fire.

It's no mystery where you and I got our affinity for drawing. Our parents were both artists. They met in art school, actually. But Dad was the talented one. Mom ... I don't know if Mom ever really found herself. Once she met Dad, she quit art school to get married and have us. She was often quiet, and seemed very nervous at times. She smoked a lot and bit her nails, even though Dad hated both habits. She was always in his shadow. He got write-ups in the paper and gallery showings (albeit small ones) and was even featured in a few magazines; she sold her work at church rummage sales for a pittance.

I wonder sometimes if you would have kept painting, and if you had, what your work would look like now. Would it be the same, even though you wear different flesh? Or would you have only drawn when you were young, as so many others do, or as a pastime on rainy days.

Your interests in those days were the common ones so many little girls shared: dancing, drawing, fairy tales, unicorns. For a time, you wanted to be a nurse. You carried around a little bag and a stethoscope, and listened to our heartbeats. "Flu," you told Dad. You diagnosed Mom with a tummy ache and me with a toothache.

I never knew you would be taken so young.

Guilt falls over me like a blanket when I remember the mean things I did to you. How I threw your favorite doll into the mud. I pulled your braids. I called you names.

I know I'm not the only one who has these sorts of regrets. Every day, people die, and every day, bereaved friends and family members regret things left unsettled, words not spoken, secrets never told. I suppose that's part of the human experience, and what it means to walk the earth encased in flesh and blood and pain.

I never knew that my good old days would be over before I even reached my teens.

We never once had a family discussion about what was happening. Our family unit fractured, and we fell away from each other. Dad dove into painting. Mom sank into the bottle. You, well, you were too young to approach things that way. And as for me, well, I sank into my own personal hell. Every night, I would wake to find dark shapes in my room. Every night, I suffered horrible, bloody nightmares.

Mom and Dad tried, in their own ways, to make it easier on us. Dad regularly brought us new toys. Your room was filled with dolls: every week Dad brought you something, a new doll or a stuffed animal, or a toy horse. My shelves were overflowing with action figures, games, and toy cars. They also bought us things we could share, like a table hockey set and a Viewfinder, which we used to watch old cartoon strips. We got new Atari games as soon as they were released, and I had subscriptions to all my favorite comics. The garage and shed were filled with bikes and skis and sleds and skates. Most weekends, Mom took us somewhere, so we could use these things; we skated on frozen ponds, skied at Sugarloaf and Sunday River, spend hours at the roller rink. We went to movies and arcades, and to every museum in the state. You got to take tap, ballet, gymnastics, and horseback riding. I took karate and sports. We both were in Scouts.

Looking back, I think that Mom was deliberately trying to limit the amount of time we spent at home. She became the ultimate soccer mom, hosting and chaperoning events, making cookies for our scout troops, and spearheading a bake sale for your gymnastics team. But, despite her efforts, these things only bought us a few extra hours' reprieve each day.

We still went home to that place every night.

Chapter Eighteen

I want to tell this tale as I lived it, and so I must proceed by memory. It is hard enough to keep that path, to stay focused, stay coherent, stay sober. There are things I have forgotten, and things I refused to think about. And some things I did not learn until years later. I am glad for that, for had I known the truth at the time, I would have been even more terrified.

Believe me, little sister (I hope you don't mind me calling you that) ... I have seen things that will make your hair stand on end. And I must delve into them now, at risk of my own sanity. Perhaps if I manage to expunge, to exorcise these grim memories by putting them in writing, I will cleanse myself, and in doing so, finally be free of this hell.

That fall, as the leaves changed, I started sleepwalking.

I had never done this before.

The first time it happened, I woke in the night to find the full moon shining bright in the sky. I was walking into the woods, but I couldn't control my body. I was a puppet in my own flesh. I felt something else controlling me. I don't know what it was. I don't know how else to describe it, but to say that someone—or something—else was driving me.

I found myself at the path that led to the decrepit cabin.

There was only darkness within, but I could sense something there. Then I saw a flicker of flames, and made out the outline of a campfire burning on the little island on Dead Man's Pond. The water was deeper this time: it was more of a pond than a marsh. I saw shapes moving, and made out the forms of naked women dancing around the fire. The primal beat of a drum thudded through the woods like a heartbeat. I heard the drumbeats quicken behind me as I ran back to the house.

That wasn't the only time I saw the witches dancing around the fire, calling to the moon. I only found out later who their leader was: Sarah. Jeremiah's daughter.

Another night, shortly after that, I again woke on that path. I don't recall waking, or leaving my room, or going outside. I came to awareness as I was walking through the forest. I had no control of my body. The part of me that was *me* was locked deep inside myself. I wanted—needed—to scream, to turn around, to go back to the house, but my legs just kept walking. I soon found myself standing before the cabin, which stood whole again, though decrepit. I sensed a malevolent presence within it.

Then, as I watched, the door slowly creaked open.

I told myself it wasn't real. I told myself I had read too many scary stories. I told myself it was a trick of my imagination.

A branch cracked behind me, and the woods grew still and silent.

And I heard a voice. It was fairly loud, and seemed to come from both above and around me.

"Ave Weresh."

I jumped. The spell was broken, and I was once more in control of myself. I turned around slowly, holding my breath. I couldn't see anything, but it was so dark it was hard to say.

Something moved in the shadowy forest. I couldn't see what it was: I just saw the light changing.

I started running, heading for home as fast as my legs would take me. Only a few moments later, I heard the distinct sound of a voice calling my name.

I stopped and turned around, only to find that somehow, the path behind me had been blocked by a massive tree. Dead branches rose from it like spikes. There was no way I could have missed it: it lay right across the path. I couldn't possibly have gone past it without climbing over it or going around it.

Needless to say, that scared the shit out of me.

The next time it happened, I awoke in the field across the street, before the flat stone. The moon came out from behind a cloud and struck the stone. I heard a drum and a flute, and mesmerizing music cut the night.

But there was no one there.

There were many more such occurrences. I found myself in the cellar, curled up in the darkest corner. I woke in the attic and in the cubbyhole in my room, in the dining room, and in the yard.

One night I found myself in the Kent cemetery, on the twins' grave. It was a full moon, and I was in my pajamas. It was chilly, though the bite of winter had not yet fully closed its jaws. I didn't know why I was there. I didn't remember leaving the house. I just remember looking around and realizing, with a slow, mind-numbing terror, that I was in a place of the dead, and I didn't understand why. In the moonlight, the gravestones looked even more foreboding.

As I went back across the road, first walking and then running toward the (relative) safety of the house, I sensed that something was following me.

ABODE

I looked back and saw, clear as day, a man standing in the moonlight watching me. He wore a dark suit, and a wide-brimmed hat.

Jeremiah.

In the time it took me to blink, he was gone, and I was alone again.

From the forest, I heard the wail of a wild animal. It sounded like a wolf. Records will tell you that in that era, wolves in Maine were extremely rare. But I know what I heard. I saw a flash of dark wings above me as a murder of crows took to the sky, flying below a bright moon. They settled in the cemetery.

I still remember the fear, how it started at the base of my spine and clenched my bowels in a tight fist, how shivers of terror lightly tickled my skin. My heart beat faster, thudding like a drum in my chest. I sped my steps, my little arms and legs pumping as hard as they could, and I ran faster and faster and faster through the darkness until I felt my lungs would burst.

Inside the house, it was dark and quiet. The relief I felt at having made it home was immediately replaced by the uneasiness of being in that place. There's no comfort at going out of the frying pan and into the fire, only a brief reprieve before the terror starts up again.

I never remembered leaving my room, during these episodes. I never remembered walking out the door, or crossing the yard. Like most sleepwalkers, I was unaware of what I was doing. I only remembered these things in bits and pieces. Sometimes I remembered nothing at all. I would wake with mud or grass or dirt on my feet or burdocks in my hair, with no idea where I had been or what I had done. A few of these incidents scared me so badly I almost could have convinced myself they were nightmares.

The mud on my shoes and the scratches on my skin said otherwise.

* * *

I have never told a single soul about these events. I tried telling one of my therapists, long ago but they didn't believe me. That's how I almost ended up with the label schizophrenic. In time, I learned to keep my memories to myself, to let the doctors try to convince me that the trauma of the events I'd experienced had messed with my mind. Most of them just chalked it up to imagination, determining that my childish brain had concocted fantastic stories to deal with the pain and shock of my little sister's death.

There are those among us, know better.

What we faced was real. I have no doubt of that. I've spent a lot of time watching paranormal reality shows, and I see myself in those folks. I understand the distress that fills their eyes when they talk about their experiences, because it's the same expression that I see on my own face when I look in the mirror.

I have realized that I shouldn't include my present struggles in this text. They're not relevant to you. I apologize, and will try my best not to burden you with my problems. I'll go to a meeting as soon as I finish writing this out. But first, I have to finish my tale. I am more than ever bound to write this, purge it, to make you understand.

A few things have happened that make me fear it isn't over.

ABODE

Last night, I heard footsteps, walking across my ceiling. No one lives above me. There is nothing over me but a steep, slanted roof. No one could walk normally across it: you'd have to crouch and crawl like a spider to get from one side to the other.

There was no mistaking the distinctive *thunk* of that heavy tread.

After I finally fell asleep, I dreamt that I was back in that house, looking for you. I could hear you, but I couldn't see you. A veil of falling snow hid the world outside from view. I heard you crying, but try as I might, I never found you. I woke feeling weighted down, as though a heavy blanket of sorrow had settled over me.

I am driven to complete this recollection. I am going to just barrel through it, and hope that when I reach the end, things will return to what in my world passes for normal.

Chapter Nineteen

Autumn in New England is a magical time. The ancient cycle
of the seasons is so prominent here, so pronounced, so
vibrant, that it seems dull in comparison elsewhere. The world
dresses in red and orange and gold, and the changing leaves turn
the forest into a vivid palette of fiery, blazing color. The air is
crisp and clean and cool, laced with the scents of wood smoke,
pumpkin pie, and cinnamon. We have stunning autumns in
Boston, of course, but Maine has a slightly different feel. Boston
is intellectual, cosmopolitan, and diverse. The Revolution clings
to its busy streets and red brick buildings like old perfume. Maine
is woodsier, more primitive, more rustic. It's a world of hunters
and fishermen, of lumberjacks and farmers.

That fall was a very exciting time for me, despite my growing
apprehension about our new house. Like any kid, I looked
forward to Halloween candy and the cartoon specials on TV. At
school, we drew construction-paper ghosts and pumpkins, drank
apple cider, and studied the Salem Witch Trials. Our autumn
play was a watered-down version of *The Crucible*. On weekends,
we went to harvest fairs and hayrides and pumpkin patches, and
picked apples from local orchards. You and I helped Dad build
Buster a doghouse, and helped Mom plant garlic in the spot she
said would be our garden. We drove to Acadia and Camden and
Boothbay, and bought little trinkets in shops that were just about
to close for the winter. Dad carved a jack-o-lantern for the porch,
and Mom fried the seeds. I still remember our excitement when
we got to go shopping to pick out our costumes. They were

horrible, with flimsy material and fake plastic masks, but we were over the moon with glee.

I was a pirate. You were a space princess.

Lane and I went to a Halloween party at Jody Thibodeau's house. We all dressed up in tacky costumes, ate orange-and-black candied corn, played games for candy prizes, and bobbed for apples. They ordered pizza for us, and after supper, we had hot cider, baked caramel apples, and cupcakes with orange and black frosting for dessert. Then we gathered around the fireplace and told ghost stories from a book Lane proudly pulled out of his backpack. We passed the book around, each of us choosing a story, most of which were only a few pages long and had silly names like *The Tale of The Bouncing Eyeball* and *The Headless Nun.*

When Lane's turn arrived, he looked at the book, and then dramatically closed it, declaring that he had a better story, which was especially scary because it was true.

He told us about the water monster of Pocomoonshine Lake. I forget the story, but it was about two shamans battling and changing form. One of them turned into a vast snake, which left trails around the lake that Lane swore could still be seen. We hung onto his every word, rapt and wide-eyed.

Lane had an amazing talent for storytelling, even then. That collection of kids' ghost stories wasn't the only scary book he owned. He also had a big book of local ghost stories, which he had pretty much memorized. He used to practice telling these tales, with me—and sometimes you—as his captive audience. Lane was a great little actor: he played Puck in our school play, *A*

Midsummer Night's Dream. He also loved trying to imitate Wolfman Jack.

We were hooked. When he finished, we all clamored around him, begging for more.

"That's not real." Jody said.

"Is too," Lane said. "I know more, too. Lots more."

"My turn!" Jennifer said, and we all turned to her while she told the story of a witch that had cursed a family and caused all their sheep and cattle to run away.

But it was Tommy Mathieus who told the story that still, to this day, chills me. He took the flashlight and shone it up over his face for added effect.

"Those are all really scary," he said. "But the creepiest thing of all is the old Kent house. The one on Murder Road." He looked directly at me. "The house is really, really old, almost as old as the pilgrims. One winter they ran out of food. Jeremiah Kent sold his sold to the Devil for corn and bread and flour. He became possessed by a demon, and then" —here he paused for dramatic effect— "he ate his own children."

A chorus of gasps and 'ews' echoed through our little circle.

Rage bubbled up through my veins. I felt sick.

Tommy continued. "But that wasn't the end of it. His wife's sister was very angry, and she cursed his family to the end of time. And most Kent children die before they grow up. Even now. And the demon is still there. A hundred years later, it possessed David Kent, and he went crazy. He killed his whole family, and then killed a bunch of kids in town. Now they are hungry ghosts, waiting to eat people. And the demon is still there." He suddenly raised his hand and pointed at me with a thin, reddish finger. "*He* lives in that house. He wants to eat us!*"*

The next moments were—and still are—a blur. I flew at Tommy and started punching him, pummeling him as hard as I could. Jody's parents rushed over to break up the fight. We were soon sequestered in the kitchen. Jody's mom pressed a bag of frozen peas to Tommy's face while his father called our parents.

A short time later, Dad knocked on the door to collect me, his face hard and cold.

End result: I was grounded for a month.

So, on Halloween, while you went to a slumber party, and Mom and Dad went out with some friends from the mill, I had to stay home alone.

I amused myself for a time by doing everything I wasn't supposed to do: drinking milk from the carton, looking at Dad's tools, and sliding down the banister. But these things soon bored me, so I decided to venture into the only room that was forbidden to us: the cellar room Dad had turned into his studio.

I opened the hall door and stood looking down into the shadows. I remember feeling both scared and exhilarated as I crept down the stairs and opened the door to the studio. To be honest, I was hoping to find some dirty magazines, or, at the very least, pictures of naked women.

Instead, I found evidence of madness.

Dad's early paintings were stacked along the western wall. (I know it faced west because when I looked out the small, grimy window, I could see the sun setting through the trees.) Some were the type of paintings I expected, things that went perfectly with the seashore and apple tree ones Mom had framed and hung in our living room. Old Orchard Beach in winter, a phantom of its bustling summer self, its shoreline cold and empty, its carnival rides abandoned. A half-eaten apple, sitting beside a hunk of cheese and a loaf of bread. A river, winding through a birch grove in autumn. Shawnee Peak. The White Mountains. Cape Cod. The Boston skyline. These things were familiar. These were the kind of art you find in any of the hundreds of tiny galleries and brick storefronts that line New England's harbor towns. They were the types of paintings cheerful, eccentric women in fishermen's sweaters do on snowy afternoons, with chubby cats curled up at their feet and herbal tea steaming before them in hand-crafted, ridiculously expensive artisanal mugs. Some of them had hung in our old house.

Dad had always dealt in landscapes, particularly oceanscapes and mountain vistas. He would take Polaroids of national parks or any view he found scenic, and use those photos as his models. The colors and paintings of that time were bright and vivid, bearing the vibrant green and blue hues of spring and summer, the brilliant reds and oranges of picturesque autumns. They belonged in a world of light and laughter, where the smell of fresh-baked goods mingled with the fragrances of wood smoke, pine trees, and barbeque grills. They belonged in art galleries, in cozy dens and living rooms and doctor's offices, in people's hallways. Dad had sold several of them to tiny, cutesy shops, the kind of places that sold handmade scarves, expensive earrings, and souvenir jewelry boxes covered in shells. Touristy Maine, the place of lobster rolls and rocky coasts, loved his work.

Then I found his newer work.

ABODE

These images still bore Dad's faint, slightly rounded style, but they felt very different. There were bleak winter forests, half-imagined. A baseball player lining up for a pitch at Fenway, his arm trailing off into nothingness, his eyes empty. A broken ship, lying battered on a peaceful shore, the sea waves beyond a stunning juxtaposition of placidity and rage. A lump lying underneath a blanket of fresh snow, making the vague outline of a human form. A dog, staring out sadly from behind the bars of a barren cage.

These made me sad, and I felt the weight of sorrow descending over me as I looked at them. They felt like lost children, or pets that had been loved for a day, only to be abandoned. These were muted, mostly greys and browns with only light traces of color. One painting of a forest was almost complete in the center, but the details of leaves and branches faded into nothingness, like a world slipping into the mist, or a memory fading into oblivion. Another was an empty bassinet on a grey day, perhaps a memory of a child that died in infancy. A fluffy orange cat that looked too familiar not to be Lucky, walking away into a field that vanished into nothingness.

None of them were finished. I knew, looking at them, that they never would be.

I found another series. These were finished, but they would never grace a dentist's waiting room, as some of his earlier work had. These were dismal, at best. They had an eerie, forbidding quality to them that made me uneasy. Night-bound rivers snaked between imposing snow-capped mountains under a full moon. Skeletal trees silhouetted against a dreary autumn sky. Gloomy, forbidding northern bogs where dead trees, stripped of bark, stood sentry like skeletal warriors amidst pools of dark water and patches of yellowish, dead grass. Remote ponds and streams that were almost entirely colorless, as though the vitality had been drained from them. A dark, mirror-calm lake, its placid waters split by two huge rocks and a single, unoccupied rowboat. An apple orchard in early winter, the trees twisted and shriveled against a barren field. There was one of the woods behind the house. A shadowy figure in a wide-brimmed hat standing at the edge of a winter forest, just behind the tree line, out of the reach of sunlight.

I put the paintings back and tiptoed back up the stairs, brokenhearted, unable to stop the tears from blurring my vision. I kept remembering the old Dad, the one who tossed me in the air and taught me how to tie knots.

I felt unseen eyes watching me that whole time, but nothing happened.

I guess my current misery was sufficient.

Chapter Twenty

For some reason, Mom and Dad lifted my grounding early. I guess they probably felt bad, and didn't want to make things worse for me. A few weeks later, I invited Lane over to play. We were fast friends by then. We hung out together at every recess, and teamed up for school projects whenever we could. We traded matchbox cars and baseball cards, borrowed comics from one another, and regularly discussed our favorite shows: *The Bionic Man, Battlestar Galactica, Star Trek,* and, of course, *The Incredible Hulk.* Lane was always curious about the house, and his fascination with it made living in a haunted house seem almost cool.

We went up to my room, and he was immediately intrigued by the little stairway alcove in my room.

"You should make that into a secret hideout," Lane said. "A pirate cave."

"I was going to," I said. I trailed off, not wanting to talk about the scratching noises.

"What's in it?"

"Just some old junk. Dad hasn't cleaned it out yet. He's going to do that soon, though."

I knew as I spoke that Dad would never get around to cleaning that space out, but the lie sounded nice. To me, at least.

"Can I look?"

I shrugged. We got the tiny half-door open, and I went and got Dad's flashlight, and shone it inside. Most of the debris was at the far end, so I scooted in a bit further to get a better look. I felt the hair-thin tickle of spiderwebs brushing against my skin, and shuddered.

The contents hadn't changed, though it seemed like some of them had moved. I remembered the old chair and the big dirty milk jug. The cubbyhole also contained a suitcase, two trunks, a few farm tools, some canning jars, and, further back in the shadows, a wooden box filled with old dishes. I reached for the suitcase and dragged it out into the room.

It was full of baby shoes. Old ones. They were made of hand-stitched leather, and I knew at a glance that they were from a different era, a time long past. There had to have been at least a dozen pairs.

Somehow, that sticks out as one of the creepiest things about the house. It was sort of sad. I just had the feeling, looking at those shoes, that the kids who had worn them never got to grow up. I thought of all the graves across the street, and hoped that none of the children had been buried barefoot.

We pulled the trunks out next. The first one contained an old shirt, a lace tablecloth, a watch, and some books. There were some unremarkable antiques; dishes and silverware, old postcards, lace tablecloths, the kind of thing you find at yard sales and antique stores throughout New England. At the bottom of the trunk, I found some books. Most of them were about hunting, fishing, gardening, and the like. I remember seeing a few works from Shakespeare, Yeats, and Dickens. A few were, well, a bit more interesting.

Such as Isabelle's diary.

The fact that I have it still is one of the things I cannot explain. I know it was lost. I know I didn't have it with me at

ABODE

Aunt Kathy's. But years later, when I was unpacking my bags in a dorm room, I found it with my things.

I tried to burn it.

It came back.

I locked it in a box and buried it.

It came back.

I don't know what she wants. I recently reread it, wondering if by revisiting it as an adult I would read more into her tale than I had before. Just the other day, I thought about scanning the pages and sending them to you as an attachment. But to be honest, most of the diary is pretty boring. Actually, excruciatingly dull would be a better description. It's filled with intelligent but bland reflections on trees, leaves, ice carving, cheese making, canning methods, clothing, and gossip, as well as page after page of love-struck ramblings about her fiancé, Gerard, who had gone off to war. Only a few entries caught my attention.

In one:

The time is coming. Father says It will be returning soon. He says the coming winter will be a bad one. It has already begun to gather strength. The shadows in the forest seem deeper and darker now, stranger, more ethereal. I hear unusual sounds at night. I should fear these things, but I do not. They seem only natural, part of the dark beauty of this place. I can sense that the forest is aware, awakening, but I am not afraid of it. I feel one with the moonlight and the shadowy, silent woods.

Every morning, Father asks us to tell him our dreams. I of course daren't say the truth of mine, for they are private thoughts of Gerard and I.

A few entries later:

We had quite a row yesterday morning. Father is not happy with Josephine and her séances. He threw her jars into the fire, and she was distraught at the loss of her Axiom Hominis, which she insists would have healed poor Elizabeth. But, after the last incident, I can hardly blame him! The foolish girl is completely obsessed with Sarah's book and story. I'm glad we are so isolated here, as were we any closer to town, the entire village would have heard the commotion.

It started at breakfast. Father asked each of us to tell him our dreams. Elizabeth refused. A terrible fight ensued, which ended with Father becoming forcible on the silly girl. In time, she confessed. I cannot repeat what she said: it brought shivers down my spine. Her dreams were filled with blood. I was so horrified at what I heard that I fainted, and they rushed to give me smelling salts. Martin insists that she is dangerous, and is entirely convinced that she should be brought to an asylum. But Father only locked her in her room.

I hope the post brings a letter from Gerard. When he last wrote me, they were moving toward Philadelphia.

ABODE

Rumors are that the enemy is approaching them. I must go: I have to make butter before dinner.

And a third:

Last night I saw Elizabeth walking into the forest, through the falling snow. But when I went to look, she was still locked in her room, raving like a lunatic. Sometimes, when she screamed, I could swear I heard the wolves singing to the moon in answer.
Father is quiet today, and pale.
The wind smells of snow.

The diary ends there. I don't know if there was a second book. But I did find that the 20th Maine Volunteer Infantry Regiment was stationed at Little Round Top, at Gettysburg. A man named Gerard Michaud from Mersport died in that battle. He is buried at Togus National Cemetery.

Lane and I dragged the second trunk out, and pawed through its contents. He was hoping we would find something really cool, like an old gun or sword, but no such luck. This trunk contained a random mix of odds and ends: knick-knacks; bottles and jars with antiquated, yellowed labels; costume jewelry; spoons; handkerchiefs; buttons; and the like. There were a few pamphlets about a magician who visited Boston in 1881, and a newspaper clipping debating the 'fad' of séances. As for the books, most of them were cookbooks and recipe books.

The last book was by Aleister Crowley. I just did a Google search, and, based on my memory of what it looked like, I believe it was *The Scented Garden of Abdullah the Satirist of Shiraz*. A

1910 edition of this tome recently sold for something like $8000. I will never know for certain, though: the book, like the rest of the house, is ash now.

These things made me uneasy.

Lane, of course, thought they were the coolest things he'd ever seen.

He really wanted to see the attic. I had never dared go up there by myself. Somehow, having someone with me made me braver. Of course, Lane was all about it. I wouldn't be surprised to find him on one of those paranormal reality shows, excitedly charging into dank, haunted castles with an arsenal of modern devices, eyes bright at the thought of capturing a ghost.

You happened to come out of your room as we were opening the attic door, and you followed us up the stairs.

There wasn't much up there, other than shadows and dust and some old furniture. A table. Our summer things sat there, amidst cobwebs and dust. We didn't find any bones. We didn't find any strange markings on the floor, or an altar once used for Black Mass.

What we did find was another room, which was so small it could almost be better described as a closet. A single bed was set up there, along with a plain bureau and a small bookshelf.

"This is where Martin put Isabelle," you said. "She was mad, after the fire. She was burned. Half of her face was melted off. Like pizza."

Even Lane was creeped out by that.

We went through the drawers, ignoring the heavy feeling that we were being watched. There were some old tablecloths, and a few more books. One, *The Royal Gallery of Poetry and Art,* was

ABODE

from 1886. It was, as one might suspect, filled with poetry and art.

You immediately grabbed it and flipped through the pages. Someone had outlined and underlined certain passages, most having to do with death and tombs and ghosts. Others were about lovers and seasons, mostly spring. I remember you carried it carefully as we went downstairs, and you left us alone the rest of the day because you were so fascinated by it.

That book became one of your treasured possessions. You spent hours and hours reading it, poring over every word. It was—or should have been—far too advanced for you. I doubt you knew what most of the poems even meant. But you began quoting some of them. I heard you in your room at night, reading aloud, correcting yourself when you mispronounced something. Your reading improved drastically while we lived there. While I buried myself in comics, you immersed yourself in Nancy Drew, The Wizard of Oz, and The Black Stallion series.

It wasn't until later that you told me, quite casually, that you were reading to the twins. Entertaining the dead.

Chapter Twenty-one

I recently got copies of our school photos. In your class photo, you're in the front row, wearing a brown-and-yellow dress and white knee socks. You're smiling, just like all the other kids. In mine, I'm in the middle row, wearing a hideous brown and orange striped shirt, standing next to Lane. We were shoving each other and giggling, and Miss Bouchard snapped at us to behave. When the photographer snapped the picture, we looked happy and mischievous.

There is no hint, in either photo, of the shadows that were falling over us at home.

For a time, we lived in two worlds. Home was tense at best and terrifying at worst. But at school, we were surrounded by friends, books, and construction paper art. You and I both liked learning. I was better at English, but you were a whiz at math. We went on field trips, played sports, and ran and laughed with the other kids.

But every day, when the final bell rang, we climbed onto a big yellow school bus, and rode home to hell as the light faded from the sky.

The bus turned at the bottom the hill we lived on, and you and I had to trudge the rest of the way back. It wasn't a long walk. I doubt it was much more than a quarter mile. But that quarter mile wove through uninhabited land, until we came to our property. The eastern side of the road had been cleared, but the west was wooded and wild. And those woods were not a small patch of forest, dissected by road or river. They went on for miles, into primal, unbroken wilderness that still, to this day, remains mostly untamed.

Whenever I passed that stretch of woods, I always felt like something was watching me. I could never see anything there. But I felt it. That one day, it was particularly strong, an unexplained malaise that hung in the air. My uneasiness became more pronounced as we drew closer to home. The skin on the back of my neck prickled. I turned, following some instinct, and saw a big black dog behind us.

This was not some friendly, goofy pet that had wandered off. It looked mean.

"Lexi," I said, trying to keep my voice calm. "Give me your book bag."

You looked at me, puzzled. "Why?"

"So you can walk faster. And if I tell you to run, run."

You slipped it off your shoulder and handed it to me, still confused. "What is it?"

"Don't look back," I said. "Just be ready to run."

I glanced over my shoulder. The dog had drawn closer. When I looked back, it stopped and crouched, hackles raised, and bared its teeth at me, emitting a low growl. The sound sent shivers down my spine. My heart started pounding in my chest.

I glanced at you, then into the woods, looking for a sharp stick. There was nothing, at least nothing I could get to before the dog reached us.

Sometimes I was mean. I admit that. But at that moment, I was looking out for you. "When I say run," I told you. "Go. Don't look back, and don't stop until you reach the house."

I heard the thing growl again. "Run!" I yelled.

You took off, sprinting for the house. I spun around, holding the book bags, as the sound of your footsteps grew fainter.

There was nothing there.

When I got to the house, you were inside, waiting for me, your hands pressed against the glass of the window. "What was it?" you asked.

I told you it was a skunk.

* * *

It was around that time that the last angel broke. Mom and I were in the kitchen, when we suddenly heard a thud and the telltale tinkle of shattering glass. I followed Mom into the dining room.

The curio door was open, and the last angel lay in pieces on the floor.

We both stood there, looking down at the mess, neither of us speaking. No one else was around. Buster was outside. Dad was at work. You were in your room upstairs.

"That's the last of them," Mom said quietly. Her hands were shaking, and her face was white, but she said nothing else, just got the broom and swept up the pieces. She worked vigorously, as though wishing she could sweep up all the bits and pieces of the dark mystery that was descending upon us.

I saw Mom's shoulders shaking, and realized that she was crying silently. She wept a lot by then. I felt bad for her, so I quietly took the broom from her and swept up the last few pieces of the broken angel. I felt bad just throwing it in the trash. It was a pretty thing, and it had belonged to Grandma.

As soon as that angel broke, things escalated rapidly.

ABODE

This is one thing I've battled with. I'm not Christian. I've no use for religion, and don't think that religion and morality are the same thing. In fact, I think they are often at odds. I don't subscribe to the theory that some bearded old dude is sitting on a cloud monitoring the words, thoughts, and deeds of every human being on the face of this earth. I do, however, believe in a higher intelligence, and suspect that the Great Spirit—the source of all matter and energy—is both conscious and interactive. I've come to the conclusion that this being can present itself in many guises and forms, and responds with and through energy. But although I cannot stomach organized religion, with its ridiculous, outdated rules and mantras, I can't deny that sometimes things like crosses and prayers do have an effect on the demonic, even though I didn't experience that myself. I've also come to think that such relics represent the massive amounts of human faith in a force of the greater good. This, not the symbolism, is why such things repel such beings. They work perhaps because people believe they work. Because they are connected to the light. They create a border in the mind, and the border itself is valid.

I believe in chaos.

I believe in evil.

And I must, therefore, subscribe to the fact that these things have their opposites. But, though Mom attempted to pray, and even dragged us to church, religious beliefs or items had no effect on the being that dwelt in that house.

If anything, they only angered it.

Chapter Twenty-two

I still remember the first time it snowed that year. Many of my memories are vague, but every detail of that experience is burned into my brain, crystal clear.

I was watching *The Jeffersons* and eating dinner when the snow began. I vividly recall going into the kitchen and putting my glass and my plate, which was decorated with big yellow flowers, into the sink. I turned to face Mom, who was sitting at the table. She shot me a disapproving look, so I reluctantly poured soap onto a sponge and began scrubbing away traces of the canned Spaghetti-O's I had heated myself on our ugly yellow stove. I heard the downstairs door opening, which was followed by the sound of Dad's footsteps. I watched his reflection in the window as he opened the fridge, grabbed a beer, and joined Mom at the table.

I'm not sure why I looked up. Perhaps it was a feeling, an impulse. Maybe it was just natural, given that the window was right over the sink. As I started washing my glass, I glanced out into the yard, and glimpsed something through the falling snow. I looked closer, and realized what I was looking at.

It was you.

You were walking across the yard, barefoot, in your pink pajamas. I was so startled I dropped the glass, breaking it.

We went through a lot of dishes in that house.

I turned around, panicked, cutting off whatever Mom was about to say about the glass. "Lexi's outside," I said. "She's going into the woods."

ABODE

Mom and Dad exchanged glances, then got up and joined me at the window.

Only a light dusting of snow covered the yard, so we all saw the fresh footprints leading from the side door into the forest. Further out, beyond a curtain of falling snow, we glimpsed a flash of pink (your pajamas) moving into the darkness.

"She must be sleepwalking," Mom said.

Dad cursed under his breath, then grabbed a flashlight, put his boots and jacket on, and went out into the frozen night. Mom and I went out onto the back porch, watching, as he headed off after you. He was staggering slightly. I guess he had already begun his dive into the bottle by then.

Dad shouted for you, but you didn't stop. You didn't turn around. You just kept walking, your movements slightly jerky. Then the forest and the night drew a veil over you, hiding you behind a curtain of shadow and falling snow that blocked you from our view.

The hills behind us echoed Dad's voice calling your name.

Lexi

Lexi

Lexi

Lexi

And then I heard a small, familiar voice behind me. "What?"

I turned. You were standing there, rubbing your eyes, your pale hair mussed from sleep.

Mom rushed back into the kitchen and knelt before you, grasping your shoulders. "Why did you go outside? What were you thinking?"

"I didn't go outside, Mommy," I heard you say. Your voice was muddled with sleep. "Can I have a grilled cheese?"

Searching for a rational explanation, I told myself that you had come back in the side door. I even went to check, sure that I would find it unlocked, that I would see tiny wet footprints on the floor. But it was locked, not just at the knob, but also at the chain. You couldn't possibly have unlocked it. No offense, but you were simply too short.

I went back into the kitchen and looked outside again. That's when I saw it. I saw *you*, standing there, at the edge of that malevolent wood, looking at the house. But I knew it wasn't you. That thing out there, whatever it was, had red glowing eyes. I could see them in the night, two crimson coals, glaring at me.

Suddenly, it was gone, so quickly I wasn't sure if I had seen it or imagined it.

Mom guided you into a chair. "Go get your father," she told me. "Hurry, before he gets too far."

You got comfortable, tucking your feet underneath you, and then looked up at her and calmly asked again for a grilled cheese.

"Mom, I don't want to go out-"

"Go!" She snapped. "Now!"

"But, there's something out there!"

She stood and went to the window. There was nothing there, only the night and the forest and the falling snow. "Go," she said again. "There's nothing out there but wind."

I didn't want to go out there, into the blackness, into the woods. But I clearly didn't have a choice. A sudden thought crossed my mind, the fear that if we left Dad out there, he would never return. So I put on my boots and my puffy coat and walked out into the night, following my father's footsteps into a frozen wood, my heart pounding in my chest.

As I stepped off the porch, my gaze followed the line of tiny footprints to the tree line. There were no return tracks. The night was completely soundless, so quiet you could almost hear the snow falling. Only the sound of my feet crunching on the fresh snow broke the silence. But this wasn't the calm, peaceful quiet of a serene winter night. It was the silence of the grave, the eternal, numbing stillness one senses in a cemetery. The trees were like black skeletons, an army of dead things surrounding us, isolating us, reaching bony fingers into a dead sky. The snow had a grayish tinge, as though the flakes were bone dust. I remember thinking for a moment that the clouds above us were teeming with the ashes of the dead.

Somewhere ahead of me, Dad's flashlight created a wavering, bluish beam of light. I heard the faint, murky echo of his voice as he called to you. He was getting further away. I yelled for him, but my voice was little, choked by youth and fear, and it didn't carry far. I decided that I would rather be with him than alone in the woods, so I started in that direction.

And then the flashlight went out, and I was left alone in the dark.

I heard the distinct crunch of a branch breaking underfoot, and then a clear inhale and exhale as something unseen drew deep breaths. I felt a thick sense of something evil, something menacing, right behind me. Then the snow crunched as whatever it was stepped closer to me. Cold, foul breath fell onto the back of my neck.

I started running. I didn't dare turn around until I reached Dad. I only looked back once, to see a thin outline of shadow in the forest, a pale thing with red, glowing eyes.

Dad was staring at the tracks. "They just stop," he said. "It doesn't make any sense."

We didn't talk about what we had seen. But I felt again that something was watching, as we walked back inside.

The dictionary definition of a doppelganger is as follows: *An apparition or double of a living person.* I had never heard of one at the time. I don't know if I would have been more or less scared had I known what was standing there, watching us. What I saw, when I looked out that window, was you, my little sister, in your pink and white polka dot pajamas.

But what I was looking at was something entirely different.

None of us said anything, but I saw Mom looking out the window, staring into the woods as though entranced. She was filling the sink with water to do dishes with, and only when the water spilled over, soaking her shirt, did she jump and snap out of it.

The tracks were still visible the next morning.

That night the scratching sound grew louder.

Chapter Twenty-three

I've had to stop for a time, to get a hold of myself. You won't see that time in the document. Time and space are warped in the world of emails and electronic documents. A single space between words can represent seconds, weeks, months, or even years. It makes no difference in the end. We think that time and space are impenetrable, undefeatable, unconditional. We think that these things rule our lives, that they have absolute power over everything else.

But, in this strange world we live in, nothing is what it seems.

There is so much in the universe beyond what we can see, touch, hear, feel, and taste. There are things that walk this earth that are not subject to the same laws that we are bound by. Things that do not play by human rules, or the laws of physics as we understand them. These beings must belong to another plane, another realm of existence. I am quite sure that they have never been human. Maybe the property itself is a sort of vortex, a gate between worlds, a place where life and death, future and past, natural and supernatural, all collide.

I begin to worry that in revisiting these events, I am doing more than telling my story. By digging into these frightening memories, I am slowly but surely digging up the grave where I had buried them. Each episode, each event, becomes real again to me as I relive it.

I do not want to pass the burden I bear onto you, this choking terror, this dread and anxiety. But I have researched you online, and I know you have a family. There are steps you must take to protect yourself. To protect them.

I have learned one thing, throughout this ordeal, and in my studies in the years that have passed since. These things, these beings, be they ghosts or demons or something utterly alien ... they feed on fear. Human fear. They feed on rage and pain and misery. They feed on violence and hatred and all of the ugly things a human being can feel, be, and cause. That energy—the vibes, if you will—that we put out when we feel these things, that is nectar to them. As the bottle once was to me. The more terror they can evoke, the more 'food' they have. And while any fear will feed them and make them stronger, fear that is specifically directed at them gives them even more sustenance.

It becomes a vicious cycle, at that point.

Last night I dreamed of Jeremiah. The nightmare was vivid, painfully clear. When I woke, I felt a dark, unnatural energy in my apartment. I chalked it up to my own foolish imagination, but I am very much afraid that the things that stalk my nightmares are still out there, somewhere, seeking entry, seeking whatever portal they can find to get into this world.

I have no answers. Only memories.

There are places where the boundaries between the living and the dead are thin. Rips in the fabric of space and time. The dead dwell beyond the reach of such things. Minutes, hours, centuries ... these things mean nothing to the lost. The next time you look to the night sky, know this: there are things that lurk there, in that eternal darkness. Things that were never human at all. These beings hate us for the things we have that they will never know: the touch of sunlight on our faces, the feel of wind in our hair, the taste of cool fresh water on a hot day. They despise us, simply for being alive. And these things are not bound to this world by flesh and blood and bone, but by fear and dark magic and hatred itself, and by rules and borders we cannot even hope to comprehend.

We dealt with such a being.

There is more than one kind of haunting. I've done my research: what I've learned matches perfectly with what I remember. First, there are human ghosts, the echoes of flesh and blood beings, usually, the restless dead, or whatever part of their energy is left behind after the spirit has left the flesh. We had our share of those, which is no surprise, given the bloodstained history of the property we claimed. But ghosts cannot generally do much harm. They may knock a painting down, open a door, or break a cup, but they haven't the strength to do much more. However, when several spirits are trapped in one place, something strange happens. They gain strength. They grow darker, more sinister. Perhaps they meld into one being. I suspect that they can open portals, and attract other beings.

Demons are a whole different story. I know that's what it was, though it took me years to admit that blasphemous truth. I do not at this point dare discuss it in depth, for such knowledge is dangerous, in and of itself. It opens a line of communication, you see.

We had both, and something that was neither truly human nor demon, man nor beast, natural or supernatural. Something primordial, that stalked the northern woods. A thing born out of a time when the First Nations still ruled this continent, before we came here and tamed the wild, stomped out the guardians of this land, put shining steel cities where there were once only forests and open plains.

These events took place over thirty years ago. I have moved on with my life, for better or worse, tried to make something of myself. Tried to stay afloat. And I have done ... okay, I guess. I'm still here, and physically whole.

But I have always felt a shadow over me. Sometimes I am afraid to turn around. I'm afraid of what I will see there, behind me.

I will not dwell on my personal issues. The ones I face today are almost —dare I say it?— normal. Relationship issues, sobriety issues; at least these are problems I share with millions of other people.

But I will never be whole.

I wonder now if that is what he wanted all along.

You were reborn, after the flames took you. We both were, in a way. But while you found yourself encased in a newborn's body, pure and innocent again, safely wrapped in flesh and blood and bone, my transformation was the opposite. I was reborn as a living ghost, a haunted, bitter soul. I have already been shaped, like a tree or a stone. I cannot be remade into a whole human being any more than I can be transformed into a fish or a bird.

My dreams, this week, have been of the cold northern woods. Autumn, on the edge of winter, in that time when the colors have bled from the leaves and the grass, leaving the world dull gold, forest green, and grey-brown, and the wiser beasts flee or close their eyes against the coming cold.

Chapter Twenty-four

My next meeting with Jeremiah remains, of everything that happened before and since, one of the most terrifying things I ever experienced. The memory still, to this day, raises the hair on my neck. I am shaking now, writing this, because I cannot shake the feeling that he is standing behind me, staring over my shoulder, and that if I turn, I will see him.

And I will go mad.

I have already recounted the scratching sounds I often heard coming from the space under the stairs, and the fact that we had heard footsteps several times. I often heard them at night, and they generally seemed to be coming from the attic, which was right above me. I would wake up at the sound of a strange, heavy tread, and fear would clutch me in an icy cold hand. I'd hold my breath, hoping that the noises would stop. Sometimes, they would. Other times, the steps continued.

By this time, it was happening almost every night. I slept with a radio on to try and drown out the noise. It worked, for a while.

And then, apparently, it angered him.

This is what I recall of that occurrence:

It was late, and we were all in bed. I was almost asleep when I heard the distinct sound of footsteps walking up the stairs to the attic. Because of the setup in my room, I heard not just the sound but the movement of the sound as it ascended. The wood creaked.

I froze. My heart pounded in my flesh. Terror traced a chilly finger over my skin, raising goosebumps.

There was a door at the top of the attic stairs, and one on the bottom. Dad had put a bolt on the top one after the first incident of mystery steps. That bolt never opened. The door remained shut. But I heard the steps cross the threshold, going *through* the closed door and continuing up into the attic. They moved, slowly, deliberately, from one end of the house to another. And then I heard them returning. I lay there, frozen in fear, as they drew closer and closer.

The steps stopped directly above my bed.

Slowly, so slowly, the shadows in the corners of my room moved, shifting, morphing, and melding into one another. Blackness rose and pooled in the center of the ceiling, as though night itself was gathering there. I saw the darkness swirling above me, turbulent and roiling, and had a sense that that inky nothingness was hungry.

Slowly, a shape took form in the shadows. And then I saw a face come through the ceiling, staring down at me. Jeremiah passed through the barrier of the ceiling/floor as though it were water. He did not push his body through, just his head. He wore a dark, wide-brimmed hat, rather like those the Amish wear. He had a mustache, and the vaguest outline of a dark suit was visible. His skin was so white he glowed almost blue in the dark.

He stared at me. He wasn't looking just at me, but into me, into my thoughts. I felt his presence reach in my mind, parasitic. Those burning eyes are seared into my mind. I've heard the saying that the eyes are the window to the soul.

These eyes were not windows to a soul, or to anything human. They were windows to the abyss. To that black void of death that waits beyond the grave.

ABODE

I tried to look away, but I could not. I was trapped, a deer in headlights.

He took a deep breath and exhaled, slowly. The air he breathed out was freezing. The room temperature dropped immediately. My windows frosted over. My breath made clouds in the air. And still he continued to exhale, not stopping. No human being could possibly have contained that much air.

I felt the room growing colder. I could not move, could not scream. I just lay there, frozen and helpless, holding my breath. For a moment, the room was still and silent. Then I heard tiny clinking sounds, as though the knick-knacks and toys on my shelves were moving. The noise wasn't coming from one distinct spot, but all around me. I closed my eyes again. At last, room grew quiet. For long, long, moments, everything was still and silent. I told myself that when I looked back, he would be gone.

He wasn't.

When I finally dared to open my eyes again, he was standing at the foot of my bed, a silent figure cloaked in cold shadows, just watching me.

Watching me.

Then he turned and walked through the wall that connected my room to yours. As soon as he was gone, I regained a little control of my muscles. I opened my mouth to scream, but nothing came out. At least, nothing came out of my mouth. In my terror, I wet myself. As I felt the sickening trickle of warm liquid running down my legs, soiling my pajamas, I clenched my fists and forced myself not to cry.

Next door, in your bedroom, Buster started barking frantically. A moment later, you let out the most bloodcurdling shriek I have ever heard in my life. The sound of it still rings through my nightmares.

A blur of motion followed: Mom and Dad waking, lights coming on, footsteps. You were screaming and crying, and I somehow got myself together enough to move and turn on my light. My pajamas were soaked. I opened the door and stood there, ashamed and frightened.

Dad saw me and cursed me out. "What the hell is wrong with you? Why would you piss yourself when there is a bathroom right across the hall?"

"I was scared," I whispered.

"Scared of *what*?" Dad demanded.

You answered before I could even open my mouth. "The man with the black hat," you said.

I looked at you, and knew you had seen him too. The fear in your eyes was tangible, and it broke my heart.

"Jesus," Mom said. She walked past me, going into my room, then looked around, rubbing her arms. "It's freezing in here."

The glass of water on my bedside table had frozen solid.

"There's nothing to be scared of," Dad said. "Go back to bed, both of you. Now."

We all jumped at the sound of a sudden thunderous crash from upstairs. The walls shook. The light fixture danced.

"That's it," Dad said. He took a few steps toward the door at the bottom of the attic stairs.

"What are you doing?" Mom cried.

I spoke up at the same time she did. "Don't go up there!"

But Dad ignored us both, and opened the stairway door. I heard him go up the steps, which confirmed beyond a doubt that it was not his footsteps I had heard before. We heard him trying the door to the attic, but it wouldn't give. After a few moments, he came back down the stairs. "That door's sealed shut," he said. "Weather makes the wood move and settle. Something probably fell over. There's nothing in this house."

At that moment, our parents' bedroom door slammed shut. The force shook the walls.

I began screaming at Dad. "That's not weather! Are you stupid? Are you dumb?" I went on a rampage, calling him every name my nine year-old brain could muster.

I thought he was going to hit me. I was sure I was going to get beat. But he only looked at me, his face seeming sad and defeated and suddenly old, and quietly told me to go to sleep, because I was scaring you.

Again, the memories are bubbling up to the surface. Things I have buried are rising up through my thoughts, staining the daylight hours with terror. I become more and more certain that if I drove there now, I will find the house still standing, and that if I were to look up at your window, I would see you there, staring down at me. And if I dared to walk around to the back yard and look into the tree line, the path would be there again, waiting for me.

Chapter Twenty-five

Some of the things that happened blur in succession. I can't always remember dates or times of specific events. I don't know the exact order of the things we saw and experienced. I have the date of the night we saw the doppelganger, because it was the first snowfall of the year, so I was able to look it up. Other incidents aren't so clear, or easy to pinpoint. There are things I don't remember at all, things that Mom told me about later, in her lucid moments. And then there are the things that come to me in dreams, and the memories that those visons jar and awaken.

One night in particular stands out in my memory. I woke from the grip of a nightmare, which I fully remember but cannot bear to recount. Afraid to fall asleep again, I turned on my light and tried to distract myself with comics. After a while, I grew thirsty, and went downstairs for a glass of water. The downstairs was thick with shadow, livid but silent.

Too silent.

When I headed back toward my room, you were standing at the top of the stairs. You looked straight at me, as though you were going to speak, but you said nothing. I called your name, but you didn't reply.

That was when I saw them behind you. Shadows, in human form. Pieces of night, that bore the shape and silhouette of human children. They crowded around you, behind you, and two of them moved forward to stand beside you.

They were growing. These were taller than the last ones I had seen. More human-like. I often saw figures out of the corner of my eye, moving bits of darkness that emanated menace. But they were always fleeting, gone so quickly I was never certain they had been there at all. I guess it was around this time that they began to change. The ones I saw after that night were much bigger than the ones I encountered in the beginning, and more human-like.

I heard you speak. You whispered, and your voice, tiny, childlike, cracked the stillness. You said only two words.

Ave Weresh.

And then the shadows surrounded you, and pulled you back into the hall.

I tried to run up the stairs after you, but I met an invisible barrier. Hands that I could feel but could not see held me back. I turned, and saw shadows moving in the blackness behind me. I dropped my water glass, and it broke on the stairs. I remember feeling as though I were drowning: at least, that is the closest comparison I can make.

And then he stepped forward.

Jeremiah.

He materialized right in front of you, and walked slowly, deliberately, down the steps. His footsteps rang out like shots, though the stairs bore no physical weight. He drew closer to me, until we were standing face to face. I could see the ghastly blue-white color of his flesh, the details of his hat. He no longer looked entirely human: it was a ghoul, I saw staring at me, a tall, thin, thing, with long fingers, pallid skin, stringy white hair, and blood-black eyes.

His eyes were the abyss of eternal night.

He came closer to me, and I was paralyzed.

And then he went *through* me. My senses fell into static, fading into white noise like a television set that wasn't picking up any channels. I heard only buzzing, and saw a flickering chaotic dance of shadow and light.

Then there was nothing. Just a cold, primordial blackness.

I woke safe and sound in my bed the next morning, as though nothing had happened. It was a Sunday, so we didn't have school. I immediately remembered the night's events. Fearing for you, I jumped out of bed and immediately checked your room, only to find that your bed was empty. I ran down the stairs and into the kitchen.

You were sitting at the table, eating French toast, quiet and sullen. Mom was at the sink, washing dishes, tense as a marionette, her movements stiff and jerky. You looked up at me, your eyes glazed and glassy. And then you smiled, and asked if I wanted to play cards.

Mom's shoulders shook, as though she was weeping. Her face looked strained, like a mask that was about to crack. And in her eyes, I saw anguish.

I've always felt that something else happened, something perhaps you and Mom experienced, but I never found out what it was. I never asked. I didn't want to know.

Something odd just happened, as I was typing this. A glass in my kitchen fell off the counter and shattered.

I would love to blame the cat, but Gizmo is curled up on my bed, in plain sight.

My heart is pounding in my chest so hard I feel it is going to burst.

Chapter Twenty-six

At the time, although I had a library card, the thought of trying to research our house really never occurred to me. I only recently started searching public records. I've joined several ancestry sites and societies, and information about the Kents is slowly trickling in. So far, the details I've uncovered are fairly bland: dates of births and deaths, military service records, marriage and divorce documents, that sort of thing. Back then, the majority of the information I got was simple rumors and urban legends. I tried to find out more about the tale Tommy told me at the party, but only ended up hearing about a dozen wildly varying versions of the same story.

It was Lane's aunt, Phyllis, who told me about the history of the home.

Lane had a bout with mono right after Halloween. When he went back to school a few weeks later, he was still pale and weak, and he seemed a bit tired. As soon as his mom gave him the all-clear to have company again, I started visiting him. We were both eager to catch up on our comic book and baseball card trading, but we also just liked hanging out. I often went to his house on weekends, and sometimes after school. He visited me occasionally, and always seemed disappointed when no ghosts or ghouls materialized. I was quietly relieved at this: if something had happened, he probably would have wanted to come over more often. I preferred to going to his house anyway. In large part, this was simply because it kept me out of my own home. But I also thought his house was really cool. He had a pool and a playroom, and his dad had built him a treehouse. Also, Lane had his own TV. I did as well—you and I both did—but Lane had cable, which was a big deal back then. We used to sit in his room and watch R-rated movies late into the night.

We were sitting in his room one day, playing with action figures and watching *Fantasy Island*, which he had taped on his very own VCR. The episode we were watching featured a cursed Egyptian tomb, which got us talking about mummies and werewolves. Eventually, the conversation led to ghosts, which of course meant that the subject of my house came up.

"So have you seen anything weird?" Lane asked casually.

I hesitated. We didn't talk about anything that was happening at home, even amongst ourselves. At first, I was reluctant to open up, even to a friend. But, after a moment, I decided to test the waters.

"I hear footsteps in the attic," I said. "And my Grandma's angel collection all broke into pieces."

We had experienced more than that. Much more. But, even at the tender age of nine, I knew better than to reveal too much too fast.

Lane's eyes lit up. "Anything else?"

I shook my head. "Not really. Things fall off the walls sometimes."

"Have you ever found the cabin?"

I stiffened. "What cabin?"

"There's a haunted cabin on the property. Used to belong to a witch."

"Who told you that?"

"Your move." Lane pointed to the card deck. "My aunt. Her husband grew up there."

"In the cabin?"

"No, the house. The one you live in."

"You never told me that."

"Yes I did."

"Did not."

"Did too."

We went a few more rounds with that.

"Wait." I frowned. "I thought the place always belonged to one family."

"It did." Lane said. "My aunt married one of them. We should go see her. She lives right down the street. She reads Tarot cards."

"Now?"

"Yeah, why not? She has kittens, too. I'm going to keep one of them. He's black and white, and his name is Oreo."

"Sure," I said, a little annoyed that he'd never told me this before.

Lane yelled to his mom that we were going to his aunt's house, and we headed for the door.

I wasn't sure what to expect from Lane's aunt. I half-expected an eccentric, gypsy woman with a lot of incense and candles, perhaps a Ouija board. Instead, I found a lady with kind eyes and dark hair wearing a bright yellow dress. When we arrived, Phyllis was in her kitchen, crocheting a scarf, chain-smoking cigarettes, and listening to country music on the radio. We happened to time our arrival perfectly, as a fresh-baked batch of Whoopie pies was sitting on the counter.

The kitchen could have been a time-capsule model of the 70's, with its mustard-yellow appliances, dark brown cabinetry, and hideous vinyl flooring. Phyllis apparently really liked mushrooms and owls, as these things were the motif on various jars, decorations, and macramé pieces. The house was old, its floors and doors slightly warped from time and weather. But it was warm and cozy, and smelled of cinnamon and baked goods. Looking into Phyllis' smiling face, I immediately felt safe.

Lane chatted with his aunt and asked about her kittens. She let us play with said kittens for a few minutes. They were, like any kittens, absolutely adorable.

Then Lane asked about the house. "So, what do you remember about the old brown house? The one on Murder Road?"

Phyllis stiffened. I saw the tension come over her immediately. "Why would you ask that? I told you to stay away from that place."

"He lives there," Lane said, jerking his head at me.

She looked at me, suddenly very still.

"Lane said your husband grew up there," I said. "Is he here? I'd like to ask him some questions, if it's alright."

Her face became very blank, as though she was deliberately suppressing her emotions. "Emmett passed on," she said tightly.

I felt like a fool, and cast Lane a withering look.

"I guess I forgot to tell him that," Lane said. "Sorry."

Phyllis sighed and shook her head slightly. "It's alright," she said, with slightly forced cheer.

"I'd really like to know about the house." I said, using my most polite voice. "Please, ma'am?"

Phyllis was quiet. I imagine she was reflecting on things, mentally debating what to tell us. I know she probably held things back: after all, we were just kids. But after a few moments, she nodded, motioned us toward the table, and told us to sit down.

ABODE

She set out a plate of Whoopie pies and poured us glasses of milk, then got herself a cup of coffee and sat down with us. Lane held Oreo on his lap. Another kitten, an orange and white one that reminded me of Lucky, attacked his shoelaces.

"You boys are young," she said. "And if your mom tells me I've given you nightmares, I'll never hear the end of it."

"We won't have nightmares," Lane and I spoke up together.

"And if we do," Lane added, "we won't tell. Promise."

Phyllis got up and went to the counter. A moment later, she came back with a brown glass ashtray. She lit a cigarette before speaking. "I'll tell you this much: that house has a long history. It's a bad place."

My eyes were glued to her face.

Phyllis sat down and took a sip of her coffee. "The Kent family always owned that house. They weren't very well-liked around here."

"How come?" Lane asked.

"Well ..." Phyllis hesitated, puffing on her cigarette. I could tell she was choosing her words carefully. "There were a lot of rumors of drinking and fighting. They weren't a friendly bunch. Kept to themselves, mostly. Emmett's mother nearly shot my brother once for trespassing. It didn't help that they didn't go to church, which was unusual. The kids all started work young: none of them stayed in school long enough to finish. And the stories didn't help, either. There were always rumors about that piece of land, you know. Some said it went back to the Algonquian tribes, that even they avoided that place."

"Why?"

Phyllis shrugged, stubbing her cigarette out. "The Algonquian thought that if a thing had an idea, it had a soul. Apparently, they

160

believed that something evil lived there. My husband's mother mentioned that a few times." She drew a deep breath. "There are a lot of old tales about the Kents, but most of them are really just different versions of the same tale. Jeremiah Kent came over with one of the first colonists. His wife, Marie, also came over from France, with her mother and sister. Some say Marie's mother fled accusations of witchcraft, and brought her daughters to the New World to escape the gallows. I also heard that it was Marie herself who was accused of witchcraft but escaped before she was arrested. I don't know which version is true, if either. In any case, Jeremiah and Marie got married young, and they came here, and claimed this place of land. Now, in those days, Maine was sort of a No-Man's Land. We were going to be New Ireland, as we were between New England and New Scotland, or Nova Scotia. But many of the first colonies built here failed. This isn't an easy land to survive on. The winters were cold and hard, and relations between natives and the new settlers were at times tense and bloody. But there were resources here. Jeremiah and Marie took a piece of land that the natives shunned. Some say the tribes believed that an evil spirit lived—or dwelt—there. A few years later, Marie's sister, Anne, joined them with her husband."

I swallowed.

"For a time, things went well enough," Phyllis said. "But then, one year, a terrible storm came through. It destroyed their crops, and they lost some cattle as well. They didn't have time to replant before the snows came down, and they didn't have enough goods to trade for food to get them through the winter. Their supplies ran out long before the spring thaw.

"Jeremiah set out on a hunting trip with Anne's husband and their three oldest boys. Another Nor'easter hit while they were out, a bad one. They were gone for weeks. Everyone thought they were dead. Jeremiah finally came back. But he came back alone. He came back changed. Legend says an evil spirit came over him in those woods. According to the story, he killed his brother-in-law and the boys.

"Anne cursed him, when she found out what he'd done. She cursed his whole line. Anne was a witch, like her mother and sister. Some say she killed herself to seal the curse. And ever since then, the Kents have had bad luck and a high mortality rate. They say the house is haunted, and will be until Anne has had her share of souls."

"Cool," Lane said, eyes bright.

"Anne retreated to her cabin. She never forgave Marie. They never spoke much after that: there was bad blood between them. They were known as the Two Witches of Mersport. That's where those two big boulders in Old Mill Lake got their name."

"What boulders?" I asked. I'd never heard of them. I knew where that lake was: we'd gone on a picnic there once. I didn't recall seeing any unusual rocks. But I immediately remembered Dad's painting, the one of the two large rocks breaking the surface of a pale, placid lake.

"I'll show you in summer," Lane said. "They're super cool. They're really big, and you can climb on them and jump off them."

Phyllis pointed a long, thin finger at her nephew. "Don't you even think about jumping off those rocks. You can break your neck. Just like the Millers' girl, the one that had the ski accident. Paralyzed for life, poor thing. And don't you even *think* about jumping off the ledge at the quarry."

"What happened to Anne and Marie?" I asked.

"Anne died alone, not very long after her husband and sons did. Marie never remarried. She taught her own daughters, Sarah and Rebecca, the dark arts. Legends say Sarah, the eldest, became a powerful witch. She married, and prospered. According to legend, she used witchcraft to ensure that her line flourished, and to keep the curse at bay. But when Sarah died, her grandson, Albert, began to show the same symptoms as Jeremiah. His siblings, nieces and nephews, and two youngest children paid the price."

"He killed them?"

She nodded. "So the stories say." She took a sip of her coffee. "There isn't much more to it. Just a lot of stories about the Kent curse. They kept to themselves, for the most part. But they have had quite a run of bad luck."

I swallowed deeply, and got up the nerve to ask a burning question. "Was there someone named Josephine?"

Phyllis nodded. "Josephine lived, oh, probably about a hundred years ago. She was the talk of the town, they say. In her day, séances were a huge trend. She was very much into the occult, and used to have big, fancy gatherings. She and her friends would play with the Ouija board, and call the spirits. Her sister, Isabelle, never agreed with what Josephine was doing. They fought a lot, those two. Their squabbling was well known. Josephine was obsessed with their ancestor, Sarah. Josephine used to try to contact Sarah during her séances. During one of these events, she knocked a candle over, and the house caught fire. Some say it was Isabelle that did it, and there were rumors that it was deliberate. Either way, several Kents died in that blaze, including Elizabeth and Josephine, as well as their father. They had another brother that died in the fire. I forget his name. I think there may have been another sister as well, but I'm not sure. Isabelle escaped, as did two of their brothers, Martin and Anthony. Isabelle never recovered, though. She was horribly burned, and she was mad after that. She'd just lost her fiancé in the war, so to lose her father and siblings just set her over the edge.

"After the fire, Martin inherited the property, and rebuilt the house. That's the house that stands today, the one Martin built. He married, and had children, including Emmett's grandmother. Or great-grandmother. I forget."

"What about the dead twins?" I asked.

She cast me a weird look.

"I saw their graves," I said quickly. "In the cemetery across the road."

Phyllis relaxed a bit. "They were Martin's youngest children," she said. "Jessamine and George, I think. They drowned in an accident. Fell into the well, somehow. My mother-in-law told us about it. She was always worried about Emmett getting too close to that well, so she had it sealed up."

"Was there . . . was there someone in a wheelchair?

"Agnes. Emmett's grandmother. She broke her back riding in the woods, when her horse spooked." She frowned. "How would you know that?

I shrugged. "Heard it somewhere."

I flinched then, as I felt something sharp prick my leg. I looked down and saw a fluffy white kitten climbing up my leg. I picked the little furball up. He immediately started purring and rubbing his head against my hand, begging for affection.

"He likes you," Phyllis said. "Do you want him? He needs a good home."

I thought of what had happened to Lucky, and a lump rose in my throat. I shook my head. "No," I said. "I can't. Maybe Jennifer Wilson can. Her cat just died. She brought his collar to Show and Tell." I paused, and took a bite of Whoopie pie before finishing. "He was really old."

"Is that so?" Phyllis stubbed her cigarette out, and lit another. I stared at her fingers, which were covered in heavy rings.

"Are there any other stories?" Lane asked.

"None that are fit for young ears." Phyllis exhaled, and tapped her ash into a dark brown glass ashtray. "Don't put too much stock in all the rumors. They're mostly just old wives' tales." She sipped her coffee before continuing. "These woods are filled with gossip about witches and warlocks and shamans and strange beasts. Maine's long, cold winters are made for telling tall tales."

"Do you think they're true?" I asked.

"Oh, there's a little truth in every story." She looked at me for a moment before speaking. "You ever been to Bucksport?"

I frowned, puzzled. "I think so. Why?"

"There's a tomb in town. The grave of Colonel Buck. Legend says he was a Puritan, one of the witch hunters. He sentenced a witch to hang, and as she stepped on the gallows, she cursed him. When his grandchildren erected a monument to him, the outline of her foot appeared. They replaced it twice, and the shape came back both times. It's still there to this day. I've seen it."

Lane's eyes brightened. "Can we go there?"

"Lane, you drive past that thing at least once a month." She inhaled again, blowing blue-grey smoke into the room. "You can see it from the road."

I swallowed, choosing my words carefully. "Do you know how to . . . how to keep the curse away?"

ABODE

She looked at me, and her voice dropped a bit, became more soothing. "Are you scared?"

I nodded.

"There are old spirits rattling around in half the houses in this town," she said. "Maine's old, son. And it has a long history. If you hear a bump in the night, or if you see something out of the corner of your eye, just remember that there are things we don't understand about the universe."

I already knew that, and remember feeling vaguely disappointed in her advice.

She looked at me, and her face was strangely still. "Do you have bad dreams?"

I nodded again.

"Keep the doors and windows shut tight, especially in winter," she said. "Winter is the dangerous time. Some say silver will help. And stay out of the woods."

"Tell him about the witches," Lane urged. His eyes were bright, and he hung onto her every word.

"That's just a rumor," Phyllis said. "And not one you need to repeat."

"What was the rumor?" I asked Lane.

Lane answered before she could stop him. "Witches used to eat dead babies in the woods."

"Lane!" Phyllis slapped him lightly on the side of the head. "Where did you hear that?"

"I heard you and your friend talking about it," Lane said. "You said there's a demon there."

"Don't you be worried about that nonsense."

"Can we use your crystal ball? Or your Tarot cards?"

"Absolutely not." Phyllis stood up and brushed off her dress. "That's enough, kids. I'm not going to fill your heads with silly ghost stories. Run on home, now." She picked up the now-empty plate of Whoopie pies, and put it in the sink. "Go on, skedaddle. I need to use the bathroom, and you don't want to stick around for that."

Looking back, I understand why Lane was so free with his tastes. Nothing was taboo in that family. Everything was out in the open. He wasn't sheltered at all, from anything. His parents allowed him to read and watch whatever he wanted. He could more or less come and go as he pleased: they hardly ever told him 'No,' unless he was in trouble for something. They didn't even make him go to church. Our parents, on the other hand, carefully dictated what we could or could not see, say, or do.

That's all she told me. It really wasn't much. But I've been able to piece together a bit more information through online research.

The storm Phyllis mentioned may very well have been the hurricane of 1638, which killed at least seventeen people. Without exact dates, it's hard to be sure, of course. But I did find written statements from those who lived through that storm, including an account from a man in Scarborough, who wrote that the tempest blew down many trees, "in some places a mile together," and wrecked their shallops, which were small boats. It's also worth noting that that period of the 1600's was known as the Little Ice Age, a time when Europe and North America were both much colder than they are now.

I lost track of Lane, but, looking back now, I wouldn't be surprised to find he did well for himself. He had a quiet intelligence and manner that would serve well in the business world.

ABODE

The things I learned from Phyllis and others helped, but they didn't explain everything. They are puzzle pieces, but the picture remained incomplete.

As it turned out, the story about the witches weren't the only piece of local folklore attached to the house. I heard various bits and pieces of the old legends at school. One kid said there was a worshipping pit shaped like a hoof in the woods. Another told me some stories about a haunted cemetery on the land. They said there was an old witch's cabin in the woods, and that sometimes a ghostly ship could be seen passing along the river at the edge of the property. Somebody else described a weird mound with holes in it that aligned to specific stars on occult holidays.

I have no idea where the ship came from. I never saw it. That, at least, I am happy to discount as pure myth. Except for that, all of these things fit with what I had seen, at least up to that point. I looked at the mound again, and have to admit that the theory about the stars made as much sense as anything else I could think of.

It was something else, led me to the truth.

It was you.

You came to me one night, frightened. You never liked my room, but you were crying and scared. You were afraid to wake Mom and Dad, for they had scolded you harshly the last time you tried to crawl into bed with them.

"I had a bad dream," you said.

I sat up and moved over so that you could get into bed with me. You had your teddy bear, and you were curled up in a little ball. Buster turned circles on the floor, and plopped down with his head on his paws.

I asked you what the dream was. You said that you were falling into cold, dark water, and you couldn't get out. And, looking up, you saw someone far above you, wearing a wide-brimmed hat, and glaring down at you. Then, all of a sudden, everything was covered in snow and ice, and you couldn't see anything.

"When I woke up," you said, "They were standing around my bed. It was really cold in my room."

"Who?" I asked. "The shadow people?"

You nodded. "He makes them do things," you whispered. "He makes them do things they don't want to. He made them do things when they were alive, and now that they're dead, he still controls them."

"Who?" I asked. "Jeremiah?"

You nodded. "The demon went inside him," you said. "Then he went inside the demon."

I didn't have much knowledge of demons, at the time. But I remembered what Lane had said, and a cold, terrible realization came over me, a mixture of dread and anxiety.

"It's getting cold now," you said. "And they are getting stronger."

At that moment, a tremendous crash shook the house. Four or five of Dad's paintings fell off the wall. The glass in our picture frames cracked. In the kitchen, dishes fell to the floor. Buster went nuts, barking frantically.

I heard Mom screaming downstairs: she must have stayed up, watching TV or reading. We ran to her, and huddled together on the couch, waiting for the next blow.

But all we heard after that was the rising howl of the wind.

Chapter Twenty-seven

A round this time, my night journeys became much more frequent. When there was snow on the ground, I often woke as soon as I stepped outside. It wasn't exactly pleasant to be jolted awake by the feeling of cold, wet snow against my bare feet, but at least on those occasions I woke at the door, or in the yard. But once the early snows had melted off, the coldness of the ground apparently wasn't enough to wake me.

The incidents also became far more sinister.

Once I awoke to find myself in the forest, on that trail again. I was naked, my body marked with strange symbols written in a substance I immediately knew was blood. I looked at my finger: the tip of my index finger was smeared with the same stuff.

I had drawn these things upon myself.

To this day, I don't know where that blood came from.

The temperature around me dropped suddenly. A few flakes of snow drifted down from swollen white clouds. I looked at the sky and wished, at that moment, for the sun.

My clothes, fortunately, were nearby. I grabbed them and dressed quickly, then ran back to the house, frantic. I was barefoot, however, and my feet were bloody by the time I reached the door.

But there was no safety in the house. There was only Mom, sitting at the kitchen table with a bottle of cheap wine. She looked at me when I burst in through the back door, and her bloodshot eyes had a glassy, glazed-over look. It was the middle of the night, and I had no business being outside, but she had absolutely no reaction to this.

As she lifted her glass, I noticed purple and yellow bruises on her arm. At the time, I thought Dad was responsible, and my blood began to boil. She only told me much later, during one of her lucid spells, that something had attacked her. She didn't know what it was: she had never seen her tormentor. That wasn't the first time it had happened, and it wasn't the last. She kept these things from us, not wanting to frighten us further.

We all sank deeper and deeper into our own private hells.

I continued to sleepwalk. One time I woke in the cemetery, lying spread-eagled on a grave. I think it was Josephine's, but I can't be certain. It was snowing, and I was covered with a dusting of pale, cold flakes. Another night, I woke in the yard, at the edge of the tree line. I saw the path clear as day before me, leading into the woods. Something made me look up.

The shadow children were standing on the ridge, just above me. This time I saw their faces.

Their mouths were sewn shut.

I don't know why I counted, but there were seventeen of them. Seventeen black shapes that radiated darkness the way a lamp radiates light. None of them were moving. Then I saw a paler form, standing among them.

It was you.

As soon as I saw you, they—you—slipped back into the tangled wood, and were soon lost among the shadows.

I slowly got to my feet. I was terrified. I wish I could say that I had no hesitation in going after you, but that would be a lie.

ABODE

Somehow, I found the strength to do it. But it wasn't easy. I had to force myself to walk forward into that dark forest.

I can go back to that moment in the space of a heartbeat, because some part of me never left. Some part of me is still wandering those woods, looking for you.

The path lay before me, clearly visible even in the blackness of the wood. It brought me again to the cabin, which stood whole once more, its dirty windows reflecting dim starlight. I was so terrified walking up to it that I hyperventilated. I drew great gasps of air, terrified that I would asphyxiate and pass out.

I heard whispering, and then the distinct sound of a thud from within.

I saw you at the cabin window. I know I did. I saw your face, plain as day, looking out at me from the shadows.

Then you stepped backwards and were enveloped by darkness.

There was no sound, in the forest. No bird, no wind, nothing. Just silence. I heard your voice from inside, clear as a bell, calling my name. You said you were scared. You said you were cold and hungry, and you wanted me to take you home.

I tried to make myself go in after you, I really did. But I never made it to the entrance. The terror became so intense that it completely overpowered me. I could not shake the feeling that something malevolent was waiting for me in that place, and that if I set foot inside the cabin I would never see daylight again. I simply stood there, shaking. I wasn't brave enough to go in.

I felt as though time had stopped, as though I had stepped through some vortex into another reality. Every cell of my being screamed at me to turn away. Yet I stood frozen before the cabin, as firmly rooted to the soil as the trees around me.

I don't know how long I stayed there. It seemed like forever.

Then, I felt a strange, rushing dizziness. It was almost like the feeling you get on a roller coaster, when you start down a really steep part and your stomach twists and heaves. All of a sudden, the cabin was gone. I was alone in the woods, standing before the stone foundation slab.

I took a step forward, and I heard a distinct voice behind me. *Ave Weresh.*

All Hail The Beast of The Woods.

There came a roar then, a thunderous bellowing that rose up from beneath the earth, a demonic howl no natural beast could have made. Goosebumps covered every inch of my body, and my hair stood on end.

In the distance, I heard the sound of branches snapping. And I knew that whatever it was that was lumbering toward me in the dark was nothing that should walk the earth. I knew it was demonic.

The Beast of the Woods.

The Beast Jeremiah fed.

The Beast Sarah had danced for.

The Beast that took dead children and enslaved them.

I ran all the way home. To this day, I feel as though I barely escaped with my life.

The next incident happened a few weeks later. I woke again on the trails behind the house, far past the spot where the cabin had stood. I stood there, wave after wave of terror washing over me, but the wood was silent around me.

Too silent.

ABODE

I started running, heading for home. Every now and then, I heard a branch crack, and the leaves rustled behind me, but when I looked, I saw only shadows. The woods ahead of me wore the faint illumination of starlight, but the world behind me was pitch black.

The sounds drew closer, but fell back a bit as I picked up speed.

And then, suddenly, behind me, I heard the distinct creaking of a door.

I stopped in my tracks, confused enough to let my curiosity overcome my fear. Turned slowly, I found myself facing a door. It was not attached to any building. It did not touch the earth, but hovered in midair. It was not a particularly fancy door: in fact, it was made of plain, simple wood that looked rather worn and weather-beaten. I could see cracked, peeling paint on the frame. The doorknob was rusted and dirty, antique looking.

It hadn't been there a moment ago: I would have run through it.

It creaked slowly open, revealing a void beyond it. There was no wind in the forest, but in the abyss beyond the door, a tempest screamed and howled. That infernal wind still howls through my dreams. It was as though someone had cut a square hole in the fabric of reality, a door that opened into primordial blackness that had existed long before the first star burst into being.

They say that black absorbs all colors, so that none of them are reflected back to the eye. This darkness, it absorbed not only color, but life and sound and air. I knew what I was looking at: death. The nothingness that waits beyond the palest light from the farthest, oldest stars that lie at the edge of the universe. It was primordial, and, though it was black, rather than filled with fire and brimstone, I knew I was looking into hell itself.

Hell, to me, has never been a fiery, burning inferno. It's cold and dark and icy.

The forest filled with howls and cries. And I knew what they were saying, the beasts of the northern wild. For one, brief moment, I understood their language. They were calling for their god.

Ave Weresh, the Devourer.
All Hail The Beast of The Woods.

Then something hit me from behind. I fell, and the world went black.

When I woke, my head was pounding, and I could feel something encrusted on my eye (blood—I had hit my head). And I heard something moving through the woods nearby.

I turned and found a dismembered deer behind me, its innards strewn about the path.

Shadows moved in the woods around me. I heard the sound of branches breaking. I looked toward the noise, and saw a pale, skeletal figure walking through the trees. I could not make out any details, but to see that it was very tall and very thin, and nothing that should have ever walked this earth. It looked human, vaguely, but great antlers rose from its head.

The thing moved slowly, and I could tell that it hadn't seen me.

Weresh, I thought, *The White Beast.*

As soon as the thought crossed my mind it turned toward me, and it fixed me with a hateful stare, its two blood red eyes seeming to look directly into my mind. It drew closer, and I got a good look at it.

That image still haunts my dreams, to this day.

The thing must have been at least fifteen feet tall, if not taller. Its body was roughly human like in shape, except that its legs looked somewhat goat-like, curving at odd angles and places. Its limbs were impossibly long, it's massive, hideous hands ending in sharp talons. But its head was the worst. The Beast's face was gaunt, with sickly, yellowish-grey skin pulled tight over prominent bones. That horrible visage was somewhat deer-like, but its mouth was a gaping maw, with rows of razor-sharp fangs and bloody, torn, lips. Massive antlers grew from its misshapen skull. It was pale, almost the color of snow, with a few thin strands of matted white hair falling from its skull.

I turned and raced for home. I don't think I had ever run that fast before, and I'm pretty sure that I haven't since. Behind me, I suddenly heard heavy thumps as the massive creature took chase. This was followed by the crashing sound of branches—perhaps whole trees—snapping.

Somehow, I made it home. I skidded into the yard and turned.

The Beast stopped at the edge of the wood, at the stone wall that divided our yard from the trees.

I ran inside. When I dared look out the window, it was gone.

I know this all sounds crazy, like something one would see in a comic book, or watch in a horror movie. There is no proof of these things. There is no documented evidence, save the occasional home video one may find online, which offer, at best, a 50/50 chance of being real. I will never come forward with the severed, antler-adorned head of the White Beast, to offer irrefutable evidence that my experiences were real, that my memories are based on reality rather than myth or imagination. I will never find a forgotten home movie, or anything else that could prove what I am telling you is true.

Instead, I offer doubt itself as evidence.

Do you believe that every single person who has described paranormal activity is mad or lying? Do you believe that every single unexplained phenomenon is nothing more than a trick of the light or the product of an unhealthy, over-imaginative mind? Can you honestly say that all of the thousands of accounts of hauntings and unnatural beings are fake? Are you that certain of the boundaries and rules of the world we live in?

If your answer is yes, I truly envy you. Because I have no such faith.

Faith, to survivors like myself, is only a lie at best, and a trap at worst.

Death's door opens both ways.

Chapter Twenty-eight

L ike most people with PTSD, I am prone to certain triggers, things that set off memories and bring the trauma back. For war veterans, it might be a loud boom, fireworks, or a holiday or landscape. For rape victims, it may be the mention of a rapist on the news, or a violent scene in a movie.

For me, it's, well, the late 70's. Disco. Eight-tracks. Plaid. Shag rugs. Bell bottoms. All the things I associate with those days. The most casual reference or reminder to those days strike me like little bullets. I even hate the colors and patterns of the era, the yellows, ochres, and browns, the plaids and stripes and ginghams, and the hideous geometric patterns and round, puffy fonts that were everywhere at the time.

I saw a Scooby Doo reference the other day, and it awakened another memory, one I had completely forgotten. You and I were sitting in the living room, watching cartoons, glued, as children often are, to the colorful animated figures on the TV. We had the volume up really, really loud. Mom came in and turned it down. I recall being disappointed when she did that. To us, the spot in front of the TV was a safe harbor. We would sit cross-legged on that avocado shag rug and just stare at the screen. The TV masked many of the sounds we could hear in the house . . . or at least it had, until Mom turned it down. But it could not entirely drown out the horrible scream of rage that echoed through the woods outside. Each time it rose—which happened at completely random intervals, as though the thing were bound to drive us mad—you inched closer to me.

As though I could protect you.

Onscreen, Scooby and Shaggy were investigating a haunted house. I guess the episode struck close to home. I started thinking, and I got scared.

As soon as fear touched my thoughts, the thing in the house awoke. From somewhere below us, we heard the sound of a dull thud.

I remember shuddering, and thinking *'No, not again. Just leave us alone.'*

And then suddenly, defiantly, you stood and turned up the volume again. You turned and looked at me, as Mom came stomping back in, her face creased with anger.

She turned it down again.

This time the volume rose by itself. But the sound was not the happy, circus-like background noise of a cartoon. It was a hellish, screaming wind.

The TV snapped off. And then it turned itself on again.

Mom went white.

We all heard the distinct sound of footsteps in the upstairs hall.

"We shouldn't be here," you said to Mom.

Mom frowned. She went to put her hands on your shoulders. And then something unseen shoved her. Whatever it was pushed her so hard that she flew into the TV set, which was one of those old console ones. Some of the knick-knacks on the top of the set fell off.

The set turned off again. And then on.

ABODE

Mom was shaking and crying, but she got herself to her feet, looking around warily. But the house was silent again, as though nothing had happened.

The TV screen went black suddenly. But this time the volume stayed on. Mom unplugged it.

We all heard the TV Dad kept in the basement snap on. He wasn't home from work yet, so we knew it wasn't him.

This time the lights went out. They came back a moment later. In fact, all of the lights turned on, even those that hadn't been on before.

That was the moment Mom broke. She crumpled into a frail, weeping heap on the floor, calling us to her. I went for comfort. You went because you were told, and only reluctantly. I remember that after a moment you stood up, and looked down at her. "You shouldn't have done that," you said.

"Go to bed," Mom snapped. She wiped her tears. "It's a wiring problem."

"It's the Beast," you said.

The lights went out again.

Then you went up into the darkness on the second floor, walking slowly up the stairs to your room.

* * *

My dreams changed, at this point. I'd been having nightmares from the start, but around this time, they rapidly grew worse. And these dreams were different than the ones I'd had before. In these, I was Jeremiah. I remember reaching my arm out —a man's arm, wiry and hairy— holding a knife. And, while I shall spare you the

180

specific details, I had very clear images of the butchery and consumption of human beings.

I dreamt death. I dreamt flesh and bone and blood. Vivid, crimson scenes, of hot wet liquid and vital organs spilling out onto pristine snow. I dreamt of the cold bite of winter's icy wind, and the eternal, lonely forest. I dreamt the dreams of the forgotten bones that lay, covered in time and mud, in the bottom of a cold lake that has long since dried up. I woke at the spot where its shores once were; all that remains is a murky, northern bog.

In more than one dream, I sat in a snowy glade, blood staining the snow around me. I knew that I was going to be sick, and so I leaned over a log and threw up violently. What came out of me still gives me goosebumps. Vomit, of course, is never a pleasant thing. But this, this was not your typical, foul slop of bile and partially-digested food. It was blood and meat, mixed with tiny bits of bone and hair. And I saw, in the revolting filth that spewed out of my body, what appeared to be a human toe.

It wasn't real. I know it wasn't real. But when I woke, my mouth was filled with a strange, coppery taste.

I sometimes woke remembering the specific circumstances of . . . a death. I won't recount those dreams here. They are certainly far too graphic for me to recall in detail. I don't even like to think of them, as those images entailed something so horrifying my stomach roils at the thought even now.

The shadow children were sometimes with me in these dreams. They drew closer to me in each nightmare, but never got close enough to touch me. I never let them. I knew, somehow, that if they ever managed to catch me, they would drag me through the veil that separated their world and mine. But somehow, oddly, they didn't seem malevolent. As time went on I eventually saw them as less of a menace, and more as victims. I don't know why. Maybe it was what you had said, about them being controlled. I just know that something about them made me think that they were trapped there, too. That they didn't want to torment us, but were forced to.

You too, had nightmares. They reached both of us that way, you see, and I think I understand why. Dreams do not belong in our realm: they belong to the dead and the unborn, and to things that never walked this earth, things that have never turned their faces to this sun.

It was me you came to with your night terrors, not Mom and Dad. You told me that you dreamt, over and over, of falling into the well. Of something sinister lurking down there. You dreamt of getting lost in the frozen wild, of running through cold, dark woods, knowing that something terrible was chasing you. You dreamt of dancing in the field across the street, honoring some dark deity. And you described the cabin and the lake to a tee.

I've painted some of your visions. They burn through my memory, even now. It's been a long time since my two measly gallery showings, but you can still see some of those images on my website, and you can find book and CD covers I've done online. I wonder if you would recognize any of them. The spider-being, crawling across the floor toward the sleeping child. The children, standing in a circle around a black hole. The clouds, filled with ancient faces. The shadow beings, reaching for the girl on the swing.

The Beast: an inhuman thing, a desiccated, white wraith, skin stretched taut over demonic features.

Chapter Twenty-nine

It grows dark early in the winter, in Maine. By suppertime, the sky is pitch black. In the city, the darkness might be broken by the pale pink-orange glow of lights cast against the sky. But in the woods, the blackness was absolute. We saw only a few dim, distant lights from the other side of the river. Town was a pale pink-orange glow on the horizon. Our nearest neighbors were nearly a mile away, on the other side of the hill. Only moonlight and starlight held back the night most nights. At other times, the world around us was completely black, as though we existed in some void.

By mid-December, the sun was already sinking when the bus dropped us off from school. It was pitch black by four.

As the year grew old, the nights grew longer. And as the nights grew longer, these things, these denizens of the realm beyond death, they grew stronger.

I've done enough research to formulate a theory on this. These things that haunted us, they belonged to the darkness. They faded in the summer days, hiding from the daylight and the brighter hours. But when winter came, and the nights grew long, they gained strength. *It* gained strength. And as it grew stronger, and we grew more frightened, our terror fed it.

As I said before, these beings feed on terror. And what is more primal than fear of the dark, of the unknown, of the cold, brutal winter night? That terror lies buried deep in the hearts of mankind, and it dates back to primordial times, when the shadows of the night hid predators, and perhaps even crueler terrors.

How does that saying go? One has nothing to fear but fear itself.

In the world of paranormal research, one thing that is generally agreed upon is that when many people die unnaturally in a certain place, that property begins to take on a supernatural air. In time, the deaths on the property created a vortex. Or perhaps, the property always sat on a portal. There is, somewhere in those woods, in that cabin or in a cave, a gate of some sort. A door. Perhaps this was the original source of the evil, or maybe all the deaths created it. I don't know. And I don't think I want to.

Some doors should never be opened.

* * *

As winter fell, we spent more and more time indoors. On weekends, we would go sledding or ice skating, but between the cold and the fact that it grew dark so early, we couldn't stay outside very long. By 3:30, the light was fading from the sky, and we would be ushered inside, ears and noses red, cheeks burning, to stamp the snow off our books. Once our homework was down, we were left to amuse ourselves until bedtime. I spent endless hours curled up with comic books, Matchbox cars, video games, and choose-your-own-ending adventures. Sometimes you and I played board games together, or watched TV in the living room, but a lot of times we retreated to our own rooms.

You always liked to draw. I know you still enjoy it; I saw the paintings on your website. You spend many cold afternoons on the couch or in your room with your crayons and markers and sketchbook. I preferred reading. I loved comic books. Even during the worst of it, I found comfort in those pages. If I had to believe in monsters and boogeymen and things that stalk the northern woods at night, it stood to reason that I could also believe in heroes too. It was the only way the world made sense.

I was watching TV one night, not long ago. While flipping through channels, I came across a show about the 70's. One brief snippet of the *Charlie's Angels* theme brought back a memory of you and I sitting together, holding hands so tightly our fingers had turned white. We were staring at the TV, only half-watching Farrah Fawcett and Jaclyn Smith. We really were just seeking the most basic comfort we could find: the sound of human voices.

Mom came in and changed the channel, so she could watch the news.

I don't know if I heard him or sensed him. I just know the room got very cold, all of a sudden. And the air grew … thicker? Heavier?

I turned, and Jeremiah was there.

I gasped, and whispered. "Mom," I said. "Mom."

She looked, and then quickly turned her face away from him. "It's nothing," she said. "Just this house playing tricks on you. It doesn't exist. Just watch TV."

So we all looked back at the TV.

There he was, standing in the background behind a newscaster that was covering a plane crash that had killed most of a basketball team.

Mom got up and changed the channel. This time he appeared in the audience at a football game, leering at us from the midst of a crowd of Cowboys fans. He wore his human face. Even his hat seemed barely out of place amidst a sea of cowboy hats. He looked human, but it was him.

The TV went dead. We heard a crash from the roof as the antenna fell.

The radio snapped on. But, instead of music or human voices, we heard a wailing, shrieking winter wind. And then, behind that, a terrible, inhuman roar.

Then there was only silence. Beyond the walls of the house, the wind screamed and howled, as though it, too, was hungry.

I remember one night in particular. I was asleep in my bed, when I was suddenly awakened, not by noise, but, strange as it sounds, by silence. My radio, which I always left on I went to bed, was off. The room was dark, but the starlight coming in through the window illuminated a shadowy figure in a wide hat standing at the end of my bed.

Jeremiah.

He didn't speak. He didn't touch me. He just . . . projected hatred into my mind.

He's not real, I told myself.

And then, he reached for my leg. I felt the coldness and the weight of his touch, and closed my eyes, telling myself that I was dreaming. I remember thinking: *What if he gets stronger, if I acknowledge him, if I react? What if my fear is what he wants?*

I opened my eyes. His face was no less than two inches above mine. He looked even less human this time. His skin was a sickly yellowish-white, and his eyes were a blackened, bloody color.

ABODE

When he opened his mouth, he had horrible, yellow fangs. Then he sniffed me, like a beast sniffing its prey.

Come to think of it, that's exactly what it was.

Images flooded into my brain. Images that belonged in horror movies. Images that have no business being in the mind of a child. Dead men, corpses, violence. I shall spare you the details, save to say that they completely traumatized me.

And then he took control of me. Like a puppet, I got out of bed and went to stand at the window, looking out across the cold, night-draped world below me. Through a blanket of falling snow, I saw shapes moving in the night. They weren't human. It took me a moment to identify them as wolves and bears. And, standing at the edge of the woods beside the house, a dark-haired figure, one I'd never seen before. I knew who it was, though. Elizabeth.

Here I must pause, and make a distinction for you. I do not know if you are familiar at all with the paranormal, but I must make clear that we were haunted not by one being, but by several.

Ghosts are the spirits of dead humans.

Demons are entities that have never, ever been human.

Both dwell on that property. We had, by this time, all had experiences with Jeremiah. But there was something else there as well. Something I did not, at the time, know quite how to classify.

I know it now only as The Beast Of The Woods.

Chapter Thirty

Please forgive me if the next bit is jumbled. My nerves are a wreck. My head is spinning, my thoughts manic, in disarray. Things are coming back to me that I had forgotten. No, *forgotten* is not the right word. I buried these things, hid them deep in my psyche, as though laying them to rest in a dark crypt in the center of my mind. I tried, in the interim years, to forget, or to at least accept the unknown and move on.

I am only now beginning to realize how impossible that is.

I saw your older daughter's paintings recently, the ones on display at the school. (I didn't actually go to the school; that would be an invasion of privacy. I found the story they ran in the paper, which included pictures of the paintings.)

The Flame Fairy

(Josephine)

The Farmer With The Hat

(Jeremiah)

The Pale Lady In The Wheelchair

(Agnes)

Your younger daughter has seen him too, hasn't she? Is she having nightmares too? Does she have a blue mermaid doll? I found one this morning, on my kitchen table. I did not steal it. I did not buy it. I've no use for such a thing.

I've begun, once more, to dream of those woods. Of the cabin. Of pale Elizabeth, mad Isabelle, and poor, crippled Agnes. Of Josephine, and the twins. I dream of you, dancing in an autumn forest, in a pretty white gown. But when you look at me, your mouth, dress, and hands are stained with blood.

I've been seeing—and hearing—more signs of his presence at home, too. The scratching the first night was very faint and gentle. It could very well have been a mouse. But each night, it grows louder and louder. Each night, the pattern becomes clearer.

Last night, I woke to find a dark, shadowy form at the end of my bed, watching me. It did not move or speak, but I had a sense of its energy, its malevolence. It emanated hatred. It emanated violence and loathing and rage.

His name rose up through my fear. I could not prevent the thought, that name, from crossing my mind. As soon as I did, he moved closer. My heart pounded in my chest. I was paralyzed, unable to move a single muscle.

Then he opened his mouth and screamed, and my windows shattered. My head still rings from the sound. I cannot pretend I dreamt it, for I've just finished sweeping up the glass. And not even an hour ago, I had a very awkward conversation with my landlord about replacement windows.

I don't know which scares me more: Jeremiah, or the thing that sometimes wears his shape.

It comes back so easily, the fear. It is one thing to tap into our primal emotions deliberately, by watching a scary movie, jumping out of an airplane, or walking through a fake haunted house at Halloween. But the terror these things produce is contrived, a passing amusement that never really hits the bone. I have no doubt that I—we—experienced the reality of something truly evil. That horror is another thing entirely.

It is starting again.

I was just interrupted by a knock at the door. When I went to answer it, there was no one there. Nothing at all.

The night grows chilly. The wind is howling at my window, as if it was trying to get in. The cold is seeping into my bones.

Darkness comes early, at this time of year, and these things, these abominations, they love the dark.

When I was young, I believed in heroes. I even dared to hope that someone would save us. I didn't care if our savior wore tights and a cape, or jeans and plaid flannel shirts. That hope flickered and died over the course of a few short months. And now? Now I have no such illusions. The sky is empty. The men in white robes worship and appease a myth of their own creation. If there are angels, then they are weeping and broken. One need only look at the world to know that there is nothing benevolent at work here.

I have poured myself a stiff drink, so that I may continue. I must write this, as quickly as possible. I must expunge these things, and then be rid of them forever. I have just given notice at my pizza delivery job, so that I can entirely focus on writing this tale.

Chapter Thirty-one

We had our first major snowstorm shortly after that. School was cancelled, and you and I settled ourselves in my room, playing video games. The skies were thick and dark, heavy grey. Mom baked cookies. And then it started snowing.

There is something magical about the first snowfall, but the first real storm is also special. At least, I used to think so, and I understand the sentiment in those that still do. The world is transformed. The familiar nooks and crannies are hidden by a landscape. The world changes, overnight.

As the day wound on and more and more thick flakes fell from the sky, a heavy feeling of dread fell over me. We were isolated now, trapped. The storm was a doozy, a true Nor'easter. Dad had already told us we'd be stuck until the plows came through.

The daylight hours passed in a flash. Darkness fell, and there was only the endless barrage of screaming winds and falling snow. Dad and I were constantly stoking the fire, bringing up wood from the basement. I hated going down there.

Against the howling wind, I heard another sound: a low, keening wail that set my nerves on edge. We all heard it. Even you questioned it, and asked Dad if there were monsters outside, in the storm.

"Just the wind," Dad said.

Buster started growling.

I looked out the window, frightened. But the falling snow made it impossible to see anything beyond the dance of heavy white flakes.

The sound came again. Mom jumped in her chair, and nearly dropped her housekeeping magazine. Buster growled again, baring his teeth. Throughout the night, we heard that horrible noise again and again and again. Dad at first insisted that it was only the storm.

We knew better.

We soon realized that it was coming closer. The wailing grew louder and louder, until we were all pale and trembling.

Then we heard a boom, somewhere in the woods behind us. The first thud was not that loud: it sounded like something falling off a shelf in the garage, perhaps. More thumps followed. Some of the noises were accompanied by the crack of branches. They came in evenly-spaced intervals, continuously growing louder and louder.

Footsteps.

The next THUD shook the walls. We felt the vibrations. Snow fell from the roof, and the dishes rattled in the cabinets. You, Mom, and I went to stand in the kitchen, staring silently into the storm. All three of us were shaking. You and I held Mom's hands, gripping her tightly, as though she could protect us. None of us spoke. I don't think we had the words to express what we were feeling. We just stood there, frozen in place, staring into the veil of falling snow.

We saw something moving in the woods at the edge of the yard. Something far too large to be human. I got a glimpse of a thin, pale, form, with antlers on its head. It had to have been as tall as our house. My stomach coiled and rumbled at the sight of it. I looked away, and when I looked back, the snow hid it from my sight.

A terrible, hellish roar cut through the night. The screech was absolutely horrendous. It broke the spell of silence that held us immobile. You started crying, and Mom put her arms around us, holding us close. Even Dad could not ignore it: we heard the sound of his steps coming up the stairs.

The scream seemed to go on forever. No human being could have made that noise, and I doubt any animals could have, either. Finally Mom broke, and screamed back. "*Go away!*"

The sound stopped immediately.

For a moment, everything was still and silent. Then, we heard the distinct thumping sound of footsteps again, this time retreating back into the woods. They grew fainter and fainter as the Beast moved away, and finally ceased entirely.

We were silent for the rest of the night. The only sound in the house was the surreal echo of Archie Bunker yelling insults at people, and the uproarious laughter of the audience. The comedy did nothing to ease our gloom. Jokes couldn't even break the surface of my thoughts. I felt like we didn't belong in that world anymore.

My dreams that night were of winter, of ice and sand and snow. I was caught in a blizzard, and was trying to find my way out of the forest. Something was chasing me, but heavy snow slowed my steps so that I couldn't run. The thing behind me drew closer and closer, and I could smell the foulness of it, a stench of death and decay.

And then, suddenly, there was only the storm again, an endless maelstrom of white flakes dancing and spinning in a freezing, howling wind. I stared into the blizzard, and knew myself puny and insignificant.

I woke to find Jeremiah standing at the end of my bed. He was clearer, this time.

And he was changing.

He no longer looked remotely human. His skin was a sickly bluish grey, stretched taut over a deformed skull. His face looked extremely drawn and gaunt. I could clearly see his cheekbones and his eye sockets, as well as the bones of his jaw, which seemed abnormally long. What remained of his hair was white and stringy. His hands had become elongated, now bearing seven razor-sharp nails looked more like claws than human fingernails. He looked taller, and thinner. His lips were torn and bloody, and his teeth looked more like the fangs of a wolf than those of a human being. His eyes were the worst: they were completely red, and had taken on a hellish glow. The rank stench that accompanied him filled my room with a foul odor that lingered through the next day.

He said nothing. But I could feel the force of his mind prying at my thoughts. I sat frozen, transfixed. I had the feeling that he was part of the storm, that he was in some way controlling it, or feeding from it.

I don't know how long he stayed in my room that night. It seemed like forever. And then he opened his mouth, showing ghastly rows of fangs, and let out a screech that literally shook the house. Buster started barking, and I heard Mom and Dad rouse. But by the time Dad threw my door open, he was gone. We heard heavy footsteps thud across the roof, and then everything went silent.

I cannot explain why, but I felt as though I had been judged, and found unworthy. That he didn't want me. That I, for some reason, had been spared.

Do you understand? It was never really Jeremiah, who haunted us at the house. At least, it wasn't entirely Jeremiah. It was a primordial thing, a demon, masquerading as the ghost of something that had once been bound to it. Jeremiah Kent may have been born of human flesh, but through his unholy deeds, perhaps through dealing with the occult, he became possessed by the White Beast. I do not know if the demon was there before him, or if he summoned it. I do not know which was servant, which was master. I do not care. In the end, it doesn't matter, does it?

In the morning, I went to the attic. I don't know why, but I wasn't scared of it, at least in that moment. I just remember feeling sure that whatever was up there would be dormant during the day. I felt a presence in the air, the feeling of being watched, but nothing else. I went to the grimy window that looked out over the woods, and found that I could see a path through the forest, a dark line that stood out against the frosted white of the snow-covered landscape. Whatever had approached us last night had shaken snow from the trees, marking its path with darker, snow-free branches.

No human being could have done that.

Phyllis was right about one thing. These lands are filled with legends of ghosts and witches and vampires, of strange things that walk the wilds at night. Just wander into any of those cutesy shops and boutiques that grow like weeds along Maine's coast, and you'll find a tome by some local author describing some of these incidents. I can name a few right off the top of my head. The Dead Ship of Harpswell, a ghost ship seen headed for shore at full sail on the night of the full moon. It always vanishes before it reaches land. Then, there's the Ghost Dog of Loon Pond, a three-legged dog that glows with an unholy light in the darkest night. A quick online search will reveal dozens of these, each more sinister than the last.

These tales are often written off as imagination, folklore, or allegory. Some are undoubtedly just urban myths. Others have some weight of truth behind them. I cannot say whether or not a ghost ship sails Casco Bay on certain nights, or whether a maiden who fell to her death from a rocky cliff near Camden haunts the misty forests there.

But I do know that the story of the Kents is no mere myth.

Jeremiah never returned to my bedroom after that night. I don't know why. The sleepwalking stopped. The landscape seemed to stay the same: the trails no longer appeared and disappeared.

For a time, I thought maybe it was ending.

But the worst of it had not yet begun.

* * *

Over the next few weeks, as the dark season moved forward, things intensified. The phenomena we were subjected to moved into the realm of physical violence. We were poked, pushed, and hit. We woke one day to find our things strewn around the home. Mom and Dad told us a bear had gotten into the house, but even you could see through their tense demeanor, and tell that it was bullshit.

I cannot bear to recount every single incident. I am fairly sure that there are some I have completely blocked from my mind. But the smallest, most innocent reminder of that time can send me spiraling into the depths of terror. It isn't just 70's memorabilia that does it. Even something as inane as a broken glass, papers in disarray, or open drawers with their contents spilling out can trigger flashbacks, anxiety, and, more than once, relapses.

As things progressed, it took a toll on all of us. We all changed, in our own ways. Mom grew thin. She chain-smoked so much that within the space of a few months her appearance changed noticeably. Her fingers and teeth grew yellow, her skin took on a sallow, dry look, and she developed a horrible cough. She drank heavily, as did Dad. This was nothing new: they'd always enjoyed their cocktails. But everything was different there than it had been in the old house. Before, she and Dad would have happy hours. They would smile and laugh and drink long into the night, often playing records and dancing. They argued sometimes, but they also giggled and talked for hours on end. Now, they retreated into their own worlds. We all did. Dad spent almost all of his time in the cellar. Mom sat quietly before the TV set, lost in a daze of red wine and cigarette smoke. I retreated even more deeply into the worlds of comic books and video games. You spent most of your time in your room, drawing.

I started eating canned spinach. That's how fucking stupid I was. As though we lived in a cartoon world, and my muscles would magically start bulging out, and scare off whatever was tormenting our family.

These things that sit, festering, in my memory, cannot possibly be reconciled with reality. At least, not through the rules of modern science. The 'you' I refer to, the sweet little sister I remember, is dust and bones, somewhere. I know that. But you are alive and well, reincarnated exactly one year to the date after the fire.

Do you know what happened to you? Do you remember?

Do you remember the Beast?

And I ask myself: were I to voice these questions in person, would you tell me the truth?

I do not believe in coincidence. Reincarnation? Crazy, I once thought. But I also once thought ghosts and monsters only dwelt in stories and old films. I once thought only old castles and mansions could be haunted. I once thought there was only one reality.

I once believed in God.

For what it's worth, I believe every soul travels a different journey. Sometimes many journeys. There is not only one heaven and hell, but thousands.

They are all part of the same abyss.

*** * ***

As winter progressed, Dad started acting strangely. He would wake in middle of the night, screaming about blizzards and ice. He complained almost incessantly about a burning pain in his legs, but four trips to the doctor offered no explanation, no clue as to what could be wrong. He still dragged himself into the mill every morning, but when he came home, he would immediately eat and then retreat into the basement to paint, emerging only for food and beer.

Dad was eating a lot by then. He no longer simply had meals: he completely gorged himself several times a day. I don't know exactly when his appetite changed. I think it was after Thanksgiving. I have a brief snapshot memory of him finishing that holiday meal, and saying how stuffed he was.

That was the last time I ever heard him say he was full.

I don't think any of us noticed much at first. The holidays were upon us. Despite the strange events in the house, we still carried on with our usual traditions, except, of course, the visits to Grandma's house. Dad strung lights up in the shrubs outside, and Mom hung her Santas and reindeer and snowmen around the house. You and I inspected the wrapped gifts under the tree, ate gingerbread cookies still warm from the oven, and drank hot chocolate while watching our favorite cartoon and Claymation holiday specials. We went to Christmas village downtown, and you sat on Santa's lap, and asked him for a new dollhouse. (You also made him promise to give Rudolph a cookie.) We put on snowsuits that made it almost impossible to move, and built a snow fort in the yard.

Christmas was fairly normal, one of those rare, peaceful days that nothing untoward happened. You and I both a got lot of gifts, much more than we had ever gotten before. We had a ridiculous amount of toys by then: name any 70's toy you can think of, and we probably had it. I got cap guns, sports gear, a train set, and a huge collection of toy cars. You had more dolls than you could count, but you ended up with several more that morning. We opened gift after gift, squealing with delight. In addition to all the toys, I got reversible pants, a new jacket, and sneakers, and you got sweaters, tights, barrettes, jewelry, and fashion plates. For a few, shining hours, we were in that special happy place kids experience on Christmas morning.

Mom made a turkey for Christmas dinner, and we had a true feast, complete with several courses and all the trappings of a perfect holiday meal. We listened to Mom's holiday records while we ate, and finished our meal with hot cocoa and cake. That night, there were plenty of leftovers. So many, in fact, that Mom put some of them in the big freezer downstairs.

By morning, they were gone.

Dad had eaten the rest of it, all by himself: the turkey, the casseroles, the stuffing, the molded gelatin fruit salad, the veggies, everything. Enough food to have lasted all of us for days, and he devoured it in one sitting.

That was the first time I really noticed his appetite changing. One serving was never enough for him. Before, we would help ourselves, and maybe have a second helping of something if we really wanted to. But, by the New Year, there were no longer any leftovers. Ever. Dad ate everything. No matter how much food Mom made, he finished it all. He grew ravenous, insatiable.

One image is burned into my brain. I went downstairs in the middle of the night, and found Dad sitting at the kitchen table, alone in the dark. The table was piled with food, almost as if Mom had just done groceries, but hadn't yet put anything away. And he just sat there, eating and eating and eating. I stood in the shadows, watching, equally fascinated and jealous.

ABODE

I was hungry too. I didn't think—I just approached the table, and reached for a piece of the grocery-store pizza that sat in the center of the table.

Dad reached out and clamped my wrist. "One piece," he said. He looked up at me slowly. His eyes were wild, manic. Cold. "One."

I took my piece of pizza and went back to my room. He hadn't even cooked it all the way: the middle was still cold, and the cheese hadn't melted. I didn't care, any more than he had.

By morning, there was no food left in the house. Mom went and got groceries again the next day. She bought enough food to last, I would say, about two weeks.

It was gone in three days.

The fights got bad then. Mom worried that so much money was going to food. She fretted that Dad was going to get fat, but he didn't.

If anything, he grew skinnier.

Even Buster noticed the change. He no longer ran to Dad, holding his favorite tennis ball, when he wanted to play. He watched Dad tensely, and stayed close to you and I. As though he were protecting us.

I couldn't wait for winter vacation to end, so the big yellow bus could come and take us away. That was the only time I actually looked forward to starting school again.

That night, after eating my pizza, I dared to look out the bathroom window. I saw something white moving in the shadows beneath the trees, something pale and thin and gaunt, like a human skeleton. I only glimpsed it for a moment, and then it was gone. I quickly crossed the hall and went back to my room. My own window looked out over the field across the street, so I thought I'd be safe, since it was on the other side of the house. But when I glanced outside, I saw the creature there, staring right at me. At first, I thought it was an animal. But then it stepped forward, and I saw that it stood on two legs.

It was not human.

I could see its red glowing eyes, and I could feel the hatred burning into me. I think I actually peed myself, and I was far beyond any bed-wetting incidents by then.

What happened next still frightens me. I heard something outside, and turned my head slowly.

The Beast was standing a few feet away from the house, just to my right.

It was the same creature I had encountered in the woods that night. The thing was pale and slender, almost skeletally thin. Height was its most distinguishing feature: it was almost as tall as a tree. Although its lower half looked like that of a goat, its head was somewhat deer-shaped, with features that only faintly looked human. Huge antlers curved over its head. Its mouth was filled with rows of fangs, and it had long, claw-tipped fingers. And its eyes ... its eyes were demonic, burning red coals.

You saw it too. You came into my room, scared, and we stood close together, terrified, looking out at a night-dark, snowy forest, and seeing those red eyes glaring at us. We heard a terrible thudding sound on the roof, and Buster growled. I remember looking into your face, and seeing how scared you were, and just wishing I could protect you. Wishing I could grow big and strong, so I could keep you safe.

ABODE

"It wants to eat us," you said. You spoke in a whisper. I could hear the terror in your voice.

"It can't," I said. I wasn't convinced of that at all, but I wanted to make you feel better. "It isn't real."

But in the morning, I found tracks in the snow that proved otherwise. They came from the forest, went around to the front yard, and then led straight up the side of the house. There was no mistaking them for anything else: the thing's footsteps had left distinct holes in the fresh snow on the roof.

Buster died that night. I don't know what happened. There wasn't a mark on him. Just the day before, he'd been a bouncy ball of fur, watching over us. He used to nip at our heels and 'herd' us, as though trying to corral cattle. Dad said he'd let the dog out, but when he didn't bark to come back in, he'd figured Buster had decided to stay in his doghouse. It wasn't freezing, snowing, or windy, and the doghouse was well-insulated, so Dad didn't worry too much about it.

I don't think any of us ever forgave him for that.

Buster's death upset us all, but we didn't speak of it. I know you cried in your room that night, and I did too. I felt terribly guilty, and hated myself for not playing with him more, for not being there to help him. I think the worst part was never having a chance to say goodbye. We never had an official funeral. Dad took him away, and I guess had him cremated. Our house seemed emptier, and even more dangerous, without our faithful pet, but we couldn't bring ourselves to get—or even discuss getting — another dog. It was just one more weight added to the crushing load of fear and sadness that were slowly grinding us down.

We knew of ghosts and vampires by then. We knew about zombies and werewolves and Bigfoot. We were aware of more present dangers as well, like strangers that lured children into cars with promises of chocolate and candies. We knew of killers and wars and greed, and understood the threats posed by poison and pollution. What we saw that night when we looked outside was far, far more terrifying to us than any of those things.

This had become our reality. Our world. Our hell.

I came to understand something about the unholy.

These things come in silence. They come in the quiet moments. Times when I was reading, Mom sewing or clipping coupons, when you were playing with your dolls. The stillness that hovered around it, I can only compare to death. It wasn't normal silence, filled with ambient noise. It was a numbing blanket of soundlessness, an emptiness where touch, sound, and vision disappear into the eternal void.

It waited until we were calm. Until we began, each in our own way, to hope that it had ended, that they had gone away. But it always returned to strike full force, leaving our hearts pounding and our skin clammy.

We tried to push through. To at least pass as normal human beings.

There have been others, known these truths, these terrors. There always will be. I see bits and pieces of these things that seek to claw their way in to reality. I see them in horror movies and macabre museum exhibits, in the dark pages of other mad scribes.

I see the truth in the dark, surrounded by skeletal trees.

I

Something else just happened.

ABODE

As I was typing this, I heard a very clear set of footsteps walking down my hallway. But there was no one there.

I am so scared.

Ave Weresh

I can't go through this again.

I would kill myself, except I fear that would only deliver me to them.

I must try to focus. I must tell this tale. I must vomit these dark facts up, clear them from my mind. I'm almost done.

Maybe he will stop then.

All Hail The Beast Of The Woods.

Chapter Thirty-two

I have, so far, told you about some of the things I experienced. I haven't yet delved into the things that happened to you. I know you didn't tell me everything. I wish I had questioned you more. The longer we were in that house, the harder it was just to, well, live. To go through the motions of being normal.

I know that at least some of your experiences were very different from mine. You had more encounters with the Kent ghosts and the shadow children than I did, and fewer with Jeremiah. I do know that you suffered sleep paralysis. You woke screaming every night, and through your sobs you spoke of the shadow children that ringed themselves around your bed at night, their mouths sewn shut. You were unable to move, or to even turn your head. You couldn't even scream until they released you.

Mom and Dad insisted that these things were only bad dreams.

I knew better.

Things came to you in the night, and spoke to you. The shadow children clustered around you, their tiny cold hands reaching for you. Often, when I saw them, you were in the room. They stood behind you, slipping from one patch of darkness to another.

You recounted several incidents where you could feel someone standing right behind you. You felt the presence there, a shadow that made no sound, but slowly gathered into form. Sometimes you felt its foul, icy breath on your neck. Other times, it pulled your hair. Once, it kicked poor Buster, and you cried and cried because you couldn't help him.

At other times, you would casually mention the ghosts, the dead things that dwelt in the shadows. Somehow, you knew their names. All of them. You saw Josephine and the twins, mostly, but you also had encounters with Agnes in her wheelchair, and poor, mad Isabelle. I don't know why, but the ghosts didn't seem to scare you very much. Maybe you were too young to really understand death, and to realize that the dead should stay dead. After all, you were still forming opinions about the world. You understood *scary,* but you didn't really have a good sense of *normal.* You still believed in unicorns, Santa Claus, and the tooth fairy, so the existence of ghosts, in your mind, only made those brighter beings more real.

When I think of that now, it strikes me as very sad. All of the good things children believe in—Santa Claus, the Easter Bunny, elves, fairy godmothers—are fake. But the nightmares, the ghosts and goblins, and hell, for all I know, werewolves and vampires, are real.

But even though the ghosts didn't scare you as much as they probably should have, you were tormented in your own way. There was a period of about a week when you kept hearing the hissing and rattling sound of snakes that you couldn't see. Once you swore you felt one slither over your foot. That incident sent you into hysterics. Even Dad, who was grumpy and withdrawn, did everything he could to soothe you.

You heard and felt wings flapping, and then felt the air move as a huge bird passed by you.

There was nothing there.

One time, you drew a picture for Mom. You ran to show her, all proud of yourself. As you held it out to her, an unseen hand grabbed it and ripped it into shreds.

And you, too, saw Jeremiah. But what you described was different than what I saw. The creature before you had no face. He seemed to be made of a weird substance, a charcoal-colored, swirling smoke. He had red eyes, but no mouth. But when you told me about his hat, well, there was no doubt that it was the same being.

To this day, big hats give me the creeps. I've gotten out of elevators on the wrong floor just because someone in a cowboy hat stepped in.

One incident you described to me in great detail. You woke at night, and had to go to the bathroom. You reached for the door, but your little hands weren't strong enough to turn it. You tried harder, and realized that it was locked. You panicked, and yelled for us, shouting as loud as you could and pounding on the door. None of us heard anything.

Suddenly, the door unlatched itself and opened on its own, and after a moment (still having to pee) you stepped out into the hall.

And into a snowstorm.

Cold flakes drifted down from the ceiling, and an icy wind blew through the hall. You thought maybe you'd stepped through a portal, like the wardrobe that led to Narnia, but you could see our ceiling above the falling snow.

A moment later, my door opened, and you saw me walk out of my room and into the hall. You called my name, but I didn't seem to hear you. I did not stop or even pause, but just started

ABODE

walking down the stairs. You started after me, and then you felt hands on your shoulders, holding you back. As you opened your mouth to scream, those hands dragged you back into your room and slammed the door.

Later that night, you found yourself in your bed. At first, you thought you'd only dreamt it, but when you got up to go to the bathroom, you noticed that my door was open and my bed was empty.

I've just found a few newspaper stories that I didn't see at the time. And in doing so, found another piece of the puzzle.

They found bones in the ruins, after the fire. Human bones, sunk deep into the foundation of the house. Baby's bones. I guess Matt Lessard was right about that after all. They never told me this at the time, but well, that really isn't much of a surprise. All I could think of when I read that was the baby shoes in the tiny closet in my bedroom.

I don't know why, but this seems to me perhaps the saddest thing of all. I've wept and cried, screamed and raged, but none of my pain can help those poor children.

I've attached the obituaries of all of those who have died in the house or on the property. There are several suicides, a double murder, and an unusually high number of accidents. These things are not confined to just our property, but also taint the ones nearby, which stand on what once was all Kent land.

These obituaries, they are filled with loving, desperate images of fluffy white heavens and comforting angels. They are the wishes of the living, who hoped and prayed that their loved ones had gone to a better place.

I feel only sadness when I read them. Not for the dead, but for the living.

We never ran one for you. We never knew for sure, until it was too late.

Chapter Thirty-three

I have just been struck by a terrible fear. A realization, that, in trying to inform you about these things, in trying to explain the danger you are in, I may have made a terrible mistake, and left out a crucial warning.

Do not forward these emails to anyone. Let no one, other than yourself, read them.

This is not a matter of privacy: it is about safety.

I have come to believe that Jeremiah is best able to haunt those who know of and recognize him. While he can manifest around those fortunate enough to remain unaware of his existence, he poses a much greater threat to those who know him than he does to those who don't. I cannot prove this, but if my assumption that he feeds on fear is correct, fear that is specifically aimed at him may be particularly potent.

It's all about energy. That is what magic is based on: the use of certain words, items, and symbols to manipulate thoughts and energy, the way ringing a bell sends sound waves through the air. The chances of someone discovering Jeremiah's story, or learning about him, without venturing onto that property are slim. We didn't know about him, but then, we were on his land, in the place where he is the strongest.

I have come to this conclusion based not only on my own experiences, but that of others. From what I have been able to discern, the netherworld has its own laws. The beings that dwell in the abyss have their own rules, restrictions, and boundaries. These things must be given permission, of some form, in order to come through. There are borders that bind them, perhaps the way the seashore binds the ocean creatures to the water. I have no doubt that the Kent family dealt in such things, and that they allowed—or invited—that being to cross over.

Knowledge, they say, is power. But some things, once learned, open doors in the mind, doors of perception that should never, ever be opened.

I do not feel that I have endangered you, in making you aware of these things. I would never, ever, deliberately put you in harm's way. In your case, Jeremiah already knows who you are.

The same cannot be said about your friends and family members.

I urge you, I beg you, do not, under any circumstances, speak to anyone of Jeremiah or The White Beast. The rest, I leave to your discretion. Whatever you do or do not remember, that is yours to reveal or keep secret as you choose. I will not pry. I ask nothing of you.

But please, please, listen to me when I say you are in danger.

These demons, these entities, they lurk in another realm, a dimension beyond death. They reach into this world, like mist seeping off a fouled black lake. They belong in the dark, in secret tomes hidden in underground vaults.

These are dark times, and for beings that feed on fear and hate, the world, in its present state, is a cornucopia.

I ramble. I do apologize. I am going to head out, to find something to calm my nerves, before I continue.

We are coming to it now.

Chapter Thirty-four

The next major storm we got was a true Nor'easter, a record breaker. It was, in fact, the last category-five blizzard to hit New England. The snows and winds lasted 68 hours, which is extreme even by Maine's standards. Overall, that storm killed over 100 people.

I'm still amazed that we weren't among them.

We were cooped up for days as the snow piled up around us and the storm screamed and whistled outside our windows. Beyond the howling gale-force winds, we heard again that demonic, unearthly keening that raised goosebumps on our skin. Mom and Dad kept telling us it was just the wind, but we didn't believe them. The growling grew louder and louder until it shook the walls. We put our hands to our ears, trying to dull the deafening noise. Occasionally, things would fall silent, and would stay quiet just long enough for us to hope that it had stopped. But then as soon as we thought it had ended, it started again.

I'm not sure what was worse: that terrible roar, or Dad.

He became violent, striking out at Mom when she spilled a bit of water on him. He spanked you for something trivial, and came at me with the belt for asking him a question. But that wasn't the worst of it.

He ate everything in the house. On the second day, Mom started to make us breakfast, only to find that there was no food left. We had tea and coffee, and some sort of weird flour pancake with salad dressing. There was nothing else in the house.

We had lukewarm water and powdered lemonade for supper that night.

"The storm will be over by morning," Mom told you, when you complained. "We'll go out to eat. We'll go to that big buffet, and you can eat all you want."

"He'll eat it all," you said.

Mom looked at Dad. He was just sitting in his chair, glowering. "No," she said, trying to be cheerful. "Even your father can't stay at an all-you-can-eat place all day."

We watched TV, and then went to sleep with growling stomachs as the storm raged around us. I dreamt of food: pizza and cereal and a table piled high with roasted meats and cheeses. When I woke up, the power was out. We heated with wood, so fortunately the temperature of the house wasn't affected. We read and played games while there was light, trying not to think of food.

We were all hungry, at that point. And Dad kept complaining about a smell. None of the rest of us noticed anything, but he swore that the house smelled like a sewer or a butcher shop.

The rest of the day was a blur of seemingly endless trips to the woodpile in the cellar.

The third day of the storm was the same, only more miserable. Many of the flashlight batteries were dying, and Mom was worried about fire, so we stumbled around with only the light of hurricane lamps and a few perfectly-placed candles in thick glass jars to guide us. There were no footsteps,   no thuds, no noises that night. When I dreamt, I dreamt only about snow and food. I was so hungry that the dream-food somehow seemed satisfying.

Dad retreated to his studio. We didn't see him the rest of that day, though we heard him talking to himself. Raving, more like. He kept going on about the pain in his legs and the stench in the house. Mom turned the radio up to drown him out, and we spent the next few hours listening to a static-y radio station that played mostly The Bee Gees and Abba.

Finally, Dad stopped talking. It was a relief: his complaints were, by then, driving us mad, and he was staring at us with a look that made me uneasy. Many times, when one of us mentioned food or hunger, he replied with a line about how good we would taste, or said that he was thinking of cooking us. It was the sort of thing that would have made us giggle on a summer day, when we were waiting for our burgers to come off the grill. But this time it wasn't funny.

Hours crept by. It seems like the storm lasted an eternity. The wind and the snow just never stopped. The darkness never lifted.

Hunger took its toll. We grew weak and shaky, and our tempers flared quickly.

On the fifth night, long after dark, Mom remembered that she had left a box of granola bars in the station wagon. She bundled up in her coat and boots, and opened the door.

Instead of the howling winds and darkness we'd been seeing out the window, we found ourselves staring at a bright blue sky. The driveway had been plowed; the clean, white snowbanks reached the bottom limbs on the tree in the yard. The storm had dumped a good four or five feet of snow on the ground, but it had clearly ended some time ago.

We all stared outside, blinking, completely confused.

At that moment, the power came on.

Mom turned around, a fake smile plastered to her face. "Kids, wake up! It's all over."

"I wasn't sleeping," you said.

Mom ignored this, and fluttered her hand. "Go get dressed. Hurry! We'll go out to eat."

As Mom had promised, we went to the all-you-can-eat place. Dad certainly got his money's worth: I think he made six trips to the buffet. When we came back, we found three newspapers in the box, and two in the snow below it. There were tracks throughout the yard. Dad said they were deer prints, but the tracks were too big and too far apart to have been made by any animal.

The storm officially lasted 68 hours.

For us, it lasted almost twice that long.

Five days, it held us trapped there. Five days, that thing toyed with us, weakening us.

I have only one clear memory of you after that. You were sitting in your room, drawing. I can't recall if it was snowing or not, but the winds were howling and whistling outside the windows. You had drawn a butterfly, and you held the picture up proudly, to show me. "It has to change," you said. "I have to change. The woods will be silent again when we go. The children will sleep when we go." You looked out the window, at the wild, snowy world below, and your eyes glazed over. "When we go," you said again. Then you started repeating it. I saw a tear fall from your eye, and your voice cracked a little. "When we go. When we go. When we go. When we go."

ABODE

"Lexi," I said. "Stop."

But you didn't. You just kept crying, and repeating the same three words over and over and over again. I put your teddy bear down on the bed beside you, and hugged you until you calmed down. When you finally fell asleep, I returned to my own room.

Chapter Thirty-five

There is nothing left of Dad's work. The vast majority of it was lost in the fire. There's one clipping I found, an article in a college journal, which included one of his landscapes and a painting of a dog underneath an apple tree. Those paintings look completely surreal and somehow wrong to me now. The last time I saw our father, he was a broken thing, seeping rage from cracks that ran so far into his psyche they could never be filled or repaired. He was ranting, drunk and dirty, and his words were cold and cruel. He was not the man I remember from my early childhood, the one who tossed us up into the air and made silly faces to make us laugh.

That man died long before the fire, I think.

Dad never spoke of his experiences. I suspect that he didn't know how to deal with them, any more than the rest of us did, so he turned his torment inward instead. As time passed, withdrew from us more and more. He ate and ate and ate, devouring everything in sight, but he never gained weight. He seemed taller, and paler. He talked in his sleep, shouting strange phrases that made no sense, and complained incessantly about the pain in his legs.

As he grew more and more unbalanced, he and Mom began to fight frequently. Violently. He had never been shy about switching us, but until then, he had never been one to just randomly strike out. When he hit us, it was to punish us. This was different. Now, his rage was insatiable. He slapped Mom and me regularly, with little or no provocation. He shoved you up the stairs one night, and you ended up with a huge bruise on your arm.

He and Mom went off one day on an 'errand' they said nothing about. I suspect they may have started counseling.

I found myself alone in the house one winter day. I think you and Mom had gone to a dance rehearsal, and Dad was working. I decided to go back downstairs and look at his newer work.

As I mentioned before, Dad's work changed drastically after we moved into the house. The paintings I had peeked at a few months before were quite a bit darker than his earlier pieces, and had a sinister, almost menacing feel. But they were tame, compared to his most recent ones.

Those images, too, are burned into my brain.

The newest paintings bore almost no resemblance to his older pieces, or even to the things he had drawn the previous year. These were graphic, visceral, horrible images, filled with blood and slime. No self-respecting gallery would ever host them. As I flipped through the pile, I saw depictions of hideous, cannibalistic feasts: gory, grotesque visions of death and dying, scenes ripped out of nightmare. They were terrifying. Had it not been for the familiar rounded style of drawing that was unmistakably Dad's, I'd have thought they were done by someone else.

A few of the scenes I recognized from my own nightmares. That's how I know he had the dreams too: he painted them.

He never painted the children. But the mouth of the cave, the cabin in the woods, the cemetery across the road, the strange glyphs carved on boulders in that pit I found in the woods, Dead Man's Pond, the desolate blueberry barrens. . . these things he had drawn, in muted rust and ochre, in drab grey and brown and garish crimson and yellow. They were dismal, hideous images. Even the colors he chose were ugly.

Those were bad enough. I found another series, all depicting a tall, pale shape emerging from a winter forest. I recognized the Beast immediately, and quickly flipped past those paintings.

But then I noticed another pile, discretely tucked in behind some blank canvases.

He drew bodies, bloody, dismembered corpses. He drew the Beast, eating the bodies. A man in a dark, wide-brimmed hat. His daughter, the black-haired witch. Her grandsons: Samuel, the dour, ill-fated soldier; poor, doomed Francoise; and Albert, the madman. In one scene, several people sat around a long dining room table upon which was spread a gruesome, unholy feast. I identified several of them: a sour-faced woman I recognized as Josephine, and her sisters, Isabelle and Elizabeth. Agnes was there, in her wheelchair. I even recognized the twins. Their mouths were sewn shut. In another, similar painting, they all had fangs instead of teeth, and their lips were bloody and torn.

In the last picture, I had joined them at the feast.

And then I saw the worst of them all.

He painted us. I can't …. I can't bring myself to describe what I saw, but he painted you and I in a tapestry of gore, guts, and blood, a scene meant for nightmares. He didn't show our faces, but I could tell that it was us. The color of your hair perfectly matched that of the lifeless, dismembered girl in the picture. My own sneakers sat on a table, beside a silver bowl filled with entrails. A thin, pale figure stood in the corner, near the end of the table. The being was unfinished, only roughly sketched in, but something about it rang a bell deep in my psyche.

I felt sick. My stomach heaved, and I felt a shivering sickness in my bowels. I quickly flipped to the next portrait, but it was too late: that vision of carnage had already been stamped onto my soul.

My pale, shaking hands reached for one last canvas. I flipped the one before it forward, and found myself staring at a striking likeness of Jeremiah.

That's when I heard the footsteps slowly coming down the stairs, toward me. I froze. I heard a creak as the door opened.

I turned slowly. There was nothing there. But then something unseen knocked a jar of paint down: it went flying across the room and shattered. Paint spilled out, staining the floor a garish yellow color.

At that moment, something shook the house. I don't know what it was. I only know I felt the walls shake, and jars of paint and turpentine rattled on the table and shelves. I saw a shadow move, out of the corner of my eye, slipping bonelessly, formlessly through the door, straight down into the earth.

I fled to the living room, and spent the next few hours watching the news. I wasn't old enough to understand the underlying issues they spoke about: the black majority rising to power in Rhodesia, Jimmy Carter's latest doings, or the smashing success of *Saturday Night Fever*. Nor did I care. I only knew that those shiny newscasters were my only link to the outside world.

But again, Jeremiah leered at me from the background of a live TV show.

I snapped the TV off and listened to records instead. But the music could not drown out the unholy roar of the Beast echoing from the forest.

It seemed forever before I saw the beam of light from Mom's headlights flashing across the room. I'd been waiting for hours for her to come home. And I realized in that moment that it didn't matter if I was alone in the house or not. I didn't feel any safer with Mom there.

I don't think I have ever felt safe anywhere since that moment. And I am not sure if I was ever able to look Dad in the eye again.

Chapter Thirty-six

He has seen you. There is no doubt, now.

I went to your office again yesterday. I stayed longer this time, leaning against the building next door, waiting for you to leave. When you walked out the door, I took a step after you, intending to catch up.

He intercepted me. He stepped out from behind two buildings and stood there, facing me. I felt him staring at me, though he had no eyes.

A man passed through him.

He was never strong enough to do that before, to bear the light of day for so long, to take form so clearly below the touch of the sun. Every other time he appeared in daylight, it was only for a moment or two.

How much stronger has he grown in the last thirty years? How much does the discord in the world strengthen such a being?

The wheel of the year is turning away from the sun, bringing us again into cold and darkness.

I hear again the sound of the drum ringing out through those woods. The rhythm of the scratching I heard in the walls. There are words to be put to the pattern, to make it a chant.

I shall not put them here.

Ave Weresh

Ravishing shadows the pale moon we beckon

While I can control my actions, my words, my behavior, the one thing I cannot control is my fear. The more I revisit these things, the stronger the fear gets. The stronger the terror gets, the more I feel threatened. It's a downward spiral. But knowing that ... knowing that only makes me more scared. And that leads me to a strange place. Because the more I write, the more I revisit ... the more frightened I become. And the door opens a bit wider.

My fear makes him stronger. But I feel that it is your fear he craves.

Ave Weresh

I could run again. But if I did, I would always wonder if my doing so had left you vulnerable.

Do you believe?

Chapter Thirty-seven

Well, I'm coming up on it now.

The night you disappeared.

You would think that every detail of that evening would be burned into my brain. In reality, I recall almost nothing about it. I have no idea what we had for supper that night, or what we watched on TV that night, if anything. I don't know if you and I played board games together, or spent the evening in our own rooms. I don't recall what day it was, if it was a school night or a weekend. I don't remember what any of us were wearing, or if Mom and Dad fought.

I don't remember going to bed.

I awoke to find my room filling with a thick, heavy smoke. I always heard that more people die in fires because of smoke inhalation than from being burned. It isn't that I didn't believe this, but I didn't know how excruciating it is until it happened to me. It's one of those things that you can't truly understand until you experience it. Every time you take a breath, your lungs fill with poison. You can't breathe, can't think. You start getting dizzy, and you cough so hard you see spots. But that only brings in more smoke.

I struggled to breathe, but my lungs just weren't getting any oxygen. After just a few moments, I got very nauseous and dizzy. Luckily, I remembered everything the fireman had told my kindergarten class a few years earlier. I grabbed the glass of water on my dresser, poured it onto a tee shirt, and held it over my mouth. Then I dropped to my hands and knees, crawled to my door, and felt the doorknob. It was still cool, so I opened it.

The hall was even smokier than my room. But I noticed a strange white substance all over the floor, which at first I thought was snow. Looking more closely, I realized what it was: pieces of paper.

I picked one up. It was a page from one of Mom's Bibles. Someone had ripped the book apart, and strewn page after page through the halls. There were also pages from other books, and from magazines and newspapers as well. The trail of paper went straight from your door, through the hall, and down the stairs.

At first, I was more confused than frightened. Then I smelled the gasoline, and it hit me.

Jeremiah wanted to burn the house down . . . with us in it.

I tried Mom and Dad's room. The door was locked, so I banged on it, screaming.

Mom opened the door and looked around. The smoke was growing heavier by the moment: she put her hand to her mouth and coughed. "What in the—?"

We both heard the sound of an explosion, and saw the sudden burst of light from below as Dad's studio caught fire. The cellar was full of paints, canvases, sketchpads, and chemicals: the perfect fuel.

The fire really took hold then. Tongues of flame licked the stairs only seconds later.

Mom pulled me into the room and shook Dad awake. I don't know if even the urgency of the situation completely brought him back to himself. He acted and spoke with clarity, but his eyes looked glassy and dazed.

"Get out," he said. "I'll get Lexi. Go out the window if you have to."

We all headed for the door, only to have it slam shut, trapping us inside.

The rest was chaos. When those old, wooden houses catch fire, they go up quick. The entire place was enveloped in flames within a few short minutes. The fire spread quickly, so quickly. So fucking fast. Dad tried the door, crashing into it with his shoulder, but when it finally opened, it was too late. An inferno lay before us, a wall of flame that no one could have made it through. A chunk of the hall floor was gone, having already burned away and collapsed. There was no way Dad could get to you through that. I'm not even sure a firefighter could have done it.

I'm sorry. I didn't think ... I hope you don't remember this.

We heard a crash from somewhere downstairs, and knew we were running out of time. Dad broke the window, and we jumped out. He hung me out by my arms, so I didn't have as far to drop, and did the same for Mom before climbing out himself. There is one good thing about snow: it broke our fall. We got out just in time: moments later, a massive fireball erupted, blazing into the sky with a big *whoosh*.

I later learned that the neighbors across the river saw the flames from their house, and called the fire department. But by the time we saw the flashing lights, and heard the sirens, it was too late. The house was completely engulfed in flame.

The rest of that night is a broken, fragmented mix of images: sirens drawing closer as the fire trucks and cop cars arrived, blue and red lights flashing in the night, the acrid smell of smoke. I had always thought fire trucks were cool: this was my first understanding that their presence usually signifies that something terrible has happened. I remember the first search party going out into the woods, even as the firemen battled the flames: the sounds of dogs barking, snippets of communication from the first responders' walkie-talkies and radios, flashlight beams crisscrossing the woods. I don't even know if these memories encompass hours, days, or only moments. But they play over and over in my thoughts, a loop that never ends.

I will never forget the sound of Mom's voice as she called for you. She just screamed your name over and over and over. At one point, she tried to run inside; Dad held her back by tackling her. Her wails were primal, heartfelt, the anguish only felt by a mother whose child has been ripped from one world into the other.

Aunt Janet and Uncle Kevin came to get me. I turned back as we rode away, and saw Mom collapse onto the ground, sobbing. I remember wondering when I was going to wake up. I was so, so sure that this was just another dream.

It wasn't. Or, in a way, it's a nightmare I have yet to escape or even truly awaken from, one that has spanned decades.

We went back to the smoldering ruins only once, the next day. Mom was there, but she became hysterical soon after we arrived, and I was taken away after only a few minutes. But that morning scene is burned into my mind, the way those ruined charred husks of wood are burned into the earth.

A life left in ashes.

ABODE

* * *

The weeks—even the hours—after the fire are a blur.

After the house burned down, I stayed with Janet and Kevin for a while. Things were very quiet there. There were no unknown noises, no strange smells. The shadows didn't follow me. Janet and Kevin spoke in whispers and bought me a goldfish. They fed me pizza and cake and candy bars, as though these things could replace my family.

They would occasionally, quietly, very gently, give me updates.

"They're still searching for your sister. There's a huge rescue party going into the woods."

"They think maybe someone broke in and took her, and started the fire."

"Your mom isn't well, yet. She's getting herself together."

"Your dad's had a hard time with this."

"You'll start the school year with us."

"I'm sure there's a good reason that your mom didn't come today. It was all probably just a misunderstanding."

"Have you heard from your father?"

They never found you. They searched and searched and searched.

You were officially listed as missing, but the assumption was that you had died, and the fire had consumed you. You never had a grave: Mom never wanted to really admit that you were gone. If she had, maybe she would have been found some comfort in that closure. Maybe she would have recovered, at least a little bit. She never gave up hope. She would grab the arms of little girls that looked like you and stare desperately into their faces, only to let go, whisper an apology, and turn away, tears welling in her eyes.

The kids at school sent me a card. The whole class signed it, even Tommy and Jody.

I threw it into the woodstove.

They say that when you get a limb cut off, you still feel it. You still feel pain, or heat, or cold, or itching. The same thing happens when you lose the people that form your world. You feel them there, just out of reach. You close your eyes, and expect to see them there when you open them. You wake up every day, and for a quick, blissful moment, you have forgotten. Then it comes back, and reality hits you like a hammer, leaving you cold and empty and full of dread and pain.

I went to a new school, but I didn't stay there long. At first, my classmates acted entirely normal around me. Then word got out. Although everyone was very quiet and nice, I saw them casting sidelong glances at me and whispering behind their hands. One kid approached me quietly, and asked if I wanted some of his comic books. I suppose when you're nine, that's the epitome of an act of kindness.

I told him to go away. My voice was a growl.

He tried to talk to me twice more, and met the same reaction. In truth, I desperately wanted his friendship, but I was too angry to accept it.

My time at Middler Elementary ended abruptly a few weeks after that. Everyone was just acting normal again. Their lives went on, a mix of Scout meetings and discussions about summer camps and baseball. This enraged me. Why should they walk in the sun, smiling, when my family was gone? Why should they spend hours chatting about movies and TV shows?

ABODE

I remember, vaguely, having a fit of black rage. I threw a chair at the door, and kicked a trashcan over. I don't know why. I am not sure I even knew why at the time. Another time, I bit a boy at school, just for looking at me. I fought like a wild animal when they came for me. And then the needle, bringing blessed numbness.

I never returned to that school. That night Janet and Kevin spoke in hushed tones in the kitchen. I was sent back to Maine, this time to Hinckley, a school for troubled boys. Though no one ever told me this directly, I know Kevin and Janet didn't want me back. They used to help me out now and then, but I never lived with them after that. I tried to call them once, a few years back, and they said I'd burned that bridge.

I don't remember what I did. I must have been pretty high.

Several months later, I was sent to live with Aunt Kathy and Uncle Mike.

Aunt Kathy was very, very religious. Perhaps, had I been of a different cloth, this would have saved me: I could have clung to illusions, thrown myself into something, believed that there was something, anything, looking out for me. But it was too late. I seethed in silence, a pale, sullen teen.

I burned your name into my arm.

I broke down the day I saw the newspaper article about you. I found it by accident one day, when I opened Uncle Mike's desk drawer, looking for a pen. (I've attached a scanned copy.) They suspected arson. I think that was the worst, because that one piece of paper was proof that what I recalled had been real. I no longer had the luxury of pretending I had imagined some of it. I screamed, and tried to cut my wrists. I devolved into madness. I can't tell you the details, because I don't know them. I remember only rage, and grief, and pain.

They sent me, then, to AMHI, Maine's biggest asylum. I remember Kathy praying as they took me away. The neighbors all came out of their houses to watch. They had condemned me. I saw it in their eyes. I can still see the looks on their faces, years later: a mixture of horror and fascination.

I have only bits and pieces of memory, of my time at the asylum. I suppose I am lucky to have escaped being lobotomized, which had fallen out of favor only a few years before. But I know I was still in hell. I tore at my eyes, and tried to pop them, so I could see no more. I drove a pen into my ear, and punctured an eardrum, so I would never again hear the scream of the Beast or the sound of sirens. (I'm half-deaf to this day). I bit chunks out of my arms, and, more than once, took bites of other people. I drew Jeremiah and the White Beast in blood on my walls, and hit them until my hand was a pulpy, broken mess.

I spent the next several years in therapy. They kept me drugged, most of the time. When I was finally released, it didn't take me long to realize that I couldn't handle sobriety.

Mom took me for a little while. I think we lasted a few months. She was broken by then, completely incapable of being a mother. There were too many things between us that we couldn't talk about. Ghosts. Dead things. Nightmarish memories.

Sometimes Mom got drunk and spoke of it. "That thing threw me across the room," she would say. Or she would rant about the man in a wide-brimmed hat, or the storm that never ended. She had become terrified of snow, cold, and ice. She would rave and cry about your father, and how he had changed at the end.

The worst was when she spoke about the old days, before we moved north.

Nothing supernatural happened to us in that time, but we were still haunted. Not by ghosts or demons, but by the past.

Mom sank into a bottle, and slowly fell into true madness. I found her one night in the yard, naked, screaming at the moon. She had cut herself, and there were bloody streaks all over her soft, sagging flesh. I looked at her and hated her with every fiber of my being. I looked at her and for one brief moment I saw her as an angel, tormented by fire, molded and shaped by grief. She was strong, for a moment. She looked back at me, her eyes bright and full of wisdom. Then she cracked into pieces, and started screaming about Jeremiah.

For a long time I hated, *hated* the neighbors for calling the cops. Now, as an adult, I understand, though I wish it would have happened differently.

Mom went to Danvers Asylum. When it closed, she was transferred to AMHI in Augusta, Maine, the same place I had been. While I was there, I often felt that I had traded one hell for another, but in truth, I don't think I would have survived those years if I hadn't been admitted. She was released once, but she quickly broke down again, and was sent to another institution. She died a few years later.

They said it was a heart attack. It wouldn't have happened, if her heart hadn't been broken.

Her date of death was February 18th ... the same as yours.

The rest of my teens were a dark time, a blur of asylums, foster homes, juvie halls, and, later, crappy apartments. I didn't have friends. I had dealers. And, for a time, customers. I had girls, but they were only flesh and blood, pallid and vapid and easily forgotten.

Dad was gone by then. I rarely heard from him, until I got a call from a New Hampshire cop one day. He had died in a drunk driving accident. Drove himself into a rocky embankment. February 18th.

I quietly earned my GED a few years later. And then one summer, by chance, I picked up a used art kit at a pawn shop.

I believe you know the rest.

Looking into the past is like staring into a dim, shady kaleidoscope. Brighter days fall into darkness. The golden times flicker and dim, like a candle going out in the midst of a cold, shadowy night. I think I became an artist to try and recapture those fleeting good times, the few years we had before everything went so wrong. You'll find an online gallery of my work, and occasionally, I do showings.

Then again, maybe the painting ties me to you, and Mom and Dad.

I walked on the brink of insanity for a long time. I did not understand that I was free, that the cost of my freedom was paid in blood. I knew only pain and rage.

In the years that followed, I tried to erase your memory, to pretend you weren't real. I tried to convince myself that I was just an orphan who had dreamt up a horrible tale. But it never worked. In time, I fell prey to my own delusions. The world threw reminders at me constantly, painful ones. Soup cans. Milk bottles. Your favorite cereal. Characters from the cartoons we watched every Saturday morning. The day-to-day things that reminded me of you were everywhere, and I couldn't escape them.

I wish I had died that night.

But I didn't. I walked away. Lived to tell the tale, so they say. I've never been able to speak of these things until now. I could never talk about what happened. For years, I couldn't even speak your name. Not in the brightest day, or in the darkest night. And, to be honest, I had no one to really talk to.

And so I drank. I did every drug you can name, and then some. And I went slowly inwards, falling into a downward spiral within my own mind. I shut myself into a little box. I became a walking zombie, an open, pus-filled wound on the face of the human race.

Isn't it strange, how it only takes one incident to break a human soul to pieces? I was stressed and unhappy before the fire, but after, I was seething black rage. The little boy that walked into that house on a bright August day burned away in the flames that took you from us. What remains, what I see when I look in the mirror, is a scarred, burnt skeleton, a husk. I am no longer real. When there was no one left to love me, I became a living statue, a mechanical thing, skin stretched taut over scars and pain and terror.

And thus I remain, to this day, shaped by fire and ice, by love and hate, equally.

They say time heals all wounds. I'd be lying if I said I was healed, but it's equally untrue to say that it hasn't helped. I function, in society, in my own, lonely corner of the world, but I am dead inside, an automaton with a paintbrush. I paint the demons that haunt my dreams, and the ghosts that hover around me. I paint visions of the life I wish were mine: bright meadows, beaches, flowers. To this day, I must confess, I don't think I have any true talent. I simply felt that I had to paint, for Dad, for you, and for Mom, and I threw myself into it. I hated it, and that only made me work harder.

My best seller, *The Girl with the Kitten*.

That was you, with Lucky.

People often remark on the expression in your/her eyes. That haunted, wistful, look, they say.

It is the look of a ghost staring at the world through a veil that can never, ever be torn.

Chapter Thirty-eight

There isn't much more to tell.

I'm not sure, now, that it was a good thing to revisit all of that. I never realized how many incidents I had buried until they all came back.

When I started this project, I thought that maybe at the end of it I would find peace, that perhaps this burden would finally be lifted. Instead, I only feel a sense of foreboding, of something malevolent coming for me again.

I'm not going to lie: I fell off the wagon during the course of this thing. Maybe that's a good thing, because I can at least try to convince myself that the recent events—the scratching, the footsteps, the sightings—were drug-induced hallucinations.

Maybe now I can move on. Maybe this time, rehab will stick.

I only saw Jeremiah a few times in the years between then and now, mostly in that first year. The first time was on a bright summer day while I was still at Hinckley. We went on a trip to Old Orchard Beach. I was getting onto that apple-red roller coaster, when suddenly, out of the corner of my eye, I saw a figure in black, wearing a wide-brimmed hat. Aerosmith's *Dream On* was blasting from the loudspeakers on a nearby ride, and the town, beach, and pier were packed with pale tourists. He did not move. Did not speak. He simply stood there in the crowd, just looking at me. He looked human again, so human that I almost thought he was real. But the people moved through him. When he looked at me, I felt the air cool around me. He vanished after just a few quick moments. But the chill remained with me long after the ride had stopped, although it was a sweltering early summer afternoon.

I saw him once more, looking at me from a documentary. He was in a random photo they included as part of the footage, clear as day. The documentary was about the ice cutting businesses and mills that flourished in Maine in the 19th century. Mersport was mentioned, as were several, now-abandoned places along the edges of the Allagash.

There are small details I suppose I could add to this account. But I'm not sure if they would be of any use to you. Would it help you to know that exactly thirty-three years ago today, Mom made beef stew for supper? Or she would have, but that Dad ate a good chunk of the meat raw, out of the fridge? No, probably not. How do I know that? Because we had to go to the emergency room after a glass flew off the shelf and cut your arm. After spending hours in the ER, we came home and had what was basically gravy soup with potatoes and carrots for supper that night. I got those records, and so I have the date of that visit.

I guess the only thing left unsaid is the fact that I kept a dream journal for a while, because my therapist thought it might be good for me to dredge up my innermost feelings. I still have that journal. It's written in ballpoint pen in one of those composition journals with the black and white covers. I stopped it fairly quickly, because I was scaring myself. The dreams faded fast, once I woke: it didn't take me long to realize I preferred not to remember them. But when I wrote them down, they stayed with me, and they returned whenever I read about them.

By then, I was all about finding ways to forget.

ABODE

I'm transcribing a few of the entries here, word for word, with only corrections for spelling. Most don't have dates. I'm not sure why, or if, that matters.

* * *

I dreamt about a hole in the ground that led down to hell. I had to go into the cellar, but the cellar stairs just kept going down and down and down. I was searching for someone. Lexi. As I went deeper and deeper underground, I sensed something behind me and picked up speed. It drew closer, and I found myself racing down a long spiral staircase that wound into blackness. The thing drove me further and further beneath the surface of the earth, far away from the reach of the sun. Here and there, I saw halls branching off the stairway. Sometimes I would take them, trying to get away from the thing behind me. They all only led to more stairs. Then I finally found a passageway, and I took it, thinking it would lead me out, but it only went to our old root cellar. There was a cat there, but it wasn't Lucky, and it wouldn't come to me. I tried to go back the other way, but the tunnel just ended. And I turned around and saw a man there, dressed in black. I was very scared. I woke up then.

* * *

I dreamt the back yard was a cemetery. Mom was trying to plant a garden, and we could not find a spot where there wasn't a grave. She was upset because her soup was going to be ruined. But when I looked into the pot, it was full of blood and guts and eyeballs. And when I looked back at her, her eyes had become pure white. Her flesh faded into shadow. And she became one of them. I felt the others drawing in around me. And when I woke, a ring of shadowy figures surrounded my bed. They did not move. They did not speak. But I could feel them inside my brain. They did something to my mind. Lexi was with them. My thoughts turned to ice. And when I tried to speak, only a cold, howling wind came out of my mouth.

* * *

I dreamt a black dog was in the house, the same one that followed Lexi and I home from school. It had very red eyes, and it was growling and it attacked Buster. We all had to hide, and there was nowhere to hide because the dog kept finding us. It finally cornered us all in one room, growling at us with fangs bared and hatred in its eyes, and it turned white and grew larger and larger. We all knew that it was holding us there. Other dogs appeared, and then the pack changed from dogs to huge black wolves. And through the silence, we heard the footsteps of the White Beast approaching. Thud. The house shook. Thud. A stronger vibration. THUD. THUD. THUD. Each step becoming louder, drawing closer. The sun and the moon changed places outside the window. Seasons flitted by. Still it drew closer. And then we saw it, moving through the trees, its massive figure the height of a huge pine. It turned to us slowly, a human leg in its hand. And then it reached a fist through the window, and took Mom. Dad was next. Then Lexi.

And then I was the beast, and they all lay before me in pieces, and I wept an ocean of tears that drowned the land.

ABODE

December 2, 1979

I dreamed Lexi's soul was missing and we couldn't find it anywhere. We looked in the house, but the house kept changing. There were many different doors. Some opened onto nothing but walls, while others led to dark forests, icy wastes, or fiery hellscapes. We went into the woods, and suddenly, there was nothing around us but darkness. We could feel things moving in that cold black night, but at first we saw nothing. And then we saw the pale grey of a face, and then another, and then we realized we were surrounded by countless dead.

* * *

I dreamed there were dead things in the woods and they were trying to kill us all. Lexi and I were trying to run but the earth split open and we were trapped in a deep, dark cave.

February 1, 1980

I dreamed there were spiders coming out of the cracks in the ground, and I was trying to protect Lexi because she was scared. We had to walk carefully because their legs were sticking up everywhere. We pulled one up, and it was a white spider with red eyes. Then, as we watched, it grew, its legs elongating as it transformed into something. And all the children came in a parade, bearing poles on which dripped severed heads, and they all sang, a ghostly, unhallowed chorus. Ave Weresh.

Those are all the ones I kept. The rest, I couldn't bear to write down. And I only kept those because you were in them, and something about them made me feel like somehow you were reaching out to me through dreams. Like the dreams connected me to you.

I wish my dreams of you were happier. I wish I'd dreamt you in sunlight fields or rose gardens or bright sunny mountain valleys.

I went back to that house only once, on a whim, about a dozen years ago. And when I stood in that overgrown drive, I found *famished* myself staring back through time.

The house was gone. Just *ravenous* an empty lot stood there. But I could still see—and sense—the shadows *hungering* in the forest. *Weresh* I could still sense them there.

Aside from that, well, I shall spare you the sordid details of how I spent my twenties and thirties. I sank to the bottom of a *blood and flesh and bone feast must feast* pit of substance abuse and depression, and then I started digging. It *eating and chewing flesh like pomegranates* took me years to finally claw my way back into something that *hungry* could almost be called human life.

And then I found you.

I just wish I could shake the feeling that it isn't over.

Chapter Thirty-nine

have just reread my prior emails. I have found text in them that I did not write. Or, at least, text that I do not recall writing. In my studio, there are fresh canvases depicting horrible, gruesome scenes that I do not remember painting. Scenes like the ones Dad was creating at the end of our time in that house.

I cannot take any more.

I am but flesh and blood, wrapped around a broken soul. I have little to live for: if this demon wants me enough, he can have me. I have fought and fought and fought, to survive, to heal, to become, if not whole, stable enough to function.

It's you I worry about.

You are not safe.

I cannot protect you now, any more than I could then. I can offer only paltry weapons. Sage. White candles. Salt circles. Prayer. But these things will only work if you believe they will.

I do not.

These days, there are paranormal societies that can help, somewhat, though I should warn you, that the field is full of frauds and scam artists. That isn't to say that there are no true seers; I once visited a psychic who was so terrified at what she sensed that she threw me out and made me promise never to return. I may have thought her a fake, but she mentioned a Jeremy, which was close enough to convince me.

I've taken the liberty of shipping a box of sage sticks to your home. I pray you use them. Sage does dispel negative energy, and may offer some protection. Perhaps if you were to ask for a blessing?

I just reread this and realize how foolish that sounds. Herbs and talismans. Chants. As though these paltry things could truly serve as weapons against the unholy.

I suppose I would try anything, if it could help you. Like Mom, with her angels.

I cannot make you listen to me. I cannot make you believe. I cannot make you accept the fact that there is something truly evil out there, stalking you.

I wish I could.

I wish I could give you a happy, feel-good tale instead of a ghost story. But all I have to offer you is a charnel, funeral truth.

There are many things I still don't understand. In truth, I have more question than answers, and little hope of ever changing that. I cannot explain these things today any more than I could then. However, I now have a tool at my disposal that may answer some of my questions: the internet. I don't know that I want to delve too far into things *hunger* but *blood* I feel *starving* that I have *eat* a bit further *winter* to go. Maybe I can learn *Weresh* something that will help. If you know what you face ... it may help you. Maybe you will find a solution *chew the salty flesh* where I could not. Or maybe you will only find more questions.

He can only travel so far. There are places he cannot go. I cannot pretend to know the boundaries of such things, but there must be limits.

I am thinking I may move to Tibet, or India. Maybe Australia, or the American Virgin Islands. Somewhere warm or exotic, where nothing I see will have any kind of connotations or connections to you or to him or to snow or to Maine.

ABODE

They say demons can't cross water. This one managed to cross several rivers. But I don't think it can follow me across the ocean.

So many questions.

I've only one answer.

Run.

He is coming for you. I can feel it in my bones.

Chapter Forty

I apologize for the frantic tone of my last email. I suffer from a nervous disorder and have just had . . . let's just call it a bad spell. I will never make peace with what happened to you. I know that now. But in revisiting these things, I have stirred up my own demons.

Please forgive me if my train of thought deteriorates, going forward.

I know you're scared.

I am telling you these things for your own safety. You won't take precautions to protect yourself until you believe me. You insist that you don't know me, that you don't remember these things, but I see the fear in your eyes. I see you looking behind you as you leave the office, as you rush to your train.

The security system you installed, the German Shephard you just adopted, the gun you purchased ... these things will not protect you. Nothing can protect you. You are up against something that isn't human.

I wish I had answers. I wish that I was the hero I once hoped for. I want nothing more than to help you, save you. But I don't know how. Sometimes I think I understand what I have to do, to break the cycle. Then the answer slips away, like a grain of sugar lost in bank of snow.

I get ahead of myself. Frenetic. I'm off the meds right now. They take the edge off. They dull the fear, but they also dull the world. And while sometimes I can soak in that comfort, like a blanket, like a bath, right now I need the clarity.

I need to remember everything.

ABODE

I need to think.

My dreams have been strange, of late. Nightmares of wolves and winter forests, and ravens siting beneath angry snow-filled skies. Last night I had a terrible dream. A wolf and a bear were eating the remains of a freshly-killed human. It was winter, and the snow was stained with blood. A raven flew down from the trees. And then, I saw my own bloody hand reach into the corpse, grab a chunk of meat, and raise it to my mouth. I could taste the ripeness of the flesh, felt guts bursting in my mouth like sweet fruit.

I woke up so repulsed that I vomited. My spew was bloody. The bathroom looked like a murder scene when I finished. My stomach feels uneasy, raw and unsettled. This has happened before, when I've been on drinking sprees. But I haven't touched a drop in days.

I am craving meat. I can think of nothing else. It is hard for me to even type a sentence without going to my fridge. But nothing satisfies me.

It's growing colder now. I smell ice in the wind. I feel death, bearing down from the north.

I fear one more incident will push me over the edge of madness.

It's getting colder now.

The Beast grows stronger when it is cold and dark.

I've sent you a package with the information I have compiled. I don't know why. I'm not sure what your school records and your birth and death certificates will mean to you maybe I've just dragged you back into the hell you escaped once you should run before he finds you maybe you can go to Florida I know there's cockroaches there and it's sticky and humid but there's no snow so maybe he can't reach you there.

I wish I had never contacted you.

And in the northern woods, I sense again the Devourer awakening. He is calling through my dreams now, pulling himself into this world.

It's happening again.

I sensed him behind me just now. As I was typing, I felt the presence. The room temperature dropped so sharply that I could see my breath.

And then I heard a clink. A glass in my cupboard, moving, just slightly ice cracking *Weresh.* And then a tap, from the other side of the room.

I turned and jumped up, and I saw him, in the shadow of my hallway. A shadow, nothing more. But it was a distinct shape. His shadow.

The shadow of the Beast.

I see his reflection in the mirror. When I look deep into my own eyes, I see that pallid form, moving through the trees.

Jeremiah

Jeremiah

Jeremiah

Chapter Forty-one

I have nowhere to turn now. The shadows are back, the shadow children, the shadow people there are eighteen of them now which doesn't make sense you came back maybe there is another maybe it's Mom maybe it's Dad they were victims too in their own way. I know what the beast in the woods is primordial I've seen the painting on the inside of the caves of a shaman that tried to fight him but the primordial cannot be fought, can only be contained, that darkness was there long before man ever walked those woods and Tommy was right I did some research even the tribes stayed away from that place they knew it was evil they knew it was dark something demonic waiting in the woods and the house burned but the fires never touched that thing and Anne made a deal with that thing kept it bound to the Kents she hated Sarah even before Jeremiah killed her husband and sons and ate them there was never a David his name was Daniel that story was true I found the records in the courthouse I found the scratches on the wall I saw the dreams he showed me Weresh remembers them all after Jeremiah the next one after him was Albert and then Jacob he hung himself at Dead Man's Pond before it could take him then Marc his victims were from Quebec he crossed the mountains and the frozen river then there was Matthew there was Luc there was Joseph but they had moved they weren't Kents anymore by name but their blood was still tainted Jeremiah showed me in the dreams they were freezing and Elizabeth started dreaming of flesh and after the fire Isabelle went mad so they locked her into her room and then there was the fire blood there was pain and then darkness and then the Beast oh god oh god oh

250

god its coming for me, don't you see, I was the one they wanted the path was meant for me but I was too young so he took Dad and then Josephine told you to burn the house down before Dad became a monster and you never made it out they tricked you and trapped you but you made it back I'm so glad you made it back. Ok trying trying trying to calm myself with music and pot and wine but I need more than that there are scratches in the walls now and I woke this morning with scratches on my leg and blood on my hands and my lips I ate my lips I fear for you I fear so much you have to run get far away get across as many rivers as you can sometimes running water stops these things his daughter Sarah protected herself and her children she danced and worked black magic but she couldn't get rid of it though she tried spell after spell. I've just hit *Ave Weresh* send on the first file, and you should get this one within seconds the internet is fast but then He is faster.

Chapter Forty-two

I am writing this to you from a café in Mersport. I don't remember driving up here. I don't remember leaving my apartment, or throwing my travel kit and some clothes into my old Bruins duffel bag, but I must have done that because these things are in my back seat. I recall absolutely nothing about coming up I-95.

I don't understand what happened. I have had blackouts before, but nothing like this. This time I lost ... I don't even know. A few days, at least, judging by the stubble on my chin.

The last thing I recall was standing in my apartment, cooking a steak.

The next thing I knew, I was back in the woods, those woods, along that trail, staring at the spot where the cabin once was. Only a stone foundation remains now, but I can still see the cabin in my mind's eye.

The sun was setting behind me. The woods were silent. Too silent.

The wind smelled of ice and death.

I stood there for a moment, shaking.

I heard Him before I saw Him. That horrible, keening wail again rode the icy wind. And then it rose, growing louder and louder before reaching a crescendo that sent clouds of birds into the greying skies. I looked up. Against the flutter of black wings, I saw the vortex in the sky.

My spine prickled with fear, as though an ice-cold finger had traced a path down my back. Every nerve in my body screamed at me to get out of there. I ran down the half-remembered trail as fast as I could. But the path changed and shifted. It didn't lead me out of the forest, but back to the pond. And in the spot where I had once seen the noose, I saw the figure of a man, hanging from a tree. He wore dark clothes, in an old style.

I knew his name. Jacob. And I knew, somehow, that the sight I saw before me, the noose and the tree, had been his last, desperate attempt to escape the Beast.

It was dark, suddenly. The forest around me filled with the sounds of screaming winds and terrible howling, and the night teemed with shadows that slithered and moved through the dark. I heard the beasts in the wood again, calling for their master.

I lost another chunk of time.

Daylight was just breaking as I emerged from the woods and ran into the overgrown lot where our house once stood. I was badly winded, and I gulped lungfuls of air to regain my breath. I think I was trying to inhale the sunlight.

My car sat in the drive. The door was open, but the engine wasn't running. Fortunately, I'd had the presence of mind to shut it off, or else it would have either overheated or run dry. I sprinted to it, slid into the seat, and turned the key. I felt a huge relief as the engine turned over. As I started backing out of the drive, I looked up, to the spot where the trail was/wasn't. I saw nothing. Beyond the house, I saw the Centipede tree, still standing. Ghosts—my ghosts—were interposed over that bleak landscape. Mom. Dad. You. Even Buster and Lucky. In my rear view mirror, I saw the land falling away toward the river. I beheld again the shapes in the earth, the dark path that leads to the cemetery. The old dead oak still stands in the yard, like a spectral guardian.

ABODE

And then I looked toward the wood again, and saw the shadow children, lined along the ridge.

That is all I remember. It is blurry and vague, and my head throbs when I think of it.

I peeled out, tires squealing, but I only made it a few miles before I pulled onto the side of the road and had what can only be described as, well, a nervous breakdown. When I got myself together, at least enough to drive, I only had one thought: I just wanted to go home, and check on you.

But I was not allowed to leave.

My car blew a gasket going through town. I bought it a few weeks ago, on a whim. It reminded me of a toy car I used to love, back in those happier early days. My hatred for the 70's doesn't extend to automobiles. It was an impulse buy, perhaps sparked by my recollections, which brought me back to that long-ago decade. I didn't bother getting it checked out, and I only drove it around the block before signing the papers. So, it probably shouldn't have been a major shock to find out that the thing is a gas-guzzling, leather-seated piece of crap. I am apparently stuck here overnight, until the garage opens in the morning. I got a hotel at the dinky little motor inn off the highway, and walked over to the diner across the street to get some dinner. And here I sit, trying to corral my thoughts, trying to make some sense of this all.

I hoped that by writing this all out, I'd find some logic, discover something that would tie everything together, or at least shed a little light on it all. I've been sitting here for hours, and all I have to show for it is more questions.

I'm so hungry. I'm on my fourth plate of food, but I am still famished. The waitress is giving me odd looks.

I think I will go to my room, and order some pizzas.

Chapter Forty-three

I don't understand.
I cannot put sense to it. Any of it.

I've been watching the news about your disappearance. It's foolish of me, I know, to think journalists or police would be able to answer questions that scientists and paranormal investigators and historians have been chasing for years. But I can't help it. I keep waiting for the next newscast, hoping against hope for good news.

All the horror I faced before pales in comparison to this.

You can't be gone again. You were safe, just a few days ago. I heard you answer the phone when I called your office. My heart thudded in my chest when I heard your name mentioned, and the dread that came over me overpowered everything else.

Still I hope that they will announce you've been found, that you are safe and sound.

I hope you are alright.

I'm still in Mersport. Hours and days slip by in a tangled blur. I have a feeling that you are here somewhere. I don't know what to do. I don't dare go back to the property, but I feel like going home is abandoning you, somehow. Giving up.

Maybe you ran. Maybe you took my advice and fled.

Please let me know you're alright.

Please.

Chapter Forty-four

You are fading from the news reports now. The media have moved on to other carrion.

I've just donated my life savings to the fund your sister created for your children. I sent the money anonymously. I have gone back and forth over whether or not to approach her. Did you share any of this with her? If so, then she, too, could be in danger.

They would think I was mad.

I think I am mad.

The headaches are back. Splitting, stabbing, pounding, crushing throbbing pain. I used to hate going to doctors, but a few days ago I broke down. They saw a shadow on my scan, and wanted more tests. I haven't gone back, and I don't intend to. I already know what's happening.

The memories are forming a tumor in my brain. Jeremiah's memory is literally eating a hole in my mind, and filling it with festering, toxic filth.

I don't know why I'm still here. But every time I try to leave, I can't. I feel as though that would be betraying you. Abandoning you.

I took a walk today, hoping to clear my head. This town, which was bustling when we moved here, is a shadow of its former self. The mill closed down in the late 90's, and when the work went away, so did the people. Nearly every other house has a For Sale sign on it. Many of the shops Mom used to take us to are closed and boarded up. The roller rink is now a discount store, and our old arcade has been replaced by a coffee shop. Only a few chain stores remain.

We never should have come here.
I never should have come here.

Chapter Forty-five

I have the answers now. At least, some of them. I'm still trying to sort things out. There are still a few puzzle pieces that don't make sense. But I am drawing closer and closer to understanding.

I am not sure that the answers I have now will be a comfort. But, however horrible the truth is, I decided long ago that would rather know what I am facing than continue to guess. I suspect you would feel the same.

Maybe I was meant to come back here all along. I don't know. I've had little—actually, no—sense of anything benevolent protecting us. Mom's prayers certainly didn't help anything.

But I did recently have a bit of luck.

After I sent the last email, I decided it was time to go home. I couldn't stand to stay in this drab, depressing town. I got myself together enough to pack and check out, then got into my car and started driving. As I went through town, I happened to pass the street where Lane's aunt lived. I slowed down, curious. It was a wet, dreary, grey day, and the cold rain and bitter winds had the bite of winter. The ground was still bare, but freezing rain had been falling on and off, and many of the streets and sidewalks were slick and icy. Most of the leaves had fallen already, leaving Mersport dull and colorless. I navigated up and down the small but tangled warren of bumpy back roads behind the spot where our old grocery store once stood, trying to remember exactly where the house was.

It didn't take me long to find it. The place looked almost exactly the same as I remembered. It probably hadn't changed much in the last century, never mind the past few decades.

The name Kent was still on the mailbox.

I drove another block, turned around, passed the house again, kept going, made a U-turn, drove to the park a few blocks down the road and sat there, not sure what to do. Eventually I decided that I had nothing left to lose, and I pulled into the drive.

There were lights on inside. The kitchen window was a square of glowing yellow light, an inviting picture of coziness and warmth on a grey, overcast day. I realized that I couldn't remember the last time I had felt as warm and safe as I had in that kitchen. My hand was shaking as I knocked on the door.

Sure enough, Phyllis opened the door. She had aged, but it was unmistakably her. She met me with a look that was more puzzled than suspicious. "Can I help you?"

"I'm Lane's friend," I said. "I was here, a long time ago. You fed me Whoopie pies."

This was, of course, a completely idiotic greeting. I was shaking. I am sure I looked wild-eyed and frantic. I couldn't think clearly enough to string together a more coherent introduction.

I'm lucky she didn't call the cops.

She looked at me as though I were insane. "Excuse me?"

"I used to live in the Kent house," I said. "The one on Route ... Old Murder Road. Lane brought me here once, a long time ago, and you told me some things. I ... I was wondering if I could ask you some questions."

She just continued to stare, her watery eyes blank.

"You were a Kent," I said. "You know ... you know about the house."

"That house burned down," she said slowly. I saw something cross her eyes, and she started to back away.

ABODE

I saw the door begin to close, and reached out to stop it, only barely managing to keep my fingers from getting smashed. "I need your help. Please."

I've begged for cash. I've begged for food. I've begged for forgiveness, and for second chances, and for lighters to work and cars to start and phone batteries to last just a few minutes longer. But I have never in my life spoken such a heartfelt plea for help.

She stood frozen.

I tried again. "I was friends with Lane," I told her. "We moved into the house, and, well, he brought me here, because he said you knew ... he said you knew about it."

Several expressions crossed her face. None of them were happy, but she didn't seem angry, either. "I remember you now," she said. She stepped back, opening the door. "I'm not sure how I can help you, but I won't sleep tonight if I don't try. Come in."

I stepped in, happy to get out of the cold, wet rain. She took my jacket, and hung it on a rack beside the door. The years that had passed since I had seen her had greyed her hair and etched lines into her face, but they hadn't been entirely unkind. She looked worried, but gentle.

She offered me a spot at the table, the same one Lane and I had sat at when we visited her nearly four decades ago. The kitchen was warm and bright. They'd done some remodeling in the interim; the 70's geometric patterned vinyl flooring had been replaced by plain white laminate, and they'd upgraded their old Formica countertops to granite ones. The pine cabinets and stainless-steel appliances also looked fairly new. But the layout looked exactly the same. Looking around, I recognized a few of the owl and mushroom knick-knacks. I smelled vanilla, and noticed a candle on a shelf.

A lump rose in my throat. This small kitchen was a home. Something I would never know.

A small grey cat appeared at the kitchen door. I remembered the kittens then. I suppose those tiny balls of fur had grown old and died in the intervening years, their nine lives spinning quickly through the cycles of my adulthood. I hoped they had been loved and well-fed and happy.

It seemed only yesterday that Lane and I had sat there, eating Whoopie pies. It seemed a million years ago.

I sat quietly for a moment, perfectly caught between past and present. I half-expected to see Lane come out of the bathroom.

"Coffee?" Phyllis asked.

I nodded. A few moments later, she placed a steaming mug before me, set a tray of butter cookies on the table, and sat down across from me. Silence settled over us like a blanket. Outside, I heard the rain pick up force, dark clouds lashing out with a frozen, icy mix that seemed to curtain us off from the rest of the world.

"Well," she said finally, "Do you want to tell me why you're here?"

"I know it's unexpected," I said. "I'm sorry. It's about the house."

"I gathered as much," she said dryly.

"You told me some things, long ago, about the house. But . . . I think you held back. I understand why. I was a child at the time. But as an adult, I have to wonder if you knew things that you wouldn't share with a fifth-grader. Things you can maybe tell me now. Things that could maybe help me understand why my family died."

ABODE

"That house burned over thirty years ago," she said. "Why are you asking now?"

I clutched my coffee cup, and tried to keep my voice steady. "I just ... I need to know. To put it to rest."

Her eyes burned into me.

"You asked me about my dreams." I raised my eyes to her face. "Why?"

Her face was unreadable. "Legends," she said quietly. "Myths. Things I overheard, when I was young, myself... Things I..."

I cut her off. "Did you ever see him?" The question was a whisper.

After a moment, she nodded. "Once," she said. "But Emmett ... Emmett grew up in that house."

Just the thought of growing up in that place made me shiver. I had barely survived ... what? Seven months?

"I wasn't from here," she told me. "So I never heard the stories growing up. I was still very young when I married Emmett. Emmett never liked to go to the house. But when his brother died, we had the funeral there. It wasn't ... it wasn't a good day. Everyone was upset and crying. Joey died in the war, you know. Vietnam. So young. He was only nineteen, I think. Twenty at most."

I remembered seeing Joey's grave. But I didn't care about him, the brother of a man I'd never met. Have you ever felt angry, even though you know deep inside that your rage really isn't justified? That's what happened to me then. I felt my blood start to boil, and clenched my fists so hard my knuckles turned white. But I bit my tongue and let her continue.

She sipped her coffee. Lit a cigarette. "I went into the kitchen to get a glass of water, and I looked out into the yard. He was standing there, plain as day. Just as I'd always heard him described. Black suit, wide-brimmed hat. Tall. Pale. Thin. I couldn't see his face. I just felt, in that moment, a wave of hatred. And then I saw the others. Small, black shadows, hiding in the tree line. It was dusk, and the sun had just set. I ran out of the kitchen, and started telling everybody what I had seen. Everyone got very quiet and tense, but no one said anything. But Emmett's father ... that night he just ate and ate and ate. He had a hunger that couldn't be fulfilled. He killed himself a few weeks later."

Old Mr. Kent blew his brains out in there. Just like his father.

I felt slightly nauseous as I repeated my original question. "Why did you ask me about my dreams?"

"That's how it starts," she said. "That's how he takes over. He builds himself a gate into your dreams. And then, with each dream, the door opens wider."

Outside, the wind howled.

"You said something to me," I said. "It didn't make sense at the time. It didn't really click until now. You told me winter was dangerous."

She was silent.

"Because of the Beast," I said.

She hesitated, and then nodded. "There are other names for him. They call him-"

"I don't care what they call him." I know the words came out snarly, even though that wasn't my intent. "I want to know what it-"

She cut me off. "Maybe you *should* care," she snapped. "Because then you could just do some research on Wendigos, and leave me in peace."

ABODE

I felt as though she had punched me. I felt as though light had stabbed a cloud, and made a hole that shone only on me. I felt as though a chasm had opened below me, to suck me down into the depths of hell.

I'd heard the name Wendigo. That was all I knew. But the word struck a funeral bell, somewhere in the murkiest recesses of my soul. It rang true.

And in that moment, I remembered you, crying, choking on tears. I would have sworn you were saying, "When we go," that night, as the winds screamed around us.

You weren't. You were saying *Wendigo*.

Phyllis sipped her coffee, and fixed her eyes on me. Her next words were colored by the rage and emotion of someone whose spouse had committed suicide. The decades that had passed since his death hadn't made it easier on her. The pain was still there, just below the surface.

As was mine.

"You're right," she said, tightly. I noticed that her voice was raspy. When she coughed, I heard a telltale rattle in her throat. "There were things I didn't say, that day. Things that weren't meant for a nine, ten-year old to hear. You want to hear them now?"

I had a sick feeling in my stomach as I nodded.

She looked me straight in the eye, as though sizing me up, and then glanced down at her cigarette as she tapped it on the ashtray. "This is an ancient land, son. And the legend of the White Beast was around long before the first European settlers set foot on this soil," she said. "It's an old Wabanaki myth. Actually, all of the Algonquian have similar stories. The First People walked these woods long before the white man came. And they had their own legends, their own mythology. The interesting—and terrifying—thing about the myth is that it is so widespread. Almost every tribe in the north, from east to west, had some version of the story. And, unlike most legends, many of them were eerily similar." Her eyes met mine. "You said you'd never heard of a Wendigo?"

I shook my head. "I think I've heard the word before."

"Well, people don't talk about them much. Some say it's bad luck to even think of them. I tend to agree. But, whereas the natives feared the Beast, the Kents ... fed it."

"I don't understand," I said. "What is it?"

Her eyes met mine. "A demon, a demi-god, a walking nightmare come to life. The Wendigo is a monster associated with winter, with howling winds and raging snowstorms and icy wastes. It craves human meat, and can never eat its fill.

"Many of the First Nations believe that thoughts hold weight. And one of the most ghastly thoughts a human being can have is of cannibalism. That is what the Beast represents. Hunger. Desperate hunger. Not the sort of hunger that makes your stomach rumble because you skipped lunch or are late for dinner. Hunger strong enough to make a man give up his humanity. A hunger that eats you from the inside out, and devours the very soul within you. The drive for food is the most basic instinct there is. That primal instinct exists even in the tiniest creature. The story of the Wendigo dwells in that hunger.

"Winter is the hard time, or it was, in the old days. Most times, people worked through the summer to store food for the cold season. But sometimes, something happened. Things went wrong. Crops failed or were stolen, cattle got sick. There were hungry winters. And there were starving winters. Hunger can drive men to do terrible things. Sometimes, in winter, people resorted to cannibalism. It's taboo, even today. It's taboo even to speak of it. But that doesn't mean it didn't happen. You've heard of the Donner party, I'm sure."

I nodded.

"Did you think they were an isolated case? That no one else in the history of humanity has been forced to make that choice?" She shook her head. "In the old myths, those that succumb to their hunger and eat human flesh become Wendigos." She reached for her coffee cup. Her hands were shaking slightly. "I've never seen the Beast. But the descriptions were enough to give me nightmares."

I felt sick.

"Tell me," I prompted.

She drew a deep, heavy breath. "I don't know all of it. Just what Emmett told me. He was obsessed with it all, before he died."

I picked up a butter cookie and bit into it. It was sweet and crumbly, but it tasted like ash in my mouth.

Phyllis continued quietly. "Tale goes way back. When Jeremiah Kent met Marie, they decided to strike out on their own. The property was in a good spot, with easy access to the river. It offered wood, game, and, once it was cleared, decent pasture and farmland. There were berries and fruit trees, and the ocean was a short distance away. Emmett said that his grandmother once told him that the tribes stayed away from that place, but I don't know if that's true. And I can't say much about what happened to Jeremiah and Marie before they met and married. Rumor says that both they and/or their parents fled the witch hunts, but we don't know that, either. What I do know is that Jeremiah and

Marie made their home here, and a few years later, Marie's sister, Anne, and her husband joined them."

I knew that much already, but I still hung on every word she said.

"For several years, things were okay. They had several children, raised cattle, and grew crops. And then one fall, there was a terrible storm. A hurricane. It ruined their crops, and they lost cattle to the sickness that followed. They didn't have time to plant again before the snows came down: it was too late. And that winter was hard, a long, brutal one. Winters here are always cold and snowy, but that year was extremely brutal. The snow was relentless: storm after storm piled on more and more misery. Long before the spring thaw, the family's stores ran out. And so, desperate, Jeremiah went out on a hunting trip with Anne's husband. They took two or three of the oldest boys with them. Legend says that they got lost, and were trapped with no food after another big storm. And Jeremiah . . . he killed and ate the others. And he became a Wendigo."

I felt sick. I thought of Dad, eating and eating and eating. My own hunger, gnawing through my memories.

Phyllis continued quietly. "When Jeremiah came back from that trip, he came back alone. And he came back changed. Before long, Marie and Anne realized what had happened. Marie must have been beside herself. Anne, however, well, she went on a rampage. Rumor has it she was a witch, and a powerful one at that. Story is that she sold her own soul to curse the Kents. She bound that thing to the Kent line, and cursed Jeremiah to hunt his own children. Jeremiah's daughter Sarah knew the black arts, and she tried to ward it off. But she was only partially successful. The thing took her grandson, Albert, next."

I shuddered. At least when we had been haunted, it wasn't our own ancestor tormenting us.

"Is there anything else?"

"Well, the stories say that the Kents have always borne this curse, that several Kents did become Wendigos. Others were killed—or killed themselves—before the transformation could become complete."

I tried to be delicate, knowing we were treading on fragile ice. "Do you believe that?"

"Oh, I don't know. It's far-fetched. But the Kents have had a lot of bad luck. The family history after that doesn't get much happier. There were at least four suicides that I know of. Two Kents charged with murder. Sarah's youngest grandson, Samuel, moved to York, and died in the massacre of 1692, when the Penobscots and a French missionary raided an English settlement. Bloody affair, that was. One of the things they don't tell you in the history books. They killed about a hundred. Emmett thought they were after Samuel from the start, but I never believed that, myself. Emmett's great-great-grandaunt, Josephine, knocked a candle over during a séance, and burned the place down with half her family in it. And even after that, things happened. Emmett's grandmother, Agnes, was wheelchair-bound after a freak riding accident. You know about the twins, and the fire. And then there was Emmett's own father."

Every hair in my body stood on end.

"How do you know all of this?" I asked. "Your husband?"

"Yes," she said quietly. "My husband. Emmett became obsessed with the place after his father died. He grilled his aunts and uncles relentlessly. Did a bunch of research on the family tree. Called every relative he could find. He compiled everything into a book." She toyed with her coffee cup, turning it slightly. "He got it in his head that the stories were true, and was looking for a way to lift the curse. Spent half his retirement money on mediums and witch doctors, and ended up with hardly nothing to show for it. That wasn't long before he . . . before he died."

I felt my interest spike. "A book?" I asked, perhaps too eagerly. "Do you have it?"

She shook her head. "I burnt it, not long after he died. I regret that now. But at the time, I wasn't thinking very clearly. I read it, first, though. What I'm telling you is what I remember. I can't remember all the names and dates, but I recall the story well enough. I read it several times before I threw it into the woodstove."

I let this sink in. "Why was he so interested in the place? Just family history?"

She looked at me. Her voice was flat and calm, still waters running deep. "Our son died there. As did his father and grandfather."

I stared at her. "I'm sorry. I didn't know. Lane never mentioned it."

"Lane didn't know either," she said. "He wasn't even born when we lost Matt, and we kept it from him. We would likely have told him when he got older, but that never happened."

I felt myself growing pale. An icy fist of dread clenched my stomach. "What? What do you mean?"

Her brows lifted. "You don't know?"

"Know what?"

Her voice fell. "Lane died a long time ago. He never made it out of grade school."

I swallowed. My throat was tight, as though my neck was clenched in a giant fist. "Was it—"

She shook her head. "Car accident," she said.

"I'm sorry," I said, sincerely.

She nodded, and quietly thanked me. We were quiet a moment.

"He wanted to go see you," she said. "After the fire. Your aunt and uncle thought you were too distraught for company."

My throat tightened. Rage washed over me, but it ebbed quickly: they were probably right.

The wind was picking up. I could hear it howling through the trees outside. Rain battered down on the roof, and splattered against the glass of her window panes in fat, icy drops.

And there we sat, warm and cozy, cordially speaking of this monstrosity over coffee and butter cookies.

"Do not think of him," she said, her voice suddenly intense. "Do not speak his name. Do not react if you see him, even if he is right before you. Do you understand?"

I sat back, my head spinning.

She stood up, and went into another room. I heard her rummaging around. A few moments later, she came back with a small chest. "Take these," she said. "I don't know why I kept them. They're the notes and resource material for Emmett's book."

I got the hint: it was time for me to go. I stood up and got my coat, then picked up the trunk.

She saw me to the door. "I'm sorry about your sister. That was heartbreaking. We read it in the papers. I said a prayer for her, poor thing."

Tears prickled in my eyes, and again, a lump rose in my throat. I saw you again, laughing and running with Buster in the sun, turning cartwheels in our old yard. "Thank you," I said quietly.

As I was about to go out the door, I stopped and turned. "How do you kill the Beast?" I asked.

She looked me dead in the eye. "You don't. You become it."

I swallowed, and thanked her again.

Then I walked out into the cold, wet, rain.

Chapter Forty-six

After leaving Phyllis' house, I headed for the highway. Then, struck by a sudden thought, I hit the brakes and screeched to a halt, then turned my car around and drove back to the property. This time, instead of going into the woods behind the house, I walked down the field across the street, toward the cemetery, careless of the freezing rain. I didn't stay long, only long enough to snap pictures of the graves, so I could have names and dates.

I spent five more days in Mersport, Wereading Emmett's materials and doing research.

Emmett told a grim tale, documenting case after case of Kents dying. Most of his reference materials are handwritten recollections of things his family members said, supplemented by birth and death records, property deeds, wills, that sort of thing. What Phyllis had told me encompassed the basics about the property's history and stories, the important parts at least. But there was much more to the tale.

It's kind of funny. They say the internet is the greatest research tool in the world. But when one starts to delve into the history of things that happened hundreds—or even just dozens—of years ago, the library is actually a treasure trove. I found quite a few records in the town library: births, deaths, old deeds. I'm attaching the records, just to be thorough.

When I felt I had gone as far as I could, I drove home in a daze, my thoughts pinwheeling into darkness. When I got home, I found that my apartment was freezing. My brand-new windows were wide open. Gizmo was outside: I guess he must have jumped out the window. The neighbors had been feeding him. I brought him in, offered him a can of tuna, and then, after a short and somewhat awkward conversation, gave him to my neighbors. He's safer with them, I think.

I shut the windows and turned the lights on, only to find that these things made the apartment unbearably hot and bright. I am sitting here now with all the windows open. Light hurts my eyes, so my laptop screen is illuminating my apartment.

My home smells of snow.

The Kent story goes back hundreds of years, to the time when white men first set foot on these lands, and met an unknown wilderness.

The history of the Beast reaches much farther back into time, into an era we know little about.

The First Nation people lived here for thousands of years before the first Europeans arrived. The very name Wendigo means 'evil spirit that devours mankind.' But the Wendigo has many names. He was known as Kee-wakw to the Abenaki, and Witiko to the Cree. The Iriquois called him Stonecoat. He has other names as well, such as Atschen, Cheno, Kokodje, Djenu, Outiko, and Vindiko, to name a few.

But to the descendants of Jeremiah Kent, he was known as Weresh.

What we faced was no mere human ghost: it was an evil spirit that has haunted these northern woods since the dawn of time.

I have done some research on the Wendigo. And in doing so, I've found more bits of lore ... all of which match up perfectly with my own memories. While the Wendigo myth as we know it originates from North America, folklore from China, Russia, Japan, and Scandinavia also have creatures with similar traits, though the names, faces, and myths are a bit different. Even the beast Grendel from Beowulf bears some resemblance to the Wendigo.

In the early days, Wendigos were accepted as a common threat. The tales of the ice wraiths are far older than any written records of this wood, but long ago, the people of the First Nations whispered about the monsters that walk the winter wild. All of the Wendigo stories were based on the assumption that any human being who resorted to cannibalism could—and would—become Wendigos themselves. Some speculate that the stories were meant as a warning against cannibalism. That may or not be true: it certainly makes sense. But it doesn't discount the evidence I hold in my memories.

There is more here than simple myth.

I've found references to several accounts of Wendigos. In 1636, Paul Le Jejune, a Jesuit missionary stationed in Quebec, wrote a letter to the Vatican about a local woman's claims that a Wendigo was stalking her village.

In another, particularly noteworthy case, a Cree hunter named Jack Fiddler claimed to have killed over a dozen Wendigos. Some were supposedly sent against his people by enemy shamans. Others, including his own brother, were men from his own tribe that developed an insatiable desire to eat long pig. At least once, Fiddler said he had been asked to basically euthanize a dying person before they could turn. Fiddler was arrested for the last of these deaths in 1907, but committed suicide soon after.

There are other accounts. Many of the stories are very similar: a group of hunters set out in winter, only to meet bad luck. They are lost, or trapped by a storm, and/or their food runs out. If a man resorts to eating human flesh, he crosses the line between human and demon, sacrificing his humanity and attracting the spirit of a Wendigo, which soon possesses him. After eating human flesh, the man—or woman—would become very sick, and vomit blood. Death soon follows.

That is when the transformation begins.

Details vary a bit from one tale to the next, but the basic description of the Wendigo remains the same. The body grows long and thin, taking on an emaciated look, with protruding bones and red eyes sunk deep into their sockets. In some stories, matted white fur covers the creature's body. The nails become talons, and the teeth grow into yellow, razor-sharp fangs. Its skull changes, too: it becomes malformed, more beast than human, and it grows massive horns or antlers. Its skin turns a sickly yellow or a blue-grey color. Some tales say Wendigos have long, split tongues and bloody, blackened lips. Most of the stories agree that the creature can grow to immense heights, and gives off the stench of death and decaying flesh.

After the transformation is complete, the thing rises in an unholy rebirth. The newly-formed Wendigo has an insatiable appetite for human flesh. It will eat nothing else, and can never be satisfied. And each time it feeds, it grows. This growth perpetuates an eternal cycle of hunger: the more it eats, the hungrier it becomes.

The Wendigo is not just a primal beast, however. It is cunning, as intelligent as a human being is. And it possesses a range of supernatural powers. Some say it can warp space and time, or cross vast distances in a split second. It can change shape, and mimic the forms of its prey or its host. Some accounts say the thing is so thin it can't be seen from the side. By all accounts, Wendigos are extremely tall, towering over many trees. The Beast has extremely sharp sight, smell, and hearing, and it can move very silently. It likes to slowly stalk its victims and toy with them, especially those it wants to possess, though it sometimes simply devours people with no such foreplay. It can trick its prey by imitating the sound of human voices, or drive them mad by stalking them. It can uproot trees, cause blizzards, and control the beasts that roam the northern forests. Its voice, a keening howl, is rumored to drive men completely mad. The monstrosity can shapeshift and can also jump from one body to another as its host ages and weakens, and sometimes even calls its victims by name. It has also been said to break into isolated homes or cabins, kill and eat the inhabitants, and then use the place as a lair. It hibernates sometimes, for years or even decades, only to arise again when a harsh winter comes along.

The Wendigo often bonds to wild beasts, such as wolves and crows. It sometimes travels with these animals, and even shares its kill with them. Sometimes it toys with its victims, keeping them alive, and killing them slowly, so it can feed—piece by piece—as it wishes. When it feeds, the souls it absorbs are trapped within it, and become part of its energy. An old Wendigo contains—or embodies—the spirits of many human cannibals. Therefore, the older the thing gets, the more powerful it becomes.

While usually a person becomes a Wendigo after eating human flesh, there are other methods aside from cannibalism. Some say that Wendigo possession starts with dreams. Others say that sorcerers and witches can turn a person into a Wendigo by cursing them. People can also willingly offer to become a Wendigo, often in return for the defeat of some enemy.

There are signs of Wendigo possession. The person will grow violent, and will become completely obsessed with eating human flesh. Next, the victim will suffer horrible pains in their arms and legs, and develop bizarre, insatiable appetites. Sometimes they complain about smelling a horrible stench, like the stink of decaying flesh, even when no one else can detect it. They often see those around them—even their own family members—as food animals, such as pigs or cows or, in olden times, beavers.

Dad had all of these symptoms. I remember him joking about eating us, and complaining about the pain in his legs.

There are a few other things worth noting.

Phyllis was right about one thing: there is no known way to kill a Wendigo. I was hoping to find something: A charm, an amulet. Holy water, garlic. Something. Anything. But the stories all say that these things are almost impossible to kill. Shoot it, stab it, hang it, burn it: the creature will only go dormant, and resurrect again. The only method that is said to work is to drive a silver stake through the Beast's frozen heart, after which one must then dismember the body and bury the pieces in several different places, where they can never be found.

It all makes sense. The pieces fit. The cabin. The children. The legends. The storm. The sounds. Dad's paintings. His hunger, his pains. Even the goddamn trail, and the games time and space played with us. Everything, even Elizabeth: they locked her into her room because she was dreaming of the thing, and in the end, Josephine burned the house down to contain it.

As did you.

I know now why the cabin appeared and reappeared. Why the landscape changed. The Wendigo was in those woods, manipulating time itself.

Only one Kent, Sarah, seemed to escape unscathed. She delved into the black arts, and fought fire with fire. She managed to keep her own children safe, but as soon as she died, it came back. Her oldest grandson, Albert, started acting strangely, and, not long after that, his brother Francoise went missing in a storm. The tale isn't complete on paper, but I have dreamt these things so clearly that I can almost smell snow and blood in the words.

Josephine sought to emulate Sarah, but her plan backfired terribly.

I thought of transcribing all of Emmett's notes, but most of them really don't matter very much. Would you care, if you knew that Martin Kent owned seven cows, 13 goats, a dozen chickens, and two plow horses? I doubt it. Do Josephine's grocery lists or household accounts matter to you? Are you interested in the fact that Sarah's youngest grandson, Samuel, fled this area, only to be killed in the York massacre of 1692?

Emmett's box also contained a handwritten book. It had clearly been rescued from a fire, because and the edges and covers were charred and blackened. Many of the pages were missing. I guess someone tore those pages out and burned them, and then tossed the book into the flames. For some reason, that person, or perhaps someone else, must have snatched it back.

According to old folklore, a witch's grimoire should be burned after her death. I think—though I am not sure—that the book was Josephine's grimoire.

The first page contains only a warning. I guess whoever ripped out the other pages didn't care about that.

This book is to be read only by initiates of our Circle. If you are not one of us, you are forbidden to read further! Be warned: you will suffer terrible consequences if you continue!

There were a few spells written in the runic Witches' language. I took time to painstakingly translate them. One turned out to be a recipe for incense, which seemed identical to the stuff you can find at any dollar store. Another was a medicinal recipe for turning blood into marmalade. The rest were . . . darker.

Tucked into this sheet was torn-off piece of paper from a different book entirely. The ink and handwriting are different than those in the diary and Grimoire. They were much, much older: the paper was yellowed with age, and the edges crumbled as I picked it up.

I cannot say for certain, but I think that is all that remains of Sarah's grimoire. In the olden days, the character they used for the letter *S* often looks like an *f*. That alone dates the parchment to early colonial times. It's annoying as hell to read, to be honest, but I transcribed it as written.

Laft night waf a full moon. We read Mother's booke, and we followed her path. We went to the circle, the three of uf, and we caft the net and we fummoned three fpiritf to protecte uf. A black bird came and fang to uf of obliteration. We faw the ftarf fhining, lighting the way to the fhining Path. And we fang our runef into the northern wind.

Every so often, the Beast resurrects, hungry. He calls himself into the world through dreams. And somewhere inside this monster, this gaunt, unholy being, is the frozen body of what was once a man named Jeremiah Kent.

Chapter Forty-seven

I t all makes sense now.
I almost missed it. In fact, I did miss it several times.

I have two accounts on the ancestry site: one for us, and one for the Kents. It took some time to realize that I was seeing one particular name on both sets: Dad's great-great-great-grandma, Alice. Her maiden name was Thibodeaux. Then she married a man named Anthony Kent, Josephine and Elizabeth's brother. They had two children. When Anthony died, Alice remarried. She took her second husband's name, and gave it to the children as well. They never lived in the house: they moved south, to Boston.

We never bore the Kent name.

But we carry their blood.

Truth is presented to us as a benevolent thing, almost like a holy relic, something wielded by the just and the brave. There are bright shiny truths, and there are serene truths and beautiful truths and harsh truths. Truth, they say, is. It brings down evil men, and avenges the victims of their crimes. But that isn't always the case. Sometimes truth is a hideous, terrible thing, that slithers through the shadows that lurk in men's hearts. And truth cloaked and veiled in legend can be a terrible thing.

The truth, in this case?

This truth is ugly, a corpse rotting in the ground. This is the truth of murder, of violence and torture and rape, and all the monstrosities humans are capable of. This truth is parasitic, toxic. Demonic. That is what I offer you; a truth you never asked for. A truth that belongs to the darkness of cold graves, to the chill of an ancient, haunted wood, to the forbidden, hideous mystery of an ancient Maine cemetery.

When we moved into the house, the Beast awoke. His lair is the cabin, but he inhabits it in a different time, when it stood whole. When he was resurrected, he stalked me at first, thinking I would be his next host.

But I was too young. He turned his attention to Dad.

It all fits.

Ave Weresh.

Now, he wants me. Am I certain of this? Of course not. But it's the only way the pieces fit together. I only wish I'd had them sooner. Though I'm not sure what I could have done. I was just a little boy, armed with knives and stones against an ancient evil. But maybe they would have listened to me. Maybe they would have run.

Maybe you'd still be alive.

We are human. We are mortal. We are flesh and blood and bone, and we are fragile. Man is an animal, at heart. We can—all of us—quickly fall back into the mindset of a primal beast. Kill or be killed. That is survival, at its basest level. There is no morality in nature.

But even animals do not typically eat their own kind.

Were the legends real? Or did Jeremiah sell his soul to something demonic, and pay the price in the flesh and blood of innocents? Are the worst beings out there all products of our own minds, our fears, somehow made real?

It doesn't matter: the answers, in the end are intangible. Irrelevant. They won't bring you back.

The hunger is gnawing at me.

ABODE

I cannot eat my fill, no matter what I do. My dreams are of ice and blood, of viscera and entrails. Crows and feral cats hover around my apartment, waiting for me to share my feast.

I have eaten my lips. I couldn't stop myself.

I think I will sew my mouth shut. That may help.

If I cannot eat, I cannot feast.

Chapter Forty-eight

I understand it all now. I finally have all of the pieces. Jeremiah was here last night. I woke to find him standing by my bed. I was frozen in place. But this time was different. This was … I think this was his true ghost, his human soul. Or what remains of it.

He reached out, very slowly, and gently touched my forehead. And it all came back to me then, both my memories and his.

The memories hit me with physical force. I remembered things I had forgotten. Even during the course of this bleak correspondence, my mind hid certain events from me. These recollections have all come rushing back now.

I know what happened when I took you back to Mersport a few weeks ago.

I understand now that the things I remembered earlier were only the 'bookends' of those events, the beginning and the end. The middle was lost.

I'm so sorry it came to this. I was so, so sure that bringing you back would end it all.

I can understand why you didn't want to go in the car. I do apologize for the way that had to happen. But I knew you wouldn't come with me, otherwise. I even had to buy an old car, one that doesn't have the release mechanism in the trunk. When I put you in there, I left you a ham and cheese sandwich, some apple juice, and crackers. These used to be some of your favorite foods. I gave you a blanket and pillow. I took care choosing these things, and bought ones that were just like your old favorites, or at least, the closest to them that I could find. I also gave you the ticket I'd bought you for the Downeaster. I put it in your coat pocket. Remember? I hoped that it would give you some reassurance, proof that I was planning to let you go. *You will be on that train,* I told you. I remember that. And I meant that promise. I even put your cell phone in the dash, so I could return it to you. I was going to give it back as soon as you walked the property with me

I only wanted you to see.

When we pulled onto the property, the first thing I saw was you, as you are today, standing on the edge of the hill. The shadow children stood behind you. The skies were overcast, the clouds thick with snow, and a few flakes drifted down.

I was at first confused (I hadn't let you out of the trunk) and then alarmed. I got out of the car and called out after you, told you to wait. When I looked at the spot where the house once stood, I could almost feel the flames reflected in my eyes.

Five minutes on the property, and already the thing had revealed itself.

When I told you that we were here, that we had arrived, I heard muffled thud from the trunk: your response. I popped the lid, my hands shaking.

I don't blame you for hitting me with the tire iron. I'm actually, despite myself, a little proud of your strength. I was taken by surprise, for, as I've mentioned, I had no intention of harming you.

You knocked me out cold.

When I came to, it was twilight. A few inches of fresh snow covered the ground. I struggled to my feet, brushed myself off, and looked into the woods.

They were still there, the shadows on the hill. Children that will never again see the light of day.

Jeremiah stood among them, outlined by a setting, blood-red sun. He wore his human form, but the shadow he cast was that of the Beast. I understand that, now. I understand why he changed, over the course of our time in the house. He appears human in the warmer months. But in winter, his true form emerges.

I felt fear clench my throat. My spine stiffened, my muscles trying to protect my central nerve column.

I jumped in the car and drove halfway home. Then I changed my mind, pulled off the interstate and got a hotel. I went back the next day, searching.

I found your purse in the woods. There was no other trace of you anywhere. When I finally gave up, I went back to the driveway and just sat in the car, shaking, growing colder, until movement caught my eye. I looked up and saw you there, running into the woods.

This time I knew it wasn't you.

I never meant for this to happen.

If you are out there, please answer me. Please. If you are reading this, let me know that you're alright. And hopefully, you will be comforted, knowing that I am not going to hurt you. I was never going to hurt you.

I'm having blackouts. Time no longer is a fluid thing: it skips days, and drags through moments.

Jeremiah/Weresh grows stronger every day. I see him everywhere now. I see his reflection behind me in mirrors, in windows. He is a shadow in a window, a step in an empty hall, the stench of death in a quiet room. I see his shadow next to mine when I turn away from the sun. I see him growing paler, taller, morphing into his winter form. His hunger reaches into me: a dark, unholy craving.

My shadow, too, is changing, growing longer and thinner.

I cannot fight him.

My mind is filled with images that weren't there before. I don't think I am remembering these things. I think the Beast put them into my thoughts. Else, I am completely mad, which would actually be a comfort compared to the alternative.

I hope I am mad. I hope those memories are not real. But I can recall every detail of my vision of you standing before that cabin in the woods.

The Beast fed that night, and grew stronger. Blood stained the freshly fallen snow.

I blocked it out. I would block it out again if I could. I can't stand to think of it. I barely managed to type this, my hands are shaking so badly. The memory makes me nauseous.

I had to run to the bathroom and vomit, just now. My puke was red and bloody, much like Jeremiah's in that vision.

I've one last vision of the Beast, standing in an open field in a winter forest, as tall as the trees, his demonic face the embodiment of menace.

A pool of blood lies at his feet.

Chapter Forty-nine

I know how to fix this now. I know what to do.
There is only one way for me to make this right.

In my dreams last night, I saw the forest open before you, blood red leaves and black branches shivering against a grey winter sky. I saw you walk into the wood. And I saw you stop before the cabin.

Those visions left me crumpled on the floor, weeping and shaking. I almost wished that I believed in God, because prayer would have been a comfort. I would have had some slim chance of help, of hope, of divine intervention. Or, at the very least, a greater purpose.

But I have no such luxury.

A friend of mine once said something that has always stuck with me. He told me that it takes all of us to make up this picture. Good people, bad people, and all of those in between. It takes the Hitlers and the Pol Pots and the Gandhis and the Mother Teresas to paint the portrait of the human race. It's not a pretty picture, by any means. But it is a realistic one.

At the end of the day, we are all humans. We're all flawed, imperfect, messy mofos. We look at the world through various filters; religion, race, age, sex, gender, class, education, experience, upbringing, personal chemistry, family traits, weight, health, region, culture. And all of these things color the world differently, so that none of us are looking through the exact same lens.

We will always live in a world that is filled with conflict and hatred and strife. We will also always live in a world filled with love and beauty and friendship.

ABODE

If you were Eve, would you eat the apple? Would you choose free will over paradise?

I find myself faced with the opposite conflict: I choose hell over submission.

I have come to some conclusions. I cannot fight this thing. It's too late for me.

But I know what to do.

I am going back into those woods one final time. I am at the property now, in the driveway. This is the last email you will get from me. My tablet battery is dying. Soon night will come, and the snow will start to fall.

I will not return from this place.

I have nothing to settle, save the matter with you. And I have handled that as best I can, by leaving all of my property and paintings to your daughters.

I just sent several batches of emails out, to the rest of the Kents. I have over four hundred email addresses for the descendants of Jacob, or at least, emails that match the names I found on the ancestry site. I paid an investigator quite a bit of money for that information, but it was well worth it. I have sent them copies of everything, including my emails to you, Emmett's notes, and the official records, in the hopes that one of them will be brave enough to end the curse.

If nothing else, I can help put the others to rest, for I know where the bones of the Beast's unknown victims are. I have listed the locations, as clearly as I could describe them. I leave it to them to do the right thing, and send the information to the authorities.

At least seven Kents have danced with the Beast. Jeremiah was the first. There are no records on Albert, but the Beast remembers him . . . and his victims. Next was Albert's grandson, Jacob, who killed himself before he turned. Then Marc, who was never caught. The Beast remembers him, too. And Daniel, who was executed for murder. Elizabeth burned to death before she could turn. I suspect Emmet and his father were also becoming possessed, and killed themselves to stop it. And there are others too, those who left this place, and took on other names.

Some of their descendants must know something. Some of them are bound to believe.

I already know what I will see, when the veil between worlds is thin. The road will return. I will see them there in the woods, waiting for me. The shadow children, Jeremiah's spawn.

Our ancestors.

The Beast can bend time. We have seen that. He can go back to that cold November day when you found yourself standing before the cabin, and change your fate.

I will go back there, and I will parley with the force that rules this wood. I will offer myself to that dark being in exchange for you. And then I will wait in the primal northern forest, as the snow comes, and I will grow hungrier and hungrier, until the hole in my stomach becomes a gate. Until my limbs grow long and white, and my teeth grow into fangs.

Until I, too, can bend time.

Until I can walk down that trail and find, not just a stone slab, not a primitive cabin where Anne chanted spells and cursed her sister, but a room full of fresh corpses and a sated, slow beast. I will go back to that moment in the forest, just before you died. If I cannot change the past, I will carry your soul to another womb. I will go into the void, and cross the rivers of time, to see you safe again.

ABODE

That is the only way to save you. I understand now. That is the price I must pay.

My choice is made, either way.

Already I can feel the Kents out there. They shine like beacons in the night. Once you are safe, I will wait for one of them to come for me and end it.

I know the sacred places this wood holds, the savage and the unholy secrets it keeps. It breathes ice, and stands in silent testimony to the unknown. I know the forest here. It speaks, not in words, but in colors and energy. Its voice is the scream of winter winds and the utter silence of falling snow.

That is death, that sound. And I know how now to open that door.

Ours is a story of fire and ice, of flesh and bone, of blood and tears; a tale of things that whisper in the night in ancient forests.

Kents everywhere will dream of Jeremiah and the Beast tonight. One of them will come, and kneel before Weresh. I regret that. But you will be safe, and that is really all that matters to me.

The Beast will always be waiting in the howl of the winter wind.

I am no longer tormented. All of this has brought me to one simple but crucial understanding: we are all caught in the dance of predator and prey.

It's starting to snow. The dead watch silently from the trees, waiting for me. Already I feel the transformation beginning. The hunger is gnawing at me, and I am changing. Soon I, too, will be a monster in the night, a pale dead thing haunting these woods.

I see the world now through the eyes of the Beast.

ABOUT THE AUTHOR

Morgan Sylvia is a metalhead, an Aquarius, a beer snob, a coffee addict, and a work in progress. A former obituarist, she is now a full-time freelance writer. She was born and raised in Maine, where a combination of long cold winters, a vivid imagination, and a librarian mother made her a bookworm at an early age. Her fiction and poetry have appeared in several anthologies, including *Forgotten Realms, Wicked Witches, Northern Frights* and *Twice Upon An Apocalypse*. Her first poetry collection, *Whispers From The Apocalypse*, was released in 2014.

Morgan also dabbles in metal journalism, and is currently writing for *Antichrist Metalzine*. She belongs to a few different writers' groups: The New England Horror Writers, Horror Writers of Maine, and Tuesday Mayhem Society. *Abode* is her first novel. She is currently working on a horror novella; two separate fantasy series; and a standalone post-apocalyptic steampunk horror novel.

ALSO FROM
BLOODSHOT BOOKS

The Specimen (The Riders Saga #1)

From a crater lake on an island off the coast of Bronze Age Estonia...

To a crippled Viking warrior's conquest of England ...

To the bloody temple of an Aztec god of death and resurrection...

Their presence has shaped our world. They are the Riders.

One month ago, an urban explorer was drawn to an abandoned asylum in the mountains of northern Massachusetts. There he discovered a large specimen jar, containing something organic, unnatural and possibly alive.

Now, he and a group of unsuspecting individuals have discovered one of history's most horrific secrets. Whether they want to or not, they are caught in the middle of a millennia-old war and the latest battle is about to begin.

Available in paperback or Kindle on Amazon.com

ISBN-13: 978-1495230004

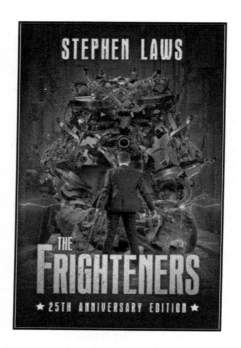

HOW MUCH DO YOU HATE?

Eddie Brinkburn's doing time for a botched garage job that left Sheraton's brother very badly burned.

HOW MUCH DO YOU HATE?

When Sheraton's gang burn his wife and kids to death, Eddie soon learns the meaning of hate.

HOW MUCH DO YOU HATE?

And that's how the prison psycho transfers his awesome power to Eddie. A power that Eddie reckons he can control. A power that will enable Eddie to put the frighteners on Sheraton...

Available in paperback or Kindle on Amazon.com

ISBN-13: 978-0998067926

WELCOME TO THE BLACK
MOUNTAIN CAMP FOR BOYS!

Summer,1989. It is a time for splashing in the lake and exploring the wilderness, for nine teenagers to bond together and create friendships that could last the rest of their lives.

But among this group there is a young man with a secret--a secret that, in this time and place, is unthinkable to his peers.

When the others discover the truth, it will change each of them forever. They will all have blood on their hands.

ODD MAN OUT is a heart-wrenching tale of bullies and bigotry, a story that explores what happens when good people don't stand up for what's right. It is a tale of how far we have come . . . and how far we still have left to go.

Available in paperback or Kindle on Amazon.com

ISBN-13: 978-0998067919

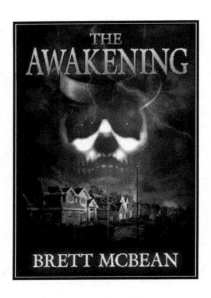

Welcome to the small Midwestern town of Belford, Ohio. It's summer vacation and fourteen-year-old Toby Fairchild is looking forward to spending a lazy, carefree summer playing basketball, staying up late watching monster movies, and camping out in his backyard with his best friend, Frankie.

But then tragedy strikes. And out of this tragedy an unlikely friendship develops between Toby and the local bogeyman, a strange old man across the street named Mr. Joseph. Over the course of a tumultuous summer, Toby will be faced with pain and death, the excitement of his first love, and the underlying racism of the townsfolk, all while learning about the value of freedom at the hands of a kind but cursed old man.

Every town has a dark side. And in Belford, the local bogeyman has a story to tell.

Available in paperback or Kindle on Amazon.com

ISBN-13: 978-0692730980

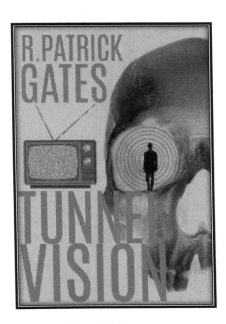

The empty airwaves of the mind...

Welcome to TunnelVision – the premium channel streaming from the imagination of R. Patrick Gates to you!

What happens when you lose sight of the forest for the trees?

Wilbur Clayton has a personal connection with Jesus – Murder! Abused for most of his life, Wilbur and Jesus are out to make amends and take revenge. With Grandma in his head and Jesus on the TunnelVision, Wilbur knows what must be done and who must be made to pay for the sins of the father...

The only thing standing in his way are a cop with a gift for details and deduction, and a young genius whose reenactments of his favorite books are about to become all too real.

TunnelVision – streaming seven days a week, 24 hours a day!

On the air and in your nightmares!

Available in paperback or Kindle on Amazon.com

ISBN-13: 978-0998067902

ON THE HORIZON FROM
BLOODSHOT BOOKS

2017*

The Raggedy Man – Christopher Collins
Those Who Follow – Michelle Garza & Melissa Lason
Sinkhole – Ken Goldman
Dust to Dust – M.C. Norris
White Death – Christine Morgan
It Sustains – Mark Morris
Red Diamond – Michales Joy
The Organ Donor – Matthew Warner
Shadow Child – Joseph A.Citro
The Noctuary: Pandemonium – Greg Chapman
What Hides Within – Jason Parent
Blood Mother: A Novel of Terror – Pete Kahle

2018*

Death Walker – R. Patrick Gates
Victoria (What Hides Within #2) – Jason Parent
The Winter Tree – Mark Morris
Happy Cage – Gene Lazuta
The Abomination (The Riders Saga #2) – Pete Kahle
Not Your Average Monster, Volume 3

2019-2020*

The Horsemen (The Riders Saga #3) – Pete Kahle
Not Your Average Monster, Volume 4

* other titles to be added when confirmed

BLOODSHOT BOOKS

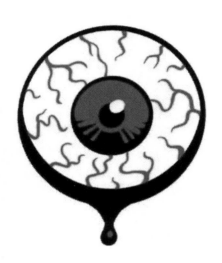

READ UNTIL
YOU BLEED!

Made in the USA
San Bernardino, CA
27 October 2017